Discovering Delilah

HARBORSIDE NIGHTS
Book Two

#LGBT

MELISSA FOSTER

London Borough of Hackney	
91300001060721	
Askews & Holts	
AF	£14.99
	5692055

This is a work of fiction. The events and characters described herein are imaginary and are not intended to refer to specific places or living persons. The opinions expressed in this manuscript are solely the opinions of the author and do not represent the opinions or thoughts of the publisher. The author has represented and warranted full ownership and/or legal right to publish all the materials in this book.

Cover Design: Elizabeth Mackey

WORLD LITERARY PRESS
PRINTED IN THE UNITED STATES OF AMERICA

A NOTE TO READERS

Delilah and Ashley stole my heart from the moment they first spoke to me. They were so real and so emotionally compelling that I knew I had to write their story. Their path to their forever love is not an easy one, but if you believe in true love, then I hope you enjoy *Discovering Delilah* as much as I enjoyed writing it.

Be sure to sign up for my newsletter so you never miss a release, and to keep up to date on giveaways and promotions. www.MelissaFoster.com/News

Discovering Delilah is the second book in the Harborside Nights series. If you enjoy this series, you might enjoy my sizzling-hot contemporary romance series, Love in Bloom, featuring the Snow Sisters, Bradens, Remingtons, Seaside Summers, Ryders, and Billionaires After Dark. All of my books may be enjoyed as standalone novels

For more information please visit my website www.MelissaFoster.com

Melissa Foster

For those who know
Love is a gift
For those who let love flourish
Without judgment
Without guilt

PRAISE FOR MELISSA FOSTER

"Contemporary romance at its hottest. Each Braden sibling left me craving the next. Sensual, sexy, and satisfying, the Braden series is a captivating blend of the dance between lust, love, and life."
—*Bestselling author Keri Nola, LMHC*
(on The Bradens)

"[LOVERS AT HEART] Foster's tale of stubborn yet persistent love takes us on a heartbreaking and soul-searing journey."
—*Reader's Favorite*

"Smart, uplifting, and beautifully layered. I couldn't put it down!"
—*National bestselling author Jane Porter*
(on SISTERS IN LOVE)

"Steamy love scenes, emotionally charged drama, and a family-driven story make this the perfect story for any romance reader."
—*Midwest Book Review (on SISTERS IN BLOOM)*

"HAVE NO SHAME is a powerful testimony to love and the progressive, logical evolution of social consciousness, with an outcome that readers will find engrossing, unexpected, and ultimately eye-opening."
—*Midwest Book Review*

"TRACES OF KARA is psychological suspense at its best, weaving a tight-knit plot, unrelenting action, and tense moments that don't let up and ending in a fiery, unpredictable revelation."
—*Midwest Book Review*

CHAPTER ONE

Delilah

"COMING OUT OF grief is like coming out of a long, dark tunnel." Meredith Garland folds her hands in her lap. Her feet are crossed at the ankles and tucked primly beneath her chair, one pointed toe touching the carpet. Her warm brown eyes slide around the room, slowing on each of the other four attendees of the grief-counseling session.

I've been coming to a grief-counseling support group for the past month at the YMCA. My friend Brooke Baker brought me to my first session, having attended herself a few years back to get over her own grief. Only she didn't lose her parents to the drunk driver of a tractor trailer like I did. She was merely getting over a bad breakup. *Merely*, because really. Can anything match the grief of losing your parents at twenty-two, on the evening of your college graduation, when you should be celebrating and making plans for your life?

Meredith is talking about the stages of grief, all of which I know by heart: denial, anger, bargaining, depression, and acceptance. When we first moved here after our parents were killed, my twin brother, Wyatt, was also dealing with his new feelings for our best friend, Cassidy. I, on the other hand, was not *dealing* with anything. I was thoroughly entrenched in denial. One night a guy forced himself on Cassidy, and Wyatt beat the crap out of him—and scared the daylights out of me. Wyatt went straight to anger, skipping over denial altogether. I couldn't watch Wyatt falling apart, so I moved in with Brooke, who has been a family friend for years. It's been a little more than two months now, and I've finally made it past denial. Now that I'm living at our beach house again, I'm trying really hard to find a way to deal with my grief as well as the personal desires that I've spent a lifetime repressing—and hiding from everyone I know other than Wyatt and Cassidy.

"You must learn to envision a future for yourself without those you have lost." Having lost her husband a few years back, Meredith says this with the confidence of someone who's achieved such a future. "Find ways to turn your memories into something you can live with and celebrate, rather than something that pulls you under."

Meredith smiles at me, but I'm unable to muster one in return because my toes are dipping in the anger pool. I'm not thinking about envisioning a future without grief. Although that would be nice, I'm pretty sure grief will be my partner for a very long time. Sometimes it hides in the shadows, waiting to swallow me whole, while other times it's front and center, taking a bow for the way it's laid me out flat.

No, it's not grief I'm thinking about coming out of, and I can't return Meredith's smile because my parents left me a legacy of fear and shame. The dark tunnel I'm thinking about coming out of feels even scarier than grief. I steal a glance at the other people in the group and envy the way they know who they are, even if they're a little lost at the moment. I envy the way Michael eyes me and the other girls in the room and how

Mark and Cathy hold hands during the entire hour. I try not to look at Janessa, because I can't help but stare, and I know how rude that is. She's a little older than me, and I don't have to look to know that her head is held higher than mine and her cocoa-brown eyes glisten with a surety that I can't even imagine how to possess. She wears shorts and loose shirts that show her cleavage, and if I look at her, I know my eyes will be drawn to the swell of her breasts and the curve of her bare shoulder as her blouse slips down, which it always does.

My attraction to Janessa is not because I *want* her. It's not the same heart-pounding, palm-sweating, I-can't-breathe attraction that I have to my friend Ashley Carver. It's more of an appreciation of her beauty *and* her confidence, and for the first time in my life I have no one standing in my way of acting on my feelings toward girls. I am free to look at whomever I please and feel whatever my body wants to feel. I'm free to *come out,* but thanks to my parents' disapproval, my desires are still tightly encased in shame, so I don't lift my eyes to admire Janessa.

Come out.

Gosh, if that isn't the stupidest phrase in the world, then I don't know what is. Do straight people have to *come out* and announce they're straight? For that matter, do they even think about their sexuality in terms of caring how others perceive them? I think the whole idea of coming out makes it ten times worse for someone like me, whose parents were ultraconservative and made no bones about their opinions against same-sex relationships. I was both elated and mortified when states began to debate same-sex marriages. Elated because, let's face it, it's a personal decision that others shouldn't have a say in, and mortified because it meant that every time the issue was mentioned in the news, I'd have to sit through my parents' lectures about why same-sex relationships are wrong. And weak little me never wanted to rock the boat, so I hid my attractions. All of them. My whole life. I even went so far as to hook up with a few guys to try to fit in and figure out if I was *sure* I liked girls. Well, I know I don't get all fluttery inside like I have over the years when I've been attracted to girls, and I definitely don't get wet between my legs over guys, like I do over Ashley. But then again, I've never been intimate with a woman, so my only validation is what I've felt toward women, and more specifically, what I feel when I'm with her.

Ashley.

Ashley. Ashley. Ashley.

I even love her name. It's feminine and confident, just like her.

After our parents died, everything about our Connecticut house, from the conservative neighborhood to the house itself, felt repressive, stifling. When Wyatt suggested that we come to Harborside after the funeral, I practically ran to the car. I met Ashley the first night after we arrived, at a gathering at our house, and I haven't been able to stop thinking about her since. She came with Brandon, and I remember thinking that she was the prettiest girl I'd ever seen, then immediately pushing that thought away because I felt like, even dead, my parents could read my thoughts. Ashley and I clicked right away. When we decided to do shots, Jesse took everyone's keys so no one would drink and drive. We have seven bedrooms, but that first night the downstairs beds weren't made up yet, so Ashley slept on the futon in my bedroom. I think I spent the whole night staring at her.

I think about her all the time, count down the hours until

I'll see her again, and I swear when she's around, gravity doesn't exist. It's really hard to stay grounded and focused around her, because I spend my time admiring her and wanting to touch her. Not even make out with, just touch, like when you sit with someone who's funny and warm and smart and you want to be closer to them. That's me with Ashley—although I *also* want to make out with her. *God, do I want to.*

My pulse quickens, and I shift in my seat. I can't even think about her without getting all hot and bothered.

I guess I zoned out because the counseling session is over and everyone's leaving. It's late summer, and when I step outside, the cool evening air stings my cheeks and clears my head. I head down the concrete steps and start my short walk home to our beach house. When my parents died, my twin brother, Wyatt, and I inherited everything—the house in Connecticut where we grew up, the beach house here in Harborside, Massachusetts, where we've spent summers since we were kids, and the Taproom, the best bar and grill in town. We've been living here and running the bar for a little more than two months, and Wyatt and I finally decided to sell the house in Connecticut this fall. Too many ghosts in that house.

"Wait up." Janessa jogs to catch up. "Are you okay? You seemed down tonight."

"I'm okay, thanks. Just thinking." We walk down the dimly lit residential street toward the lights of the boardwalk. Harborside is small enough to walk most places but still big enough that the outskirts of town are more secluded and less commercialized.

"Yeah, that's kind of what this whole grief-counseling thing is supposed to do to us, right? Make us introspective and force us to deal with our feelings."

I know Janessa lost a family member, but she was already attending the group sessions when I started, and she's never said exactly who it was that she lost. I'm not about to ask. If there's one thing I've learned in group, it's that when people want to talk about their grief, they'll bring it up.

"Yeah, I guess it is."

"Want to grab a cup of coffee at Brooke's Bytes?"

"Brooke's is so crowded at night. How about someplace else?" I try to say it casually, but the truth is, counseling leaves me feeling uneasy, and the last place I want to be is near giddy teenagers in a boardwalk café. Not to mention that my friend Brooke owns the café, and I really just want to be away from people I know while I come down from group.

Janessa's eyes drop from mine, linger around my mouth, then lift to my eyes again. Her scrutiny makes me nervous, but it feels good at the same time, and I'm not sure how to handle it, so I tuck my hair behind my ear to distract myself.

"Sure," she says. "The Sandbar, over on Shab Row?"

The Sandbar is a pub, so I know we won't be drinking coffee. Ashley is working at the surf shop tonight, and my other friends are just hanging out at home, which means I have no plans, and looking at Janessa all night is *not* a hardship, so I agree.

Shab Row is a quiet street with old-fashioned, bulbous streetlights on tall black poles, brick pavers, and only a handful of shops. Unlike the many commercial streets of Harborside, which boast bright signs and sidewalk displays, Shab Row is more subdued. The signs have muted colors of slate blue, maroon, and earth tones, and the most paraphernalia that I've ever seen outside are holiday lights on the wrought-iron railings lining the steps into the shops and pub.

The bar is dimly lit and nearly empty. We sit at a booth in the back and order drinks from a tall, slim waiter who looks like he wants to be anywhere but here. My phone vibrates and my heart skips a beat when Ashley's name appears on the screen.

It's kind of pathetic that I'm crushing on her so hard that I get excited over seeing her name on my phone.

How was counseling? I smile as I read her text, loving that she cares enough to ask.

"Boyfriend?" Janessa asks as the waiter returns with our drinks.

I shake my head and laugh as I reply to Ashley. *Fine. Having a drink with a girl from the session. Still on for sketching sunrise tomorrow?* Ashley and I have been meeting at sunrise or sunset a few times each week. She paints landscapes, and I'm teaching her to sketch. It's about the only hobby that I have, but I'm pretty good at it. The only problem is, I'm usually so busy looking at Ashley that I don't get much sketching done when we're together.

"Why did you laugh?" Janessa sips her drink as I read Ashley's confirmation for tomorrow, then set my phone aside.

Ashley's my first *real* girl crush ever—although it feels like a hell of a lot more than a crush. I have to stop lusting after her. Not knowing if Ash is straight or into girls leaves me longing for someone I'll probably never have. Besides, having absolutely zero intimate experience with girls, I can't even be sure that I'd enjoy the sexy side of being with her if she *is* into me. When Ashley and I are together, we don't really talk about frivolous stuff like hooking up with people. It's like we're so in sync with each other that nothing else even exists. I guess between learning to run the Taproom and dealing with moving in and out of the beach house—which I know hurt Wyatt's feelings—and trying to deal with the death of my parents, my focus has pretty much been on survival. And when Ash and I are together, I'm working so hard to ignore my burgeoning feelings for her that I avoid any topics having to do with dating or hooking up.

"Hello? Delilah?" Janessa waves her hand in front of my eyes.

"I'm sorry. I totally zoned out."

"Yeah, I noticed you did that at counseling, too. You sure you're okay?" She tilts her head, and her long dark hair slips over her shoulder. She reminds me of Megan Fox, except Megan's eyes look sharp and catlike, like she's always either on the prowl or ready for the paparazzi. Janessa's are a little larger, slightly rounder, and usually thoughtful or filled with compassion, as they are now.

"Yes." I down half of my drink.

"So, are you going to tell me why you laughed when I asked if you had a boyfriend?" Her lips curl up in a smile, revealing a row of perfect pearly whites beneath.

I run my finger over the rim of my glass to keep her from seeing what's going through my mind. I was always so afraid of my parents finding out that I thought I liked girls that I admitted it only to Wyatt and Cassidy.

"Okay, here's the thing." Janessa reaches across the table and covers my hand with hers. "I know you're grieving for your parents, and my heart goes out to you. It's going to take a really long time to deal with that, but I can see that something else is going through that pretty little mind of yours, and if you want to talk about it, I'm here."

Pretty little mind? She leaves her hand on mine. It's warm and soft and makes my pulse speed up. Did I misread her? Is she into me? Me? Why would she be? *Do I look like a lesbian?* No woman has ever come onto me before.

"Thanks, Janessa." I finish my drink and move my hand, feeling a little queasy.

She waves the waiter over and orders another round of drinks. "So…was that your *girlfriend* on the phone?"

My eyes shoot to hers.

"It was just a guess." She holds both hands up in surrender, then leans across the table and lowers her voice. "But your look is very telling."

"She's not my girlfriend." I feel my cheeks heat up, but I can't look away from Janessa as she arches a brow. We've spoken only a handful of times. How can she possibly guess this about me?

"But…you wish she was?" Janessa's phone rings and she holds up her index finger. "Hold that thought." She looks at me as she answers the call, and the attention makes me even more nervous. "Hi, baby. Are you going night-night?"

Night-night? Oh my gosh. I'm thinking she's into me and she's a mom? She's probably married. My radar is totally off. My stomach feels like there's a tornado brewing inside me. I look away, embarrassed that I was so far off base.

"Okay, sweetheart. Have fun with Uncle Dean." She blows a kiss into the phone, then holds up her finger again. "Hey, Dean. Yeah. She's okay? Great. Okay. I'll be there tomorrow morning." She pauses. "Okay. Love you, too." She ends the call and stuffs her phone into her purse. "I'm sorry. My little girl is staying with my brother and his little boy for their weekly slumber party."

"You have a daughter?" If I was wrong about how she was looking at me, how will I ever know when someone's really interested?

"Mm-hm. Jackie, she's three. Here, I'll show you a picture of her." She pulls her phone back out and scrolls through pictures, then reaches across the table and shows me a picture of the most adorable little brown-haired girl. Janessa is lying on a bed hugging Jackie, cheek to cheek.

"Aw, she's so cute. She looks just like you, too."

She shows me a bunch more pictures, and in every one she and Jackie are both smiling. Even in the picture of Jackie sleeping on Janessa's shoulder, it looks like the little girl is smiling.

"What does your husband do?"

She puts her phone away. "Oh, I'm not married." She locks eyes with me. "And I'm not straight, either."

"Oh." It comes out as a whisper, and the fact that I can't even answer like a normal human being embarrasses me. I wonder if she adopted Jackie. She must have…No. She could have used artificial insemination. Or maybe Jackie's her girlfriend's child? I'm not curious because I'm interested in her. I've never thought past one day having a girlfriend—which in itself seems like a fantasy. I'm curious about how it all works.

"Delilah, I'm going out on a limb here, so feel free to tell me if I'm off base, but you haven't come out yet, have you?"

I sigh, but this time I don't look away. I have to start some-where, and I've already admitted more to her verbally and nonverbally than I have to anyone else, so I force myself to answer her.

"I hate that term."

"I hate it, too," she admits. "So, are you *out*?"

I shake my head.

"Aw, Delilah. I'm sorry. I didn't mean to—"

"It's okay, really. I'm…This is all new to me. My parents

were very conservative, so…"

"So, you never told them?" Her brows knit together. "Want to talk about it?"

"I told them right before I walked for graduation, but they weren't very supportive." I feel my eyes tear up and I down my drink in one gulp. When I told my parents that I liked girls, they looked at me like I disgusted them, and it nearly took me to my knees. They never said a word about my confession after graduation, but it was chaotic. There were pictures to deal with and congratulations from friends and my aunt Lara who had come with them to watch me and Wyatt graduate.

I push the memories away and blink several times, trying to repress my tears. "I'm sorry. Can we not talk about my parents?"

"Of course. I'm sorry. I'm being too nosy."

"No, it's not that. Actually, I like talking to you. This is the first time I've had a conversation like this. It feels good to get some of it out in the open."

She smiles. "I like talking to you, too."

"I don't really talk about this stuff with anyone else. My brother, Wyatt, tries to talk to me about it, but it feels weird even though he's supportive."

"Listen, I get it. My parents were surprised to find out that my brother, Dean, and I weren't straight." Her eyes fill with sadness, and just as quickly, that sadness is replaced with something else. Determination? Acceptance? I'm not sure.

"Our parents came around, and they're very supportive, but I've dated women whose families weren't exactly on board with their lifestyles, and I know how hard it can be."

"Even around here? Harborside is so diverse. I still can't figure out why my parents had a summer house here and bought the Taproom."

"Your parents owned the Taproom?"

"Yeah, well, Wyatt and I do now." Knowing that she understands my situation puts me at ease.

"So…" She sips her drink and lifts her chin in the direction of my phone. "Want to tell me about the texter we're not talking about?"

I laugh. "Ashley. I just met her at the beginning of the summer, and she's…" My heart is sprinting in my chest, and I can feel a goofy smile coming on.

"Uh-huh. You have a major crush on Ashley. So, what's the problem?"

"Take your pick. I've *never* kissed a girl. I have no idea if *she's* into girls or guys, and oh yeah, did I say I have *never* even kissed a girl?" I know I'm blushing, but at the same time, it feels so good to get the words out that I can't seem to stop myself.

"Never? Didn't you say in therapy that you just graduated from college?"

I nod, knowing what's coming next.

"And you never explored your sexuality?"

I shake my head.

"You never got drunk and kissed your best friend, or got into a little girl-on-girl action and blamed it on the alcohol?"

I laugh and shake my head again. "That would have been a good idea, if I drank a lot, but I was too afraid of my parents catching wind of it. And believe me, they would *not* have approved. I have no idea what they would have done, but the idea of them finding out and…I don't know, refusing to pay my college tuition, or just making me feel worse than I already did…" I shrug again, unable to believe how I'm opening up to her. She's so easy to talk to, and I feel oddly safe sitting in this dimly lit corner booth, spilling my heart to her.

"Oh, Delilah. No offense, but your parents did a job on you. At least you're in the right place to figure it all out, and it sounds like your brother is supportive even if you don't want to talk to him. Believe me, support is everything." She finishes her drink and slaps money on the table. "Want to get out of here and walk for a while?"

"Sure. Thanks for the drinks." We grab our stuff, and once we're outside she loops her arm into mine, like a friend who's known me for years.

"I promise you, Delilah. It won't always feel like you're living in a fishbowl. Life has a way of working itself out, and there will come a time when you know you're on the right path, and when that happens, you'll stop worrying about what everyone else thinks."

A fishbowl. That's exactly what I feel like, even though my parents are gone. They drove their beliefs into my head so strongly that I can't get out from under the feeling of being scrutinized. Walking with Janessa is nothing like walking with Ashley, where I'm dissecting every step, every breath, searching for hints that might reveal if she's into me or not. Being with Janessa is different. Then again, no one makes me feel like I do when I'm with Ashley.

When we come to my street, I stop walking. Janessa stops, too, our arms still linked. It feels nice to have another friend.

"This is my street. So I guess I'll see you next week?"

"Yeah, sure." She steps in closer and touches my hip, causing goose bumps to race up my limbs. "Delilah, I know your heart is wrapped around Ashley. I can see that when you talk about her, and that's such a good feeling. But I've also been where you are, with no experience."

Her eyes are warm and her touch is caring, not pushy. Even though I'm crossing into new territory by opening up to her, and even though my stomach is more nervous than a fly on a lily pad, I don't retreat. And I don't feel like she's coming onto me, although there is something in her eyes, her touch, the sensual sound of her voice, that makes my breathing become shallow.

"Every woman deserves to feel safe when she has her first experience and to feel confident when they're with the woman they care about." Her eyes never waver from mine. "If you ever want to...you know...*explore* that side without the pressure of doing it right or the embarrassment of feeling inexperienced..."

Ohgodohgodohgod.

"I'm here for you, as a nonjudgmental friend. My life now is all about Jackie. I don't have room for anything more than sharing an intimate night. Or a few. Or whatever. I'm not looking for a girlfriend or a quick hookup. I'm offering to help, and trust me, there's a big difference between hooking up with someone and overcoming your fears in a safe environment." She smiles like she hasn't just sucked all the air from the world, and it's all I can do to remain erect.

I can hardly believe she's offering herself up to me, but more than that, I can hardly believe I'm considering it.

CHAPTER TWO

Ashley

I SHOULDER MY backpack and shove my hands deep into the front pocket of my hoodie as I walk across the dense sand behind my apartment complex toward the dunes to meet Delilah Armstrong. We're both artists, although not professionally. I've been painting landscapes for about four years, and Delilah sketches. She's begun teaching me how to sketch. She's incredibly talented, and sketching seems to come as naturally to her as painting landscapes comes to me. I used to sleep in, but as Delilah comes into focus, perched high among the dune grass, with the rising sun illuminating her profile, I never want to sleep in again. I have no idea if she knows I'm a lesbian or not, and I can't tell for sure if she's straight or not, but even if she is, I'd get up at the crack of dawn to see her every day if I had the chance. We don't get a lot of time together because she works a lot of hours at the Taproom, and I work a lot at Endless Summer Surf Shop. But even though we get to share only a few stolen hours here and there, during those times it seems like no one else in the world exists.

She's leaning over her sketch pad with an intense look in her grassy-green eyes as I walk up the dune. I'm careful not to disturb her. I like watching her sketch. Her pencil moves swiftly across the page, and every once in a while she smiles, like she's happy with the shading she's accomplished or the curve she's drawn. She's wearing a thick sweatshirt, shorts, and her favorite black lace-up boots with frilly white socks. Seeing her in those boots always does funky stuff to my stomach. Only Delilah could pull off black boots with frilly socks, especially in summer.

She lifts her eyes when I'm a few feet away, and her shoulders drop a hair as a smile spreads across her lips. She picks up a to-go cup from beside her and hands it to me. Her eyes sweep over me quickly and she nibbles on her lower lip, then covers her sketch.

"Hi, Ash. I brought you coffee."

She's usually too busy showing me how to sketch to create something herself. As much as I like when she's leaning against me, showing me the right angle to draw from or the proper shading technique to use, I like when she sketches even more, because it gives me time to drink her in. She's shy about her drawings, though I don't know why. They're always amazing.

"Thanks." I drop my backpack and settle in beside her, pulling out my sketch pad and pencil. "It's chilly this morning."

"I know, but after a few minutes you'll get used to it."

I lean in close and peer at her sketch pad. "Can I see?"

She spreads her hands across the page as if she's not going to show me. I know she will. She always does this, fights her shyness.

"It's not very good." She points to a boat anchored by the Harborside Pier. "I'm trying to draw that, but I can't get the waterline right. It looks like a five-year-old did it."

I want to laugh because the image is so beautifully drawn

that it's almost ridiculous that she worries, but I don't. I didn't know Delilah before her parents died, but I wonder if their death somehow undermined her confidence, or if she's always doubted her talents. She moved here right after her parents were killed in an accident on the way home from her college graduation, and even though her confidence wavers, she still seems incredibly strong to me. I don't think she realizes how managing everything she does on a daily basis requires her to be strong. Since the day I met her she's been dealing with more than any young woman should have to. As if losing both parents wasn't enough, she's also had to learn to run their business, decide about selling her childhood home, deal with attorneys and wills and other things that no one our age should have to think about.

"It does not." She watches my eyes as I reach for the sketch pad. She does that a lot, watching me. I set her sketch pad on my lap and marvel at her sketch, and when I feel her eyes leave me, I steal a glance at her.

She has the most flawless skin. Her slightly upturned nose might look snobbish on anyone else, but Delilah's image is natural. There's nothing harsh or contrived about her. She's tall and lean, but not hollow-looking, like many thin girls.

Even though Delilah is strong, she has this shyness, this vulnerability, about her that makes me want to hold her in my arms and tell her things are going to be okay. We've only known each other a short while, but she's already touched me in ways no one else ever has.

"This is so good, Dee. I wish I could draw this well." I hand her the sketch pad and pick up my pencil.

"Stay right where you are. I want to see if I can draw your profile." I hover over my sketch pad and set to work trying to create her image, but it's like re-creating the *Mona Lisa*. I know I'll never come close.

She sets her sketch pad in the sand and sighs.

"Come on, Ash. Draw that boat or something." She looks down at the sand and bows her neck.

"Boats are so boring, and you're supposed to be showing me how to draw people, remember? Now lift your chin and don't complain." *Besides, boats don't make me want to kiss them.*

She rolls her eyes, but her cheeks plump up with her smile. I'm glad she gives in.

"Tell me about therapy last night—then you won't think about me drawing you." I'm trying to take her mind off of the fact that I'm studying her. I know she won't go into much detail. She never does. But I like hearing the thoughts she is willing to share, and I think it helps her to talk it over, even just a little here and there. Most people would probably think she's moving forward just fine. She keeps her emotions pretty close to her chest. But when she does share, I can tell there are struggles she's not revealing, because along with a thread of sadness, there's an underlying layer of anger. She buries the toes of her boots in the sand.

"It's okay if you don't want to talk about it."

"No, it's fine." She sifts sand through her fingers, and I can see she's nervous.

I've come to know several of Delilah's nervous habits. If we're on the beach, she reaches for sand, but when we're sitting in the grass, she pulls blades apart in skinny strips, and when we're at her house or at my apartment, she plays with the edges of her shorts.

I go back to sketching, waiting for her to say more as the sun rises higher into the sky and catches her long blond hair at just the right angle to show off the golden highlights. Sometimes when we're together it's hard for me not to reach out and touch her. This is one of those times. I can see she's struggling to tell me something. Her eyes flick to the water, then back to her feet, and finally she meets my gaze.

"I spaced out through most of therapy, but I went out with Janessa, the girl I told you about."

Janessa. My stomach takes a nosedive as the green-eyed monster sinks her claws into my neck. My hand stills on the sketch pad. Delilah is pretty careful with her emotions, and I'm not entirely sure how to read her sometimes. There are times when I catch her looking at me like she wants to touch me, or kiss me, and at those times my heart swells with hope. I know I'm probably seeing only what I want to see. Other times I see her gazing off at guys on the beach, and I don't know what to think. I have no right to be jealous about Delilah going out with another girl, especially since I'm pretty sure she's straight, but I am jealous, and I have to force myself to push those feelings aside and act like it doesn't bother me. I've made the mistake of being attracted to straight girls before, and I'm not willing to lose our friendship over my crush on her.

"Was it fun?" *Please say no.*

Oh my God. I'm such a bitch.

She's looking at me *that* way, like I could lean forward and kiss her and she would be totally into it. *Ugh.* I know it's my own wishful thinking, but hell if I don't think I see it in her eyes. I wish I could just ask her if she's straight or not, but it's not a topic you can throw out there. *Hey, check out the sunrise. Are you into girls?* She's never brought it up to me, either. I figure eventually it'll come out one way or the other. Either I won't be able to keep myself from touching her, or she will go out with a guy and that'll be that. Only I'm not sure turning off my feelings for Delilah would be as easy as *that'll be that.*

"It wasn't really fun, but it was nice."

Her voice pulls me from my thoughts.

"We went for drinks at the Sandbar."

"Drinks? You don't even like to drink that much." I lower my eyes to keep her from reading what I'm sure my sharp response has probably already conveyed.

"I only had two, but it was nice talking with her. She's got a three-year-old little girl, and she's really nice. You'd like her." She looks out over the water again.

She has a baby. She's probably in a relationship. Relief lifts my eyes to her again.

"Maybe I can meet her sometime." Even knowing she's probably straight, I'm still a little jealous that Delilah spent the evening with her. I know she and Janessa are friends and talk before and after their group sessions, but they've never gone out for drinks before. I realize I'm gripping my pencil too tightly and the shading I'm working on is too dark, too angry, but I can't seem to loosen my grip.

"That would be great. Maybe after therapy sometime?" She reaches for the sketch pad and our fingers brush. "Can I see?"

Her fingers are long and delicate, and I want so badly to bring them to my lips and press a kiss to their tender skin. It takes all of my focus to resist the urge and release the sketch pad.

"It's not very good."

"Ash, this is amazing. You made me much prettier than I am."

I scoot closer and look over her shoulder. This is my favorite place, pressed up against her with our hips touching. We sit like

this a lot when she's teaching me sketching techni
discussing the nuances of drawing. Lame, I know, but ̶ ̶ ̶ ̶ ̶ take
what I can get, because even if she's into girls, it doesn't mean
she'll be into *me*, and I enjoy spending time with her too much
to chance losing that.

"You are prettier than I can capture on paper, Delilah." Our
eyes connect, and the air between us pulses with electricity. I
brush her hair from her shoulder, barely breathing, hoping she'll
give me a sign that she wants me as badly as I want her.

"Thanks, Ash. You're the greatest friend ever."

My heart sinks. Greatest *friend* ever.

Delilah

THE TAPROOM HAS become my safe harbor, a project that
fills my head and keeps me from thinking too much about the
loss of my parents or my feelings for Ashley. It took a few weeks
for me and Wyatt to get a system down for managing the bar.
Luckily, we had Jesse Steele to help us. He and his brother,
Brent, own Endless Summer Surf Shop, where Ashley works,
and recently purchased a restaurant in town, which they're
renovating. Before buying the restaurant, Jesse ran the Taproom
in the off-season, and after my parents died, Jesse stepped in to
help us learn the business. Now we have a system. I handle
inventory, ordering, and staffing, and Wyatt manages the
accounting and administrative end of things. We don't have a
huge staff, so when someone is out, Wyatt or I often have to fill
in.

Today Tristan is working the bar. Charley, one of our wait-
resses who also fills in as a bartender, is out on a three-day

assignment with her other part-time job, and Rusty, a waiter, couldn't come in early to cover her shift. It's just me and Livi handling tables. Livi's worked here all summer. She's an excellent waitress. She lost her mother when she was a teenager, so she understands what Wyatt and I have been going through and she's always willing to talk, although I'm not big on talking about my parents. Sometimes it's hard to separate how much I miss them with how much I hate some of the feelings they've left me with.

I hand my customers' orders to Dutch, our cook, and grab a stack of napkins to refill the napkin holder behind the bar. I stare at the box of napkins like it has answers written all over it instead of napkin sizes. It's no use. No matter how much I try to focus on those words, hoping they'll replace the look in Ashley's eyes when we were on the dunes, I can't. And it's *that* look—the look that makes me think Ashley might be into me—that draws me back to Janessa's offer.

Would it be so bad to climb between the sheets with her and figure this out? To see if I like being intimate with girls and make sure I'm not some freak who likes to check out girls but doesn't like being intimate with *anyone*? Would that be using Janessa? Is she using me? I immediately push that thought away. Let's face it—she's pretty enough and sweet enough that she hardly needs to spend a night with a lesbian virgin.

I swear being with a guy was never this hard. Even when I had sex the first time, it wasn't this complicated. Brad and I had been sort of dating for a few weeks. I was trying to figure out if I liked guys or not, because everyone I knew in Connecticut was straight, and here in Harborside I didn't know any lesbian women, only gay guys. And as if that didn't make me feel out of place, every time we saw a newscast about same-sex marriages, my parents' faces would pinch up, and Dad would make a comment about how wrong it was. I was really hoping that I was misinterpreting my feelings toward girls.

It was a painful road of discovery, because I felt like I was out in a dinghy floating in the middle of the sea with a storm brewing in the distance and no one to throw me a lifeline. It's such a lonely journey, this whole self-discovery thing we have to do. My first endeavor into making sure I wasn't misinterpreting my feelings was to be intimate with a guy. What a mess that was. I was seventeen and at least a year behind my friends in losing my virginity. We did it in the backseat of Brad's father's car, parked on a back road. The whole experience was uncomfortable and without emotion. He got all sweaty and grunted like he was in pain, and I kept thinking, *This is what girls rave about?* I still don't get it. I thought it might have just been him, so I tried again with another guy my senior year. But sex experiment number two didn't go any better than the first one. When I got to college I decided to try one last time, still clinging to the hope that it was all in my mind. Frank. I dated him for appearances' sake, which allowed me to go to parties without being hit on by guys and made me feel a little less like an outsider. Looking back, I wish I had been like every other rebellious kid and jumped into bed with as many girls as I could, even though that's not who I am. I cringe inside at the thought. I'm just not made of slutty cloth. But it would have made things easier to deal with now.

Sometimes I hate my parents.

Guilt chases that thought right out of my head.

Guilt, guilt, guilt.

Run, run, run.

My desires are always chased by guilt, because being who I

think I was born to be, who I *want* to be, goes against everything my parents believed and filled my head with. And yeah, I know they're dead, but…That's another thing I feel guilty about and the reason my guilt is always followed by the urge to run from dealing with my feelings at all.

I pry those thoughts from my mind and try again to focus on work.

Wyatt bursts through the double doors into the back of the bar. We're twins, but his hair is thicker, shaggy, and darker than mine, light brown compared to my blond, and while I'm only five foot five, Wyatt's over six feet tall and broad as a linebacker. The kitchen seems smaller with him in it. He's been in and out between meetings with accounting firms. We're hiring an outside company to audit our books because our last accountant—and our dad's best friend, whom we called *Uncle* Tim— embezzled money from the bar. I guess gambling and drinking can drive a person over the edge, but add losing your best friend and I guess I can see why he lost it. Wyatt fired him and told him to stay away from us, but Uncle Tim…er…Tim Johnson, has known us since we were born. We spent a lot of time with him and his wife over the years. He even came to our high school and college graduations. Wyatt couldn't just push him out of our lives completely, even though that was what he tried to do. After firing him, Wyatt got him into a treatment center, and I know Wyatt's visited him a few times, although he doesn't really talk about it.

"Hey, sis." He joins me at the counter, where I'm waiting to pick up a sandwich order from Dutch. "You sure you can hold down the fort?"

"Yeah, no problem."

Dutch slides the order across the stainless-steel counter and winks. His hair has grown a lot in the last month, and it looks like a curly brown Afro. He reminds me of Seth Rogan, only bigger.

"Hey, *Rocky*. There's nothing Delilah can't handle. And she doesn't have to use her fists." Dutch's deep laugh fills the kitchen as my brother gives him a narrow-eyed stare.

"The nickname's *Army*, thank you very much." Wyatt flashes a crooked smile, and Dutch shakes his head. *Army* has been his nickname since we first went to college. His friends thought that *Army* was cooler than *Wyatt Armstrong*. Most girls loved it, but me and Cassidy, whom Wyatt and I have known since we were five years old, have never cared for it. To us he'll always be *Wyatt*.

"It's your own fault for beating up that guy who was coming on to Cassidy. You'll never live it down in Dutch's eyes," I say as we walk back into the bar.

"She's right!" Dutch yells after us.

Wyatt's face grows tight. He's not proud of that fight, and I think the fact that it was the catalyst for my moving out still bothers him. Our parents' death hit us both equally as hard but in totally different ways. Wyatt seems to have moved past most of his grief, but I'm still knee-deep in quicksand.

"I'm heading out to meet with another accounting firm. Rusty's coming in to relieve you soon, and Jesse's coming by later to check over the books and inventory. You know, gotta make sure we're still on target and all that."

In addition to helping us with the Taproom, Jesse has taken on the role of watching over us, too. I think my father would be pleased that Jesse has stepped in, even though he's only about ten years older than us. And he doesn't act like a father, but more like an older brother. He hangs out with us when we have parties and makes sure no one drinks and drives.

"I'm fine, Wy. How are the interviews going?"

"Eh. You know, it's a lot of numbers talk, but I really liked one guy, so we'll see. You'll have to meet him before we make any decisions, of course." Wyatt scans the room. The bar runs the full length of the wall across from the door. We have a dance floor toward the back of the bar and a small stage where our friend Brandon Owens's band plays a few times each week. Two girls are sitting on barstools drinking cocktails and eating sandwiches. One of them runs her eyes over Wyatt. He's so into Cassidy now that he doesn't even notice, or he doesn't seem to. There are two couples sitting at tables in the middle of the room.

"Looks like you have a customer." Wyatt nods at a booth, where—*holy crap*—Janessa is sitting. She has one leg stretched across to the other side of the booth as she studies the menu. "A very pretty customer."

My pulse quickens at the sight of her. "Hey, you have a girlfriend."

"She's not for me." He winks, and I grab his arm and move in really close before he can walk away.

"How can you tell she's into girls?" I whisper. I really want to know, because to me she looks just like every other girl in the bar, only prettier. Wyatt and Cassidy are the only people who know that I like girls, even though I know our friends here would be supportive. My parents are no longer here watching over every move I make, but I still feel like they are. Yes, my parents have messed me up *that* badly.

"Want me to take the booth?" Livi asks as she hurries behind me.

"No, I've got it, but can you take these to that couple over there?" I hand her the tray of sandwiches and squeeze Wyatt's arm. He rolls his eyes.

"Really, Delilah? Look at the people she's eyeing. It's not me or Tristan, the two hottest guys in here."

"Tristan's also gay." We've known Tristan Brewer since we were kids, and he's bartended for the Taproom for the last three years. He moved in with us a few weeks ago, after breaking up with his boyfriend, Ian.

Wyatt nods across the bar to six-foot-two, dark-haired, hard-bodied Tristan. "So, you're saying he *looks* gay?"

"No! You know I don't think that, but…"

"She's checking out Livi's ass. She's scanned every woman in here, including you, but she's not looking at the guys in the same way. I could be way off base, but even though I'm taken and would never cheat on Cass, a guy knows when he's being checked out, and *that* woman is not checking me out." He pulls out of my grip and whispers, "Maybe you need me to be your wingman."

I smack him. "*Ugh*. No, I do not. Go talk accounting."

The few feet I have to walk to get to Janessa's booth feel like a mile. My stomach is knotting up, and ever since she offered to…help me learn, I keep picturing her without any clothes on. I must be crazy. She's wearing skinny jeans and a tank top, but I swear she's sitting there in lacy underwear and no top at all. I feel my cheeks flush as I reach her table.

"Hi."

She smiles up at me. "Hey there. You know, I've been in here a million times, but today it feels different."

Oh God. Maybe I'm in over my head.

"Knowing you and Wyatt own this place makes it more comfortable."

Whew. I let out a breath I didn't realize I was holding. I thought she was *really* coming on to me, and that would have made things even more uncomfortable.

She wrinkles her brow. "Are you okay? You look nervous."

"Yes. Fine." I hold up the order pad. "Do you want something to eat?"

She looks me up and down, and her eyes fill with concern like they did last night. "You didn't think…Oh gosh, Delilah, I'm sorry. I didn't mean it like a come-on. Seriously, I really like you, but I'm not here to hit on you. I just thought since we were becoming friends, it would be fun to come over."

I move closer to the booth and rest my hand on the table for stability. I feel like everyone in the place is looking at us. *Thanks, Mom and Dad.* They've drilled how wrong it is to be a lesbian into my head so deep that I can't even act normal.

"It's fine. It's me." I lean down closer to her and angle my body so my back is toward the bar, blocking us from the rest of the customers. "I'm a little like a deer in headlights with all this stuff. I feel like I misinterpret everything." I'm not sure why I reveal this to her so easily, but I can't seem to stop. And I'm not sure I want to. Every time I uncover a hidden fear, I breathe a little easier.

"Did you give any thought to my offer?" she asks with a straight face and a smile, as if she's asking me if I liked the sandwich I had for lunch.

Part of me wants to turn to liquid and slip through the floorboards, but another part of me, the part I've been burying deep inside for years, wants me to grab hold of this brass ring and cling so tight that it forces my parents' disapproving eyes from my memory.

My response sounds far more confident than I feel. "I haven't thought of anything but your offer and Ashley since last night. I was with Ash this morning, and it's so hard not to tell her how I feel, but…I don't even know…you know. If I like *being with* girls." I'm whispering, but I can't squelch the urge to turn and make sure no one heard me.

Tristan raises his chin in my direction and smiles as he wipes down the bar.

I feel exposed and slide into the booth across from Janessa. She puts her foot on the floor, resting it against mine, causing those knots in my stomach to tighten even more.

"I'm thinking about it, but what will it do to our friendship? I mean, I really like being able to talk to you about this stuff. What if it makes it weird?"

"Then we'll talk about it. We're both adults, and Delilah, it's sex—it's not like we're robbing a bank."

It's sex. She says it like it's not that big of a deal, and for most twenty-two-year-olds, it isn't a big deal. But it still feels like there's a billboard strapped to my back that reads *I'm about to have my first sexual experience with a girl!* I hate that it feels so all-consuming. I tell myself it's not a big deal. *We're not robbing a bank.*

Why was it so much easier to give my body over to a guy than to do this?

My thoughts turn to Ashley and how much I wanted to kiss her this morning. I'll lose my mind if I have to go any longer pretending that I don't have feelings for Ashley, and being with Janessa will give me the answers—and the experience—I need to know if I'm doing the right thing.

I look across the booth at Janessa, and nothing about this situation makes sense in the conventional way. It's the weirdest offer I've ever received and definitely the strangest one I've ever considered, but for whatever reason, I feel like this is also the most important decision of my life. I trust Janessa. Something in the way she's looking at me, like she wants to help me, not like she wants to devour me, makes me feel comfortable, and I've *never* been comfortable with my sexuality. That means something, doesn't it?

I *want* to do this. I don't want to make a fool of myself with her or Ashley, but if it is a choice, I pick making a fool of myself with Janessa. Because if I totally screw up, or don't end up liking making out with a girl, then I'll definitely want to run away afterward. And I could never run away from Ashley.

The sooner it's done the better.

Assuming I enjoy the sexual side of things, this will give me enough confidence to talk with Ashley about how I feel, and on the off chance Ash is into me, then I won't be fumbling through the rest. Or maybe I will, but at least it won't be like it's my first time.

Thinking it through is making my stomach feel like the inside of a whirring blender.

Before I can chicken out, I blurt out, "I want to do this."

"Okay." She smiles.

"Okay." *Oh my God!*

Janessa shrugs. "Jackie's staying with Dean again tonight. I guess she couldn't get enough of their fort last night."

Tonight? "Okay." Not one single part of me believes I'm going to go through with this, but the affirmations keep coming—*This will help. I'll finally know for sure*—and Janessa is looking at me with such compassion that I start to believe I just might follow through.

She scribbles down her address on my order pad as I rise from the seat. When I reach for it, she covers my hand with hers.

"No pressure, okay? If you decide you don't want to do this, just call and let me know. And if you do…" She smiles, and her eyes go dark. "Then I promise we'll have a nice night together and you won't be disappointed."

CHAPTER THREE

Delilah

AT NINE O'CLOCK I'm standing on Janessa's front porch with my heart jackhammering in my chest and my phone fisted in my hand. I have no idea how I made it up the front walk, but now that I'm standing on her porch, I'm stiff as a statue. Petrified. I couldn't knock if I wanted to. That would take moving my hand, and my hand is not going anywhere. I still can't believe I'm standing here beneath her porch light. I'm doing this. I'm about to give up my lesbian virginity. Is that even a thing?

I look down at my outfit one last time. I wore a sundress and my favorite pair of black lace-up boots. My mom bought me these boots about three years ago, and they're my go-to comfort shoes, even in the summer. I wear them with every-thing from shorts to dresses, and I *usually* feel confident in them. I'm still waiting for the confidence to kick in. I've already nearly chickened out three times.

I inhale a lungful of cool air and look at Janessa's one-story home.

This is where it's going to happen.

So much better than the backseat of a car. Inside I laugh a

little at the thought, but my nerves swallow that laugh before it has time to come out.

Oh God! Am I really doing this?

Her house is cute, with blue siding and white trim. It looks cozy and comfortable, unlike our houses, which are both way too big. I prefer smaller places, like Ashley's apartment. My nerves go a little crazy when I think of Ashley. For some reason I feel like I'm cheating on her, which is totally nuts. She probably doesn't even like girls.

She did give me *that* look.

Wishful thinking, Dee.

She *was* checking out Wyatt the first day we met, although she did say that was because she was an artist and interested in the human body. What if she isn't into girls? Do I still want to do this?

I turn and look at my Jeep, nibbling on my lower lip as I debate making a run for it—*but I really want to do this!*

My phone vibrates and I turn it over. *Janessa.* Goose bumps form on my arms, and with a shaky finger I open the message.

Should I open the door or are you considering bolting?

Gulp. I lift my eyes to the door. Janessa waves from behind the glass. Instead of opening the door, she shrugs, smiles. I text her back, too nervous to open my mouth.

Open it fast and I'll stay.

She pushes the door open. All the air rushes out of my lungs as she reaches for my hand and I take the first step inside. The door clicks softly closed behind me.

There's no turning back.

"Hi." She leans in and kisses my cheek. She smells freshly clean, like spring, and as her eyes roll down my body, my mouth goes dry. "You look incredible."

"So…" I clear my throat, wondering if I'll be able to speak at all tonight. "So do you." She's clearly not wearing a bra beneath her dark tank top, and I can't seem to drag my eyes from her taut nipples poking against the material. I finally force my eyes to drop, but they hang on her supershort miniskirt.

I can't believe this is really happening.

I can't believe I'm here.

I tell myself it's like a booty call and to just relax. People do this all the time. But I've never been a booty call. I've never had a booty call. Relaxation went out the door with her bra and the rest of her skirt. I'm a nervous wreck.

She presses her hand to my lower back and leads me into the living room. I can't believe my legs are working. They feel like Jell-O. I look around, in need of a distraction from rattling nerves. The room looks lived-in and comfy, with children's magazines on the coffee table and a miniature recliner, which must be for Jackie. The couch is dark brown, and the room is decorated in warm earth tones. There's a small fireplace across from the couch, with several pictures of her daughter on the mantel.

"You can sit down if you'd like." She walks into the adjoining kitchen, and the space she vacated feels cold. I want her back. Somehow I felt safer with her close, which is weird given what we're about to do.

What we're about to do.

Oh my God.

Janessa holds up a bottle of wine. "Wine okay?"

"Um, sure." *Lots of it, please.* I distract myself with the photos and force myself to speak so she doesn't back out, because I'm a silent, nervous wreck that she doesn't want to help after all. "Jackie's adorable. Are you still in touch with her father?"

Janessa carries two wineglasses into the living room and hands me one. I take a big drink to calm my nerves. She stands close as we stare at the pictures, me trying to talk myself off the ledge and her probably regretting her offer. I inhale deeply, and the scent of CK One fills my senses. I know it well, since I used to wear it. Ashley wears Obsession by Calvin Klein. *I guess I'm a Calvin girl.* The thought that I'm an *anything* girl makes me smile.

Janessa's arm brushes mine, and the room gets ten degrees hotter.

"Jackie's dad, well…Do you want the truth or what I tell everyone else?"

She doesn't sound nervous at all, and when I steal a glance at her, I realize she doesn't look like she regrets her offer either. Her easy smile reaches her eyes, and it makes me feel a little better.

"I guess whatever you feel comfortable telling me."

She takes my hand and we sit on the couch facing each other. Her touch makes my nerves go wild again. She puts down her wineglass and I cling to mine like a shield.

"I'm bisexual, Delilah, and there's a guy in my life that I've had an on-again off-again thing with for years. We're really close friends and we make great lovers, but we aren't made to be in a monogamous relationship with each other."

I nod as if I understand, but I really don't. She had his *child.* "Why not?"

She sits back and places her hand on my thigh, like she's touched me a hundred times before. Like it's natural, normal, and easy. I hold my breath, desperately wanting it to feel normal and easy instead of new and exciting and scary at once.

"Because I like women," she explains. "Being with a guy

isn't enough for me. I enjoy it, and I enjoy him. But it's different being with a guy than a girl, and I'm not ready to give up being with women."

She slides her hand up my thigh as she sits up again and leans in close.

I'm doing this. Here it comes.

Her fingertips slip beneath the edge of my dress, and her soft hand feels so different from Frank's calloused palm and rough fingers. I immediately understand what she meant. Her touch is gentle, not hurried or forceful. My body inclines toward her despite my nerves.

I lean back again, feeling disjointed, too nervous, and swallow hard to distract myself from how good her hand feels and the thundering of my heart.

"Does Jackie know he's her father?" I say this to distract myself, but my voice is shaky, like the rest of my body.

I finish my wine in one gulp, and she takes the glass from my hand and sets it on the coffee table. I can feel myself trembling. I hope she doesn't notice, but how can she not? She's so close I feel her breath on my skin. She's even prettier up close, and as she gazes into my eyes and brushes my hair from my shoulder, it reminds me of when Ashley did it earlier that morning. It's a good reminder that I'm doing this for Ashley. Not that I don't want to feel Janessa's full lips on mine. I do. God, I really, really do. But I'd be lying if I didn't acknowledge that I wish it were Ashley opening herself up to me right now, despite how nervous I am.

"Jackie knows him, and she knows he's her daddy," she says just above a whisper. "You're shaking. Do you still want to do this?"

I've never been this nervous before, but I'm glad I didn't

chicken out.

My answer comes as softly as her question. "Yes."

She smiles again. "Is it okay if I kiss you?"

Now? She holds my gaze, taking control.

I nod, and she touches her left hand to the nape of my neck, drawing me closer. When our lips touch, the first thing I notice is how soft hers are. She's patient, kissing me carefully. Her cheeks touch mine, soft and pliable, not at all like a guy's rough, stubbly skin. This is so much better. Her tongue slips between my lips and strokes over mine with the same unhurried tenderness. Her fingers tighten around the back of my neck as she deepens the kiss, and I feel myself letting go, relaxing into the kiss, into the taste of her, into finally—*God, finally*—doing what feels natural.

When our lips part, I lean forward, trying to reconnect.

"Okay?" Like her tone, her eyes are soft and warm.

"Oh my God, yes." Years of curiosity and repressed desire surge forward. I wrap my arms around her neck and run my fingers through her hair as our lips come together again.

Hungrier.

Harder.

And suddenly I'm not trembling anymore. I'm not thinking, barely breathing. Letting my body take over and do what feels good. What feels right. And it's so much better than when I was lying beneath a guy with his hand pressing too hard, his cheeks scratching mine.

My hand plays over the gentle curve of her shoulder, and I have the urge to kiss it, taste her smooth skin. I draw back, and we're both breathing heavily, but not panting roughly like guys do. It's softer, hotter, sexier than anything I've ever experienced.

"It's okay, Delilah. You can touch me."

I can't respond, I'm too focused on how good this feels. Being with her, finally being touched by a woman. I press my lips to her shoulder. Her skin is warm and soft. I open my lips and stroke her with my tongue. Her skin has a taste all its own. It's tangy, not salty like Frank's. I wonder what Ashley's skin tastes like. Janessa's fingers slide beneath my hair, and she cups the back of my head, holding me to her. My body vibrates with anticipation. Her touch is encouraging, not pressuring or hurried. I bring my mouth to the curve of her neck, the dip beneath her ear. She makes a mewing sound, and I know she likes it, so I do it again, feeling empowered, gaining confidence by the second. I trail kisses along her jaw and tease her lips with my own. She moans against my mouth, *and God*, I never knew a sound could turn me on so much.

I seal my lips over hers and bring my shaky hand to her breast, feeling her taut nipple against my palm, and I feel myself go damp. I've wondered what this would be like for so long that I'm still in a state of disbelief, a little detached, like I'm watching it happening. And I don't want to stop. I want to see what else makes her breathing hitch, but it's one thing to touch her above her clothing, above the waist, and a whole other thing to venture below.

As if she read my mind, she pulls back. Eyes steady on mine, she takes off her tank top and shakes her head. Her hair tumbles over her breasts. Any ability to restrain myself disappears with the sight of her tousled hair and bare breasts. Her nipples are pink and upturned, her breasts are full and so beautiful it's impossible for me to look away. I lick my lips, wondering how she tastes, if she'll mind if I use my mouth instead of my hands. She takes my hand and brings it to her breast again. I have a fleeting thought about how I'm not sure what to do, but my hand seems to know as it explores her body. She slides her hand beneath my dress and rubs my hip as I give in to my desires and bring my mouth to her breast. Her nipple is sweet and tightens as I tease her with my tongue, palming her other breast as she strokes me through my underwear.

Holy hell this feels good.

Wayyyy too good.

My body is on fire. There's no way in hell this is wrong.

I push the thought away, unable to get enough of her and unwilling to go down a guilty path. I don't know what I want more, to lean back and be touched or to take my fill. Our mouths crash together, and there's no choice to be made. She leans in to me, and we paw, grope, taste with wild abandon. Her fingers push beneath my underwear and slide inside me. I moan into her mouth as my hips rock, begging for more. She moves in and out of me in the same urgent rhythm as our tongues mash together. She does something that feels so good that my head falls back, and I have to bite my lip to keep from crying out. She sucks on my neck as her talented fingers work their magic, and in seconds I feel pressure mounting inside me. My insides are reaching for her. My legs tingle and my hips fly off the couch as my eyes slam shut. Lights explode behind my closed lids, and she keeps probing, stroking, keeps open-mouthed kissing my neck, as my body bucks and my inner muscles squeeze her fingers over and over again. Her fingers remain inside me until the last pulse of my climax shudders through me, and as I open my eyes, she kisses me softly.

Even in my fantasies I never thought something could feel this good. The student in me awakens, and my focus turns.

"I want to do that to you." The words escape before I can stop them, but I do want to learn to do that. I want to learn how to make Ashley feel that good. Hell, I want to feel that good again. Guys have nothing on Janessa. I wonder if all women other than me know how to do that.

She smiles. "I was hoping you would."

"God, Janessa. How'd you learn to do that?"

"Practice."

She wraps her arms around my neck and leans back against the arm of the couch, bringing me down on top of her. I kick off my boots and settle my body between her legs. We're hip to hip, and again I notice the difference between Frank's hard muscles and the soft pillows of Janessa's breasts, the feel of her tender hands on my arms. The lack of a hard rod between us, pressing into my stomach. There's only soft femininity. I kiss her lips and let my mouth travel south, paving the way for my hands, lingering, exploring her breasts again with shaky hands. I'm nervous, but it's different this time. I'm in student mode, and somehow that makes it a little easier. I'm even more detached, taking mental notes of what makes her hips meet mine, what earns me a moan or a gasp.

"That feels so good." She holds the back of my head, keeping my mouth over her breast as I lap her nipple, then take her breast into my mouth again.

I kiss a path down the flat plane of her stomach. It's nice not to have to battle with a man's chest hair. I never thought about how many things I didn't like about being with guys, but it's all coming to the forefront. From their heady scent to the roughness of their skin. I can't help but wonder what Ashley's naked body would feel like. I play her image over and over in my mind as I explore Janessa's stomach, her ribs, her hips. When I get to her miniskirt, I lick above the waist of the material, which is right above her pubic bone, and then I lean back a little, pressing my hands to her thighs, and I stop.

I don't know how to do this.

I'm going to do it wrong.

"It's okay," she whispers. "Don't feel pressure, Delilah. You don't have to do anything."

"No. I want to. I just…" *Don't know how.*

She sits up and presses her hands to my cheeks, then kisses me softly. "You can't do it wrong. Just do what you want Ashley to do to you."

A dreamy sigh escapes before I can stop it. Hearing Ashley's name linked to something so sexual makes butterflies take flight in my stomach. I want to be with her so badly I ache.

I'm so thankful Janessa understands. We don't say anything more. She eases onto her back and closes her eyes, which makes it much less stressful for me. I lower my lips to her belly and allow my hands to feel the softness of her thighs, the heat between her legs. I use both hands to lower her thong. She smiles as we maneuver around each other to get it completely off, and then she eases back down. She's so patient, which makes me a little less embarrassed. Everyone should have someone like Janessa to walk them through their first time.

I close my eyes as I explore her body and think, *Do what I want Ashley to do to me.* My hands splay wide across the tops of her thighs. I slide them up until my thumbs touch, feeling the heat of her sex. I brush over her wetness, marveling in the slick, warm feel of her skin. I move my thumbs up, nimbly find her clit, and caress it gently, stroking her with my other hand. When my fingers sink inside her wetness, she breathes harder.

I hardly breathe at all.

Her eyes are closed and her head is tilted back, lips slightly parted. I'm still unsure about my skills, but when her hips rise off the couch and she grips the cushions in fisted hands, I guess I'm doing something right. My head is in a strange place, learning, watching, wanting to take her to the mind-numbing place she took me.

I try to find the spot inside her that will make her lose control, and I feel like I'm fumbling and losing confidence. She's writhing like she likes it, but I know I'm not getting her there. She's not lost in sensation like I was, and I desperately want to learn this. Somehow I know this will be my only *lesson*.

I can do this. I have to do this. I have to ask. I gather all the courage I can possibly hold on to in the three seconds I give myself and plead, "Show me."

Her hands unfurl. "Yes," she says in one long whisper.

"I'm sorry." I draw away, embarrassed to have asked for guidance.

She sits up and kisses me. "Delilah, you're perfect. You're wonderful. If Ashley's into girls, then you're going to make her a very happy woman. This—like anything else in life—is perfected with experience. Every woman's body is different."

I deflate a little. Is she trying to tell me that she can't teach me? I imagine googling *How to Make a Girl Come*, and I shift my eyes away.

She kisses me again, but I'm so focused that I'm anxious and I push her gently away.

"Can you—" *Show me, show me, show me.*

She nods. "When you put your finger inside, put it all the way in, and then do this." She turns her palm up and moves her finger in a *come-hither* way. "As you...*explore*...you'll find a spot that feels different from the rest. Ridged, or rougher. That's the G-spot, but some women don't respond to it, so if you can't find it, don't worry. Chances are it's not something you're doing wrong, and honestly, that's like an added bonus. You can get a woman over the edge by just doing what you were doing, so don't stress over this, okay? Your touch is amazing."

That makes me feel a little more at ease. Even though this explanation should embarrass me, it doesn't. I'm a good student, and I'm going to nail this.

"You have a look of determination in your eyes." She smiles. "It's really cute."

"I'm kind of a competitive student." I always had to be, to meet the grades my parents expected, but I don't tell her this as she relaxes back onto the couch again and brings her own hand between her legs.

Holy crap, that's so hot.

"Touch me," she whispers.

I stroke her around her finger, then press mine into her all the way and crook my finger. Just as I feel the spot I think is right, she moans. My heart skips a beat, knowing I accomplished this. Watching her face flush and her teeth trap her lower lip as I repeat the move over and over while she strokes her clit and comes apart right there around my fingers is the most exciting thing I've ever seen. She reaches for me and I think she wants to kiss me, so I move quickly up to meet her lips, my fingers still buried deep inside her. She tucks her forehead against my neck, thrusts her hand into my underwear, and takes me up, up, up, and we spiral over the edge together.

Questions. Answered.

I don't know how long we lie together on the couch, but sometime later we bring the wineglasses into the kitchen and I carry my phone and boots to the door, knowing I look as freshly fucked as she does, and not caring. Her hair is awry and her lips have that kissed-too-hard look. I'm no longer embarrassed, and

I don't feel funny standing with Janessa at her front door. It's hard to imagine that a few hours ago I was standing on the other side of the door debating leaving. Thank God I didn't.

I feel so much freer than I have ever felt and so much gratitude toward her. It's a little overwhelming. My body is still humming from her touch and from the confidence she's given me. From knowing, once and for all, that I'm *definitely* into girls.

"Thank you, Janessa. I don't know how long I would have gone before ever..."

She cups the back of my head and presses her lips to mine. "You're amazing. Just be careful, you know. Be smart. Respect your body."

I nod.

"Are you okay? Are *we* okay?" Her eyes get serious.

I nod faster than I mean to. "I don't feel weird. Oh gosh, do you?"

"No. No, Delilah, I don't. But I've been with lots of women."

"I'm fine, really. I'm so thankful. And you're so beautiful, and so nice, and I just hope that when we see each other again we won't feel funny." I bite my lip. "And I'm rambling and nervous and excited, and...I'll shut up now."

She laughs. "I think we were pretty straight up with each other. I'm not looking for a girlfriend, and hopefully now you'll feel confident enough to go after the one girl you really want."

"*If* she's into girls." I roll my eyes like it's no big deal, but I hope and pray Ashley is not just into girls, but into *me*.

"You won't know unless you try, and life's too short not to go after what you want."

After we hug goodbye I head to my Jeep. The air feels lighter and my head feels clearer than it ever has. I start up the Jeep, and as much as I want to drive straight over to Ashley's and share this feeling with her, I don't. It doesn't feel right to be with her after being with Janessa. I drive home with the windows down and the cool night air blowing through my hair. It isn't until I reach my house that guilt sneaks in, stealing the excitement of my newfound pleasure like a thief.

CHAPTER FOUR

Ashley

ENDLESS SUMMER SURF Shop is located a block away from the boardwalk. It's painted bright yellow with a huge sign out front featuring a surfer riding a wave. Every morning we line up a display of surfboards out front and wheel one of the sale racks out to the sidewalk. We have a bike rack out front for customers to chain up their bikes while they shop. Between the brightly colored surfboards and the yellow building, our shop is easy to spot, even from a distance. One of the coolest things about working here is that when we aren't busy, Brent Steele, the owner and an amazing surfer, lets me set up a chair and paint in front of the store. Some days I just leave my easel there and go outside for a few minutes here or there.

I'm sitting out front of the shop now, thinking about Delilah. Ever since we began meeting on the dunes, I wake before the alarm, and on the mornings we don't meet, like this morning, the day is not nearly as bright.

I leaf through my sketch pad, trying to find the picture of Delilah I started yesterday morning. At least I'll see her tonight. Cassidy and Brooke planned a birthday party for my friend Brandon Owens. He's the one who introduced me to Delilah at the beginning of the summer.

Brandon and I went to college together. We met the first week of our freshman year, and we clicked right away. He's a tough nut, all attitude and hard edges, but there's a softer side to Brandon that I don't think many people get to see. I don't know why he let me into his inner circle, but I'm glad he did. I would never have come to Harborside or met Delilah if it weren't for him. Brandon's from Harborside, and after I had a really bad breakup, Brandon suggested that I move to Harborside instead of going home to Rhode Island. I love my family, but nothing beats living at the beach. I've been living in an apartment down the road for almost a year and have fallen in love with everything about the town and all the friends I've made.

Brandon's sort of living at Delilah's now. He crashes there almost every night. All of Brandon's friends, many of whom are also Delilah's friends, accepted me into their group pretty easily. And now that Delilah and Wyatt decided to sell their house in Connecticut and stay in Harborside, I like it here even more.

I find the sketch I was working on and begin refining the arch of Delilah's slim eyebrows. Her hair is blonder than mine and silkier. Mine's dirty blond and longer than Delilah's. Sometimes the urge to run my fingers through her hair is so strong that I have to shove my hands in my pockets, or if we're on the dunes, I have to put them beneath my thighs. And when we're at my place? That's the most difficult, because while we're watching movies or sitting on the balcony overlooking the ocean, all I can think about is taking her into my bedroom. It's really bad. If I knew she was a lesbian, I'd feel better, because I'd just do all those things I want to do. Not knowing is killing me.

Ugh. I hate this feeling.

I gaze at the sketch and move from her delicate eyebrows to the shading around her expressive eyes—the eyes that I nearly fell into yesterday morning. I tell myself the same thing I've been telling myself all summer. *The next time she looks at me like that, I'm just going to kiss her.*

Give up my fear of her being straight and just do it.

I look up at the sound of a motorcycle and see Brent's twin brother, Jesse, parking in front of the shop. He's good friends with Delilah, too, and very protective of her. I imagine myself kissing her and Delilah pushing away, her green eyes wide and appalled. And then I imagine Jesse's thick dark brows lowering into an angry slash.

Okay, so I won't kiss her.

It was a stupid idea anyway. You don't just kiss a girl, especially if you aren't sure if she's straight or not. Been there, done that. It's an embarrassing situation that there's no easy way out of, like asking a woman if she's pregnant when she's not.

"Hey, Ash. Is my brother around?" Jesse's tall and broad with shoulder-length dark hair, several tattoos, and a well-manicured beard and mustache. Although he and Brent are twins, Jesse's face is harder, his expressions more serious than Brent's. Jesse also always wears jeans and boots, which I don't understand given that he lives at the beach. But then again, I don't understand the leather band he wears around his thick wrist or the chain that hooks to his wallet, either.

"He was in the back when I came outside." I notice a guy heading for the shop and tuck my sketch pad and pencil into my backpack. "I'll go in with you."

"Are you going to Brandon's party tonight?" I ask as he pulls the door open.

Jesse's dark eyes run over the racks of clothing and surfboards lined up against the far wall and finally land on his equally tall and long-haired brother helping a customer in the back of the shop.

"I wouldn't miss it. You?" He's watching Brent intently as he asks.

"Absolutely. See you there."

He's already on the move toward his brother.

The guy I noticed outside comes into the shop talking on his cell phone. He's tall, with sun-streaked blond hair, lean and muscular, and walks with a definite surfer swagger. He shoves his phone in the pocket of his board shorts, and I do my job.

"Hi. Is there anything I can help you find?"

"Nah, just checking out the longboards and some clothes." His eyes take a slow roll over me, and then he turns toward the boards.

It never really bothers me when guys check me out. I think it's the whole long blond hair and fit body thing they're attracted to. Guys are so cursory. It's like they have a mental checklist that can be marked off in three seconds: *A face that doesn't require too many beers to look good, boobs, nice ass.* Whereas with girls, at least with me, when I check a girl out, it goes much deeper than looks. The first thing I notice is a girl's eyes. Are they cold and wary or intense and seductive? I like them to be somewhere in the middle. Wary enough to be careful, but sexy in the right moments.

Like Delilah's.

Gaaaahhhhh! Stop!

I've never been interested in guys. Never even kissed a guy. I do like to look, though, from an artistic perspective. Sometimes that gets me in trouble and guys think I'm checking them out, so I've learned to be discreet about it. I can't help it if I find the human body fascinating. I'm an artist. It feels natural to notice sleek curves and taut muscles. It's not like I'm Brandon or anything. He practically undresses guys and girls in a single glance and would sleep with either or both at the same time. I've never felt a need to flaunt my sexuality. I don't even like to talk about it, but after dating Sandy Andraka for a few months, I realized that I also don't want to be someone's dirty little secret. Sandy acknowledged me only as a friend in public, because she wasn't *out* yet. Because I was sensitive to her feelings, I overlooked all the telltale clues of a liar. We saw each other only on weekdays, at my place, and never after ten at night. It was only after we broke up that I found out she was living with a guy and our relationship was nothing more than a fun distraction for her.

"Excuse me." Blond surfer guy waves in my direction.

I push thoughts of Sandy away and go to help him.

"Hi. What can I help you with?"

He holds up a shirt. "Do you have this in XL?"

"I'll check." I go in the back room and retrieve his size, and when I bring it to him, he's on the phone again, having a heated discussion as he watches me approach.

I hand him the shirt and he holds up a finger, asking me to wait.

He covers the mouthpiece and asks, "Isn't it easier for girls to surf than guys?"

"Um…" I notice Brent and Jesse come out of the back room.

He raises his brows.

"You're asking the wrong person. I don't surf." I hate admitting that to customers, but it's true. Brent hired me because I'm organized, a hard worker, and really good with people. He said it would be good if I learned to surf, and I had planned to learn when I first moved here, but then I got busy. "Ask him." I point to Brent.

"Dude, I'll call you back." The guy ends his call and leans on the clothing rack, like he has all the time in the world. "How can you work in a surf shop and not surf?"

"I know the mechanics of it. I've read up on it. I've just never taken the time to learn."

"Do you *like* working here?" he asks.

I can't tell if he's asking because he's interested or trying to figure me out. He's looking at me so intently that I think it's the latter. "Yeah. I like working with customers, and I'm not one of those people who could sit behind a desk all day, so for now, yeah, I like it." I'm hyperaware of Brent and Jesse just a few feet away, and although Brent knows that one day I hope to make a living with my art, I'm careful not to reference it.

"Drake!" Brent and Jesse join us. Brent high-fives Drake. "I see you met my best employee, Ashley."

I laugh. I should have known Brent would know him. He's one of the best surfers around. I'd bet he knows every surfer in Harborside.

"Ashley." Drake holds out a hand. "Nice to formally meet you."

Jesse pats Brent on the back. "See you at the party. I've gotta run." He waves to me. "See you tonight, Ash."

"Party?" Drake asks.

"Yeah, for Brandon's birthday," Brent explains. He and Brandon play in a band together all over town.

"Cool. Is it an open party, or do I need to know someone besides you and Brandon to get in?" Drake asks as we walk toward the cash register.

Brent turns to me. "Think Wyatt and Delilah will mind?"

"How should I know? But based on their past parties, probably not." Parties at Wyatt and Delilah's house are always crowded with Brandon's friends.

"You know Brandon never misses a chance to play. Our band is playing tonight, so I can't really introduce you to Wyatt and Delilah." Brent joins me behind the counter and pats me on the back. "But Ashley…"

I roll my eyes. "I'll introduce him around, sure."

By the time I've rung him up, I learn that Drake likes working with his hands, doing metal and construction type work, and grew up in Harborside.

"In exchange for introducing me tonight, I'll show you how to surf," Drake offers. "You really should learn. Don't you think, Brent?"

"Absolutely. Ash, take him up on the offer. He's the best surf instructor around." Brent hands Drake his purchases.

"You're a surf instructor?"

Drake nods. "Yup. Leave it to me. I'll have you up on the board and comfortable within a week. You'll love it—you'll see. What's your schedule? Can you make dawn patrol tomorrow?"

Dawn patrol is when surfers catch early-morning waves. That's usually when I sketch with Delilah, but we haven't planned anything for the next few days, and honestly, maybe the distraction would be a good thing. It's getting progressively harder to resist Delilah when we spend mornings together, and until she and I fall into a conversation that naturally transitions into talking about guys or girls, I'm keeping my lips sealed. She's got so much going on, and she never talks about hooking up with anyone. I know it's the last thing on her mind.

"Sure, but just so you know, I might suck."

"Or you might be awesome," Drake says.

We exchange numbers, and after Drake leaves, Brent convinces me that Drake is the greatest surf instructor around and a trustworthy guy, which is good, considering we plan to meet here after work and go to the party together. He'll be a welcome distraction, much easier to handle than drooling over Delilah—or worse, accidentally on purpose kissing her.

CHAPTER FIVE

Delilah

WHEN THE SUN goes down the temperature always drops, but tonight it's cooler than normal—even so, I'm hot. *Hot, hot, hot.* I've been hot since I left Janessa's last night. I'm all nervous energy and anxious anticipation. I hear Brandon's band playing on the back deck, and I'm upstairs, pacing in my bedroom, waiting for Ashley to get here. I'm too nervous to wait outside, because now that I know I'll *like* kissing her, I can't stop thinking about the possibility.

I'm probably going to wear a path in the hardwood. I've been pacing for more than half an hour. My bedroom is spacious, so there's a lot of room to pace. I love this bedroom, with the double bed and the futon over by the doors to the deck. I'm glad I moved back in. Nothing compares to living right on the beach, and it's easier to be here now than it was those first few nights when we arrived after my parents died. Back then I felt like their ghosts were everywhere. Maybe it's because time has passed since they died, or maybe it's because I spent several weeks living at Brooke's and the memories had time to skitter away before I moved back. I don't know, but it feels good to be back, and every day it feels more like home.

I walk out the glass doors to the deck and look down at the people dancing and laughing on the beach. There are lots of people dancing on the deck while Brandon's band plays. We live at the end of a private road, and the closest house is about half a block up the road. The beach is private as well, so we don't have to worry about party crashers or bothering neighbors.

Cassidy is taking pictures of the party—she's always taking pictures. She's been working with Brooke all summer at Brooke's Bytes, and they just started a party-planning business. In addition to helping with the business side, Cassidy is the photographer for their events. I watch as Wyatt comes up behind her, wraps his arms around her waist, and nuzzles against her neck. She puts the lens cap on her camera, and her long brown hair swings as she turns in his arms and presses her lips to his. I long for that. The ease of being in a real relationship with someone I care about. Being able to hold and kiss and nuzzle without the guilt of who I want to do those things with.

I want that with Ashley.

Brandon's band starts another song and, thankfully, it nearly drowns out the guilt raging in my head. People begin to *whoop* at the song choice. I don't know most of the people who are here, but this is Brandon's birthday party, and because his band plays all over Harborside, he knows tons of people.

As I descend the steps to the side yard, I see Janessa come around the corner of the house from the front. I invited her, but she'd said she couldn't come because she was picking up Jackie from Dean's. She's scanning the crowd, and I know she's looking for me. I hurry down the steps and weave through the crowd, expecting to feel strange around her, or at least embarrassed, but when I spot her in front of a guy and make my way around him, I don't feel either of those things.

She turns, and when our eyes meet, she smiles and throws her arms around me. "Hi."

Her perfume brings back memories of last night. I'm not sure what it says about me that while the memory floods me with good, sexy feelings, I also feel detached from it. Janessa was right. It was *just* sex. It didn't create the type of feelings toward her that I have toward Ashley, but I also don't feel ashamed of what we did. I don't feel like a slut. I think I've compartmentalized our night as a learning experience, just as it was intended to be. Memories of my parents make me feel ashamed enough, for my thoughts, my desires. *Ugh.* For the life I want and am afraid to have.

"Hi. I'm glad you made it." She looks great in a pair of jeans, a cami, and an open sweater.

"I only came by to see how you were. I can't stay." Her eyes roll over my face, looking for an answer.

"I'm good."

"Delilah!"

I spot Ashley waving from behind a group of girls. I wave and she turns and grabs some guy's arm and leads him over. I look at Janessa, who must read my mind—or maybe the floored look I'm sure is on my face gives away my disappointment.

Janessa touches my arm, and as Ashley approaches, she leans in close and says, "Don't jump to conclusions. They're probably just friends."

"Hi." Ashley smiles, still holding that tall, good-looking, towheaded guy's arm like he's hers. "This is Drake."

"Hi, I'm Delilah." I force a smile, but my stomach is tying itself into a knot.

Drake says hello, and the feel of Janessa's hand on my arm

brings me out of my jealous head and back to the moment.

"Oh, and this is Janessa," I say loud enough to be heard over the band.

"Hi, Ashley. I've heard a lot about you." Janessa waves to the guy. "Nice to meet you." She turns her attention to me and lowers her voice. "I have to go, but I wanted to make sure you were okay. I had a good time last night." She kisses my cheek and whispers loudly, "Good luck."

Janessa waves to the others as she leaves.

My earlier hopes of telling Ashley how I feel are dashed, and for a minute we just stand there staring at each other. I've got to do something. Say something. But I'm pretty sure, *Is he yours? Are you straight? Can I change your mind?* isn't the way to go.

"Drinks are in the kitchen." *I'm so lame.*

"Great." Drake looks at Ashley. "Want me to bring you one?"

"Sure. Wine, if there is any."

"You got it." He lifts his chin in my direction. "Want anything, Delilah?"

Only Ashley. "Uh, sure. Whatever Ash is having."

He heads for the kitchen as the band starts up another song, and Ashley watches him walk away. I wish I could disappear into the night like the music.

"So, you were with Janessa last night?" Ashley steps in close and practically yells for me to hear her.

"Yeah. How do you know Drake?" I can't help but ask. I've never seen the guy before and suddenly she's holding his arm? *I guess I can assume you're not into girls.*

Her smile fades. "I...um...I met him at the shop. He's going to teach me to surf."

"He's...Oh." Maybe Ashley doesn't remember, but the day

after we met, I offered to teach her how to surf. She was nervous about the whole process and told me that maybe she'd take me up on it one day. Uh-oh. Maybe she *does* remember and this is her way of drawing a line between us because she noticed the way I must have been looking at her yesterday morning when I wanted to kiss her.

I feel my shoulders drop and pry for more information.

"How are you going to do that with your schedule at the surf shop?"

"I'll hit dawn patrol with him when I can, and sometimes I'll go in the evenings when the tide is in. Brent is all for it. He's excited that I'm willing to finally learn how to do it." She takes my hand and leads me off to the side of the house, farther away from the music.

She's held my hand dozens of times, but this time I'm aware of how our hands fit so well together, how good it feels to have our fingers interlaced, and I want that hand on my body. She stops walking and I nearly plow right into her. We're standing so close I wonder if she can feel the space between us heating up like I do. She looks into my eyes and my head is so confused about seeing her with Drake and knowing she's blowing me off to be with him that I want to look away. But I can't. I'm drawn to her even though my heart is aching.

"You don't mind, do you?" she asks.

Being this close to you? No. I want more of it.

It takes me a minute to realize she's talking about going surfing in the mornings instead of meeting me. I want to tell her, *Damn right I mind.* I want to ask her if she's seeing him, and a hundred more questions, but none of them matter now. She's definitely into Drake.

"No. It's fine. We'll sketch some other time. Sunset or

something."

I see Drake walking toward us and I want to run in the other direction, but my legs won't move. And when Drake holds up two cups, I remember he was getting one for me, so I can't very well walk away without it.

"Here you go, ladies." He hands us each a cup.

"Thanks." I watch Ashley, dissecting the smile she flashes him, which doesn't reach her eyes the way it does when she smiles at me. Their fingers don't brush when she takes the cup, and her eyes shift quickly back to me. I'm being petty, and I'm not proud of it, but I've gone my whole life *not* knowing what it feels like to be close to a woman. I want to be with Ashley so badly my insides ache. *If I can't have Ashley, I'm allowed to be as petty as I want to be.*

I spent the evening preparing to lay my feelings on the line, and now that I know Ashley's into guys, I'm not sure how I'll survive another second, much less the night.

"I'm going to see what needs to be restocked in the kitchen." Before Ashley can say anything, I escape into the crowd, feeling the sting of tears in my eyes. The music is pounding, people are shoulder to shoulder, leaving me to duck my head and plow right through without a bit of finesse or a care of how they're looking at me like I'm the rudest girl around. I don't know what upsets me more. The fact that I'll never be with Ashley or that I'm obviously so messed up that I can't even read people anymore. I thought she might be into me, but now I realize that I'm totally whacked in that department.

"Dee?" Wyatt touches my arm as I speed past.

I look over my shoulder at him and plow directly into a wall of muscle.

"Hey, hon. You okay?"

I feel Tristan's arms circle me and look up into his chiseled, handsome face. I've known Tristan since I was a kid, just like I've known Brandon, Jesse, Brooke, and the rest of our friends here. We've spent summers together forever. He knows everything about me, except my darkest secret, and as his compassionate dark eyes hold my gaze, something inside me cracks. I've lied to him and all my friends about who I am. I've lied to myself, my parents. *My fucking parents.* I can't stop the tears from falling, and I can't move an inch. I lean in to Tristan, soaking up the comfort of his strong arms as he holds me tight.

"Shh. Whatever it is, it's going to be okay."

Tristan just broke up with his boyfriend, Ian, and I know it's unfair for me to unload on him like this, but I can't stop myself. It's like all the excitement from last night—all my efforts at building up my courage to come out to Ashley—crashed head-on into the reality that Ashley's with Drake.

I feel Tristan guiding me across the sand. The music gets farther away and the sound of the ocean grows louder. Wyatt must not have seen that I was crying—thank God—because he'd be right here with us, and that would be too embarrassing.

Tristan lowers himself into the sand and brings me down beside him. I wipe my eyes and try to catch my breath.

"You okay?" He strokes my back soothingly.

"Yes. No. I don't know." I glance over his shoulder and see Jesse and Wyatt both heading toward us. "God," I mutter.

Tristan glances behind us. "Your saviors."

I roll my eyes. "I know I should be thankful that so many people care about me, but some things are too embarrassing to talk about."

"Dee? What's wrong? Did someone do something?" Wyatt sits on my other side and drapes his arm over my shoulder.

I close my eyes, sandwiched safely—and—annoyingly, between Tristan and Wyatt. "No. I'm fine."

Jesse plants his thick legs in the sand like tree trunks and crosses his arms. His eyes shift from me to Tristan and back again.

"Tristan? Anything I need to take care of?" Jesse asks.

"No. No. No. You guys, I'm a big girl. I can handle this." I say this even though I don't feel like a big girl right now. I'm confused, and hurt, and way out of my comfort zone. I should cry on my brother's shoulder and suck up my broken heart without going into any detail. Just let my friendship with Ashley fade away, because seeing her every day will be too hard.

I've never had a broken heart before. I always thought people were overly dramatic when they said their heart hurt. Now I know they weren't being dramatic at all. Mine feels like someone's squeezing it so tight it might pop.

"Can you just tell me why you're crying? Is it Mom and Dad?" Wyatt rubs my shoulder. He's so careful with me, always looking out for me, aware of how recently our parents died.

But this isn't something he can fix. I'm in this alone, and I feel like I did right before walking into my finals. When my head was full of information and my mind was repeating, *I have to pass, I have to pass,* and it was all I could do to remember how to sit down and write my name. My head is full of everything I did with Janessa, of the things I had hoped to tell Ashley, of the image of her holding on to Drake. It's too much. And if I hear about my parents' deaths one more time, I'm going to lose my mind. I've been so afraid of anyone finding out that I'm a lesbian for so many years that I can barely think. My mind is fucking full of suppressed worries and heartache I can't process another thing.

"Yes," I finally yell. "Yes, I *can* tell you." I'm so angry I'm shaking. I push to my feet and look past my brother, past Tristan and Jesse, who I know love me dearly and think I've lost my mind. I scan the crowd for the one and only person I *want* to share my feelings with, no matter how much it hurts. Finally I spot her blond hair. She's standing next to Drake, staring into her drink and running her finger around the rim of her cup. She's not holding on to him. She looks bored.

I've never seen Ashley look bored.

Ever.

Bored with Drake? Even better.

"Dee?" Wyatt's voice brings me back to the moment as he rises beside me and touches my back. "What's going on?"

I don't need to look at him to know his green eyes are full of worry, which makes me feel bad for shutting him out, but not bad enough to keep from doing it.

"I could tell you guys, but you're not who I *need* to tell." I stomp across the thick sand toward the only person I want. The only person I need.

I didn't spend last night exposing myself to Janessa and all day today building up my courage just to sit down and cry about it. Ashley sees me as I push my way through the crowd. I'm sure I have a scowl on my face, and if smoke could come from my ears, it surely would. My entire body is corded so tight it feels like it's going to explode as I reach for her hand and pull her behind me through the crowd. She stumbles to keep up as I break free from the throng of partygoers and head around the far side of the house. Away from the band. Away from the lights of the party and the prying eyes of our guests. I want her all to myself. Her full attention without any distractions. If I can't have that, I know I'll chicken out.

We step out of the light and into the shadow of the house, and I release her hand. She steps in close, breathing hard.

"Jesus, Delilah. What's wrong? Did I piss you off or something?"

It's pitch-black, but I still feel too exposed. I pull her into the dark alcove by the laundry-room door. The second we step onto the decking, I feel buffered from everything and everyone, like there's only me and Ashley. I don't have a plan, and I definitely don't know what I'm going to say. I'm breathing so hard I hope I can manage something intelligent. I hear her breathing at the same frantic pace as I am—probably from being dragged away from the party by a crazy person.

I step closer, trying to bring her face into focus. Our thighs touch, and fire races through my chest. It's a whole different feeling from what I experienced last night when I was with Janessa. This is hotter, sexier, more real. Ashley tightens her fingers around mine. I know she feels it, too. I want to see her eyes, and I don't know if I'm using the darkness as an excuse or not, but I step impossibly closer, pressing her against the wall. Our lips almost touch, and her eyes—*God, her incredibly sensuous brown eyes*—go as dark as the night sky.

"Are you dating Drake?" I hate myself for saying it like an accusation, but I can't stop myself.

"What? Why?" She squeezes my hand tighter.

"Just answer me, Ash. Yes or no."

"No."

Relief washes through me.

"No," I repeat.

"No. Why?"

"I..." I've never done anything like this, and fear sinks into me, stealing the courage that drove me here in the first place.

She leans forward and presses her breasts to mine. Holy freaking hell. Never in my life have I been so turned on.

"Tell me," she says in a heated whisper.

I can smell the wine on her breath and the scent of desire rolling off of her, but I still don't trust my instincts. She's here with Drake. Even if she's not dating him, she was hanging on to him like she wanted to be his. *Drake's, not mine.* My lips part, but I can barely think. How am I going to speak?

She moves forward, pushing against me until my back connects with the rough cedar siding of the tight alcove. She lifts my hand and presses it against the wall next to my head, then steps in closer so we're connected again from knees to chest, and—*oh, Lord*—I can't even think.

"What is it, Delilah? Why did you drag me over here?"

I. Can't. Speak.

My body trembles with need and fear and so much rampant lust I know she can taste it.

"You need to tell me, Dee."

I can't force a single word from my lungs. Every silent second feels like a lifetime.

"If I'm reading you right, then I'm going to do something neither of us will regret." She stares right through me. "But if I'm reading you wrong…it could destroy our friendship."

"Are you…?" My mouth goes dry, and I force myself to continue. *Now or never. Now, now, now!*

"Are you into girls?" It leaves my lips with desperation.

"No."

She holds my gaze as my heart splinters inside my chest.

"I'm into you," she says before sealing her lips over mine.

Her entire body pushes against me. I press back, wanting, needing, craving every inch of her. She nudges my legs open with her knee and grinds against my thigh. Every reservation I had last night evaporates. I don't care if I do anything right. I need to touch her. I hold her against me with my free hand, unwilling to ease the pressure, unwilling to chance her changing her mind. Her fingernails dig into mine, and the cedar siding scrapes the back of my hand. I don't care. The mix of pain and pleasure is hotter than hell, and *this*. Ashley's lips on mine, her body forming to mine, it takes me to a plane I've never experienced. It's surreal and hot and delicious and sexy at once. I push through the feeling that I'm stuck in a fantasy, because if I am, I never want it to end.

She buries her hand in my hair and deepens the kiss, still holding my other hand captive beside my head. Her glorious tongue claims my mouth, possessive and hard. Then she tugs my hair and nips at my lower lip, which makes me go a little crazy. I push my fingers beneath her skirt and fill my palms with her perfect ass. It's still not enough. I hear myself moaning, pleading for more. I need to feel her flesh, not her silky underwear. I shove my hand beneath the material and—another greedy moan escapes from my lungs into hers—her ass is soft and firm. I can't believe she's letting me do this, but she is, and she's taking, taking, taking everything I'm willing to give. She grazes her teeth over my earlobe, and I feel like I've touched a live wire.

"I've wanted you from the moment I met you," she says, fast and needful, against my ear.

"Oh God, Ash. *Take me.*"

She draws back and searches my eyes. "Delilah." It's a heated whisper. "You're...I wasn't sure."

"Neither was I."

I can't wait another second to kiss her again. Our fingers are still clutched together beside my head. She slips her free hand beneath my blousy summer top, still holding my gaze, and touches my stomach. My skin prickles with need. I want to close my eyes and revel in her first touch of my breast, but I can't. I want to see the heat in her eyes when she touches me. She presses her hand to my waist, and it feels sinfully good as her soft hands move up and over my rib cage, then higher still, brushing over the side of my breast. We're both barely breathing as her thumb lightly passes over my nipple, and I melt against her.

"You're so beautiful, Delilah. I'm never going to get enough of you."

Months of repressed desire come out in four confident words. "Take more of me."

Her eyes widen, then narrow as her lips curve into a cunning smile. Her hand presses flat and hard against my breast and moves in a slow circular motion, sending heat between my legs. She tugs my bra strap down my arm. She's still holding my gaze, and I don't know how I'm still standing. All I can think is, *More, more, more.* It feels dangerous in the dark alcove, with the party beating just beyond the wall behind us. And it makes me dizzy with desire. I *want* dangerous with Ashley. I *need* dangerous to break free of the walls I've built around myself.

She slides the strap of my shirt down next, baring my breast to the cool night air. I feel my nipple tighten, and when she lowers her mouth and laves it with her tongue, my head tips back and I close my eyes. *Heaven.* She grazes her teeth over the taut peak, making my hips shoot off the wall, and I ride her thigh as she rode mine. Writhing against her, getting wetter by the second, closer to coming apart. She frees my other breast, and my shirt falls, hitching around my shorts, leaving me bare from the waist up. I should be afraid, nervous, embarrassed to be so exposed with all those people nearby, but I'm not any of those things. I'm so excited I barely care that they're there. It helps to know that no one will come around this side of the house. No one ever does, and I wouldn't stop Ashley if my life depended on it.

I want this. I want her. Being with her feels completely different from being with Janessa. Ashley's not my teacher. I want to bring pleasure to every ounce of her body, and I want to disappear into her touch as she pleasures me. I want to memorize the feel of her skin, the curves of her hips, the taste of her. I want to figure out how she likes to be touched. I want to know about her life, her family, and—*Fuck!* My thoughts stop as she squeezes my nipple between her finger and thumb, sending a spear of heat between my legs.

"Ah," she whispers against my lips. "You like that."

I can't answer. It's all I can do to remember to breathe. She squeezes my nipple again as her lips meet mine, and I go up on my toes. My hand moves between her legs without any thought or guidance from my brain. My body knows what it wants, and it doesn't need a road map. She widens her stance, an invitation I'm not about to ignore. I slide my fingers beneath her underwear. She's so wet, my body actually shudders.

"And you like that, too," she says against my lips, then sinks her teeth into my neck and sucks as I slide my fingers deep inside her.

Her mouth feels too good on my neck, distracting me from focusing on what I learned last night. I probe and touch, letting my mind go numb and my body take over. Doing it right is off the table. I'm lost in doing it at all with Ashley. Seconds later her head falls back and she moans in pleasure as her wetness pulses against my fingers over and over again. Seeing her eyelashes flutter, hearing the sexy noises tearing from her lungs and knowing I made her come makes me want to do more, but she doesn't give me a chance. Her mouth crashes over mine and she rips open my shorts and shoves her hand down the front, fingering me as she rides my thigh again. Feeling her wetness against my flesh with her fingers buried deep inside me takes me right up to the edge.

"Ash—"

She seals her lips over mine, capturing my cries of passion as she makes me come again and again, until we're both breathing so hard we have to lean against each other just to remain erect. She presses her lips to mine.

"God, Delilah. What you do to me..." With trembling hands she rights my bra, my blouse, my shorts, her skirt—it's a good thing, because I can't move—and she collapses against me.

Ashley

PRESSED AGAINST DELILAH, feeling her heart beat against mine, her whispers across my cheek, surpasses anything I've ever experienced. I don't know what came over me when she dragged me back here. I didn't know if she was messing with me, pissed at me, or what, but when she asked about Drake, the look in her eyes left no room for misinterpretation. Whether she was going for an *I-want-you* seductive stare or not, that's what she conveyed, and I couldn't wonder for another second. I had to know, once and for all, if she wanted me or not.

Music from the party filters into my consciousness again, and I wonder how long we've been back here. It feels like a lifetime. The best lifetime I've ever lived. I lift my head from her shoulder and press my lips to hers. I can't stop myself from deepening the kiss. Even after everything we've just done, I want more of her. I want to see her hair spread out on my pillow, her naked body on *my* sheets. I want to taste and experience every inch of her. I want to walk down the street and hold her hand. I want to pull her into my arms and kiss her when the feeling hits and know that when she goes home at night, it's the curve of my hips she feels in her palms.

I kiss the corners of her mouth. "Why didn't you tell me you were into me?"

She shrugs, and now that my eyes have adjusted to the dark, I can see that her cheeks are flushed. She drops her eyes and fidgets with the edge of her shorts.

"Hey." I lift her chin so I can see her eyes. "Are you okay? I mean, you seemed to be okay a second ago, but..."

"Yes. Yes, more than okay. I...You..." She presses her forehead to my chest and I stroke the back of her neck.

"Your shy side is showing," I tease to lighten the mood.

She smiles up at me. *Thank God.* I worried she was regretting what we'd done.

"You've probably figured this out already, but I'm not very experienced at this." She traps her lower lip between her teeth, and she's so cute I have to kiss her again. And again.

Okay, one more kiss for good measure.

She laughs, a soft, feminine laugh that I don't hear nearly enough, and it warms my heart.

"I wouldn't have guessed."

"No?" Her brows knit together, and she presses her hand over my heart.

I cover her hand with mine. "No. You're perfect."

She stares at me for a long time, and I wish I could read her thoughts. Then, without a word, she moves her hand and steps out of the alcove and into the glare of lights from the party. I reach for her hand and she stops walking. The blood drains from her face, and her jaw drops open. She points over her shoulder toward the front yard.

"I'm...I'm going...inside to wash up." She turns and walks away without waiting for me.

Warning bells go off in my head, and I catch up to her, thinking more about what she's said. Wondering why she said she's inexperienced and why she's acting like we didn't just practically climb inside each other's bodies.

"Are you okay?" I ask, feeling like I've missed something she wants me to know.

"Uh-huh. I just want to get cleaned up." She goes in the front door and ignores the people milling about in the kitchen. I follow her upstairs to her bedroom. She opens a dresser drawer, grabs a pair of underwear, and then heads into the bathroom.

What the hell?

I've been in Delilah's room a dozen times, and it's never felt so cold, so lonely. I feel like I don't belong, when, if anything, what we did should make me feel like I belong even more. She comes out of the bathroom smelling like soap and scented body lotion. Three seconds ago I preferred the heady scent of desire, but right now I don't know what to think. I go into the bathroom to give us both some space to think. When I come out of the bathroom, she's sitting on the edge of the bed, fidgeting with the seam of her shorts. She smiles up at me, but it's not a real smile. It's her hesitant smile, the one that means she has something to say, but she doesn't always come forward with whatever it is.

I kneel before her and place my hands on her thighs. "Delilah, if you regret what we did, you need to tell me."

She shakes her head, and tears fill her eyes. "I don't. I promise."

Tears. Oh, Delilah, what is it?

"What is it, then? Because seeing you sad makes me sad. Please talk to me. I thought we just connected like I've never connected with anyone in my whole life."

"Me too." She blinks through her tears.

I reach up and wipe them with my thumb, then gather her in my arms. "I wish you'd share with me whatever's upsetting you. I can't help if I don't understand."

"It's everything. I feel so much for you, but I feel guilty for feeling it, and I know you deserve to be with someone who will hold your hand and hold their head high out there at that party, but…" She pulls out of my arms and turns away.

"But?" I sit beside her, trying to rein in the thoughts racing through my mind and convince myself not to jump to conclusions, which is pretty difficult given what she's just said. I'm not sure I can go through being someone's secret girlfriend again, and I get the impression that's where she's headed.

"But my parents really fucked me up, Ash." She turns pain-filled eyes toward me. Her hair curtains her face, and her voice is so soft I have to lean in close to hear her.

"I never…you know…did any of that before last night because my parents were so against it, and—"

"Last night?" *Holy shit. Are you kidding me?*

She swallows hard, and I know the answer before I ask the question.

"You were with *Janessa*?" I can't keep my voice from shaking.

"Not really the way I was with you."

That helps a little, but something tells me she's not being straight with me. "What do you mean, *not really*?" I grip my thighs to keep from fisting my hands.

"She...I..." She walks to the other side of the room and leans on her desk, her back to me. Her head drops between her shoulders. "She helped me learn how to..."

"Helped you...? So you *were* with her like that."

"No. Yes." Delilah pushes from the desk and paces. "You can't be upset with me. You and I weren't even together yesterday. I did it so I could be with *you*, Ashley. Not because I wanted to be with *her*."

I feel like my throat is closing. She's not even making sense. I pray I'm misunderstanding what she's trying to say.

I rise to my feet, and our eyes lock. "Tell me if I'm understanding this correctly. You had sex with Janessa so you could have sex with me?"

She shrugs. "I had no experience."

Just thinking about Delilah kissing Janessa, touching her like she touched me, and vice versa, makes me want to run back to my apartment, but I force myself to stay and figure it out. I want so badly to be with Delilah. This can't be happening. I'm clinging to a hope that doesn't exist rather than accepting the truth.

I force the calmest tone I can, which isn't very calm at all. "So, you *liked* me yesterday?"

"Yes. I've liked you since we first met. A lot."

"But instead of coming to me, you went to Janessa, a girl you see only one night a week at therapy? Boy, isn't she the lucky one? Did she talk you into it? Were you even into girls?

How did you go through college and...?" We've never talked about this, and now another fear bowls me over. If she's bisexual, then I will *never* be enough for her. Been there, done that. "Are you a lesbian, or are you bisexual?"

She's trembling as she opens her mouth to speak, but no words come. Her eyes fill with something that I can't read. Fear? Sadness? Finality?

She opens her mouth again and whispers, "Yes. I'm a lesbian." Her brows draw together, and she looks like she's just bared her soul.

Relief floods my body. I have to move, to give her space, to give myself space to process the enormity of what she's saying. I pace, shaking my head. "I still don't get it."

Delilah sinks back down to the mattress, and I realize that she *did* just bare her soul. "Let me try to explain again."

"No. I understand what you're saying. You never acted on your feelings toward girls because your parents were against it."

Delilah lets out a relieved sigh. "Yes."

"And when you finally decided to, you went to Janessa instead of me."

"God, Ash. That sounds really bad. I didn't even know if you were straight or not." She says this so softly it breaks my heart, but it isn't a salve for my hurt.

"You could have asked."

"Why are you putting this all on me? If you were so into me, you could have told me!" She covers her face with her hands and groans. "This is so fucked-up."

"I didn't know if you were into girls or not!" I cross my arms to try to gain control of my anger.

"I didn't either!" she yells, and pushes from the bed again. She closes the distance between us, and her eyes fill with anger, which I know mirrors mine. She's shaking as much as I am.

"I *thought* I liked girls, but how could I know for sure without ever kissing a girl? How could I know if I'd like touching a girl or having my fingers inside of her or putting her breast in my mouth?" She's so angry, I'm afraid to interrupt her.

"Damn it, Ashley. I didn't want you to be the person I fumbled with my first time. I didn't want to screw things up with a girl I was falling head over heels for with every passing second." She turns away and runs her hand through her hair quickly out of frustration.

Head over heels. The words hit me with the impact of a bullet train.

"I don't feel anything but friendship toward Janessa, and if you want the truth, I'm thankful." Her back is to me, but I hear every determined word clear as day. She faces me again, her eyes locked on mine, her hands fisted at her sides.

"I'm wicked thankful, because without Janessa offering herself up to help me figure things out, I'd still be on the corner of Lust and What-the-Fuck every time I looked at you."

"Delilah—"

"No." She lowers her voice. "Let me finish. Now I know for sure, Ashley. I may not be comfortable with letting the whole world know yet, but I know in my heart, without a shadow of a doubt, who I am, and that's a huge start for me. I feel like I've found my true self. You can't imagine how hard it is to live inside a steel box, worrying that if you let your true emotions out, your parents will disown you."

"Dee…" I reach for her hand and she pulls away.

She shakes her head. "No. Just…Don't."

I hear heavy footsteps running up the stairs. We both look toward the sound as Wyatt appears in the doorway. Delilah turns her back to him.

"Dee? Ashley? You guys okay?" Wyatt's stare is intense. His jaw is set tight as he comes behind Delilah and touches her shoulders. It kills me when she turns in to his embrace so easily instead of mine.

He looks at me over her shoulder and arches a brow. I don't even know what to say, so I drop my eyes.

"What can I do?" Wyatt asks. "How can I help?"

Delilah's fraying at every seam. I know she's mortified and hurt, and I hate that I can't fix it. She pushes out of Wyatt's arms and waves a dismissive hand at him as she wipes the tears from her eyes.

"We're fine. I just lost it," she manages.

Wyatt's concerned eyes bounce between us, and as the things Delilah said to me start to become clearer, I feel like a jerk. *I didn't want you to be the person I fumbled with my first time. I didn't want to screw things up with a girl I was falling head over heels for...*

"Can you give us a few minutes, Wy?" she asks.

"Of course. Whatever you need." Wyatt turns his attention to me. "Ashley, are you okay?"

I'm so touched that he can focus on me when his sister is having such a hard time, it's all I can do to nod.

"Okay. If you need me, just holler. But you might want to close that door." He points to the open door leading to the deck.

Fuck. If he heard us arguing, how many other people did? That's when I realize that the band must be taking a break. There's no music to muffle a damn thing. I pull the door closed, wondering if tonight could get any worse or any more awkward.

After Wyatt leaves, I go to Delilah and open my arms. "Forgive me for being jealous?"

She shakes her head and falls into my arms. Her conflicting messages have me baffled, but she's letting me hold her, and that's all I care about.

She doesn't need to know that Thursdays have now become my least favorite night of the week.

"I'm sorry I'm such a loser." I hear her smile, and I press a kiss to the side of her head.

"You're not a loser."

She leans back and searches my eyes. There's so much more I want to say, that we have to talk about, like the fact that she's not out and I'm not sure I can deal with living a secret life again. But I don't push her. I know, or I hope, we'll have time to figure this out. Even my worst fear—being someone's dirty little secret—isn't enough to hold me back from Delilah. She claimed a piece of me the first night we met, and right now there's only one thing I want to know for sure. The rest can wait.

"Do you still want to be with me, Dee?"

She nods, but fear lingers in her eyes.

"*Just me*? Do you want to be my girlfriend? Because I don't want to share. I'm not...I can't. I can't be with you and share you in that way with Janessa or anyone else."

She nods, and when our lips come together, our salty tears seep between them, slippery reminders of how far we've come and how very far we have to go.

CHAPTER SIX

Delilah

PEOPLE SAY THAT one night can change your whole life. What they don't tell you is how to deal with those changes. After being with Janessa, I thought the rest would come easily. That once I was certain I liked being intimate with women, I'd have no problem following my feelings. I know our friends will accept me. Tristan is gay, and Brandon is bisexual, and none of our friends have ever blinked an eye at either of them. But while coming together with Ashley on a physical and emotional level definitely came easily once we were alone in that alcove, the minute we stepped outside of that private space, the rest knocked me off-kilter.

To say that I was disappointed in myself for not walking back into the party holding Ashley's hand would be the understatement of the year. I hated myself for walking the opposite way. I hated knowing I was hurting her, hated knowing I was hurting myself, but no matter how much I wanted to walk into that party with her—*And boy did I ever want to*—I couldn't.

I've held her hand a million times in public. I've held Cassidy's hand, walked arm in arm with Brooke—but we weren't making a statement; we were just friends walking around Harborside.

Everything changed last night.

I felt like the minute I walked into the backyard, everyone would know what we'd done. I know that's crazy. Seriously, it's a party. There are always people making out at parties, and I wasn't embarrassed to have made out with Ashley. Just the opposite. I could hardly believe I was lucky enough to be with her. It was what happened afterward that stole my legs right out from under me.

The fear my parents instilled in me about their beliefs.

The fear of being a spectacle.

The disappointment in their eyes when I came out to them.

Right now I hate my parents as much as I hate the term *coming out*.

Waking up this morning and knowing I'm a *girl's* girlfriend for the first time in my life is a good feeling. Knowing I'm *Ashley's* girlfriend...? That makes my world spin. I smile, knowing that despite everything my parents instilled in me, I woke up feeling *good* about who I am. That might change in five minutes, or maybe it already has, but at least I had those few seconds before they crept back into my head.

It's Monday morning and I'm sitting on the back deck in a pair of boxer shorts and a T-shirt, drinking coffee and thinking about Ashley—and my parents. My mom used to sit outside and drink coffee in the mornings when we were here. I remember waking up to the smell of coffee, and I'd find my mom sitting out on the deck sipping coffee and reading a novel or the newspaper. My father would be standing down by the water with one hand on his hip, the other shading his eyes, as if he were looking at a faraway land. Morning after morning. I never knew what he was looking at, but I know my mom liked watching him. She used to smile and reach for my hand when I came outside. *Sit. Watch your father with me.* We'd both look at him, and she'd sigh. *He's so much more relaxed here, isn't he?*

Sadness tugs at the edges of my mouth, and I look down the beach, away from the place my father used to stand. After a few minutes I can think beyond them again. Grief is like that. It sneaks up when I'm least expecting it and clings for a while. The times I'm able to disengage from it, I feel thankful, and those times that I can't, I feel like I'm dying right along with them.

My mind shifts to Ashley. She left sometime after midnight and she texted me early this morning.

Miss you already.

Three simple words.

Three simple words that brought last night rushing back to me—the look in her eyes right before she kissed me, like I was the only woman on earth she ever wanted. The first press of her lips against mine, the sensuous feel of her tongue exploring my mouth. I shiver with the memory.

She's meeting Drake this morning for her first surfing lesson. I was so disappointed when she agreed to let him teach her to surf, but last night as I was lying in bed thinking about her—because my mind and body have become a sponge and I'm drenched in thoughts of her—I came to understand why she was so hurt that I turned to Janessa instead of her. She wanted to share in my first time, and I get that *now*.

I was so nervous the night I was with Janessa, trying to navigate completely unfamiliar territory while also trying to enjoy the ride. I think if I had been with Ashley that first time, while I'm sure it would have been amazing, I would have been in student mode, like I was with Janessa. It wouldn't have been nearly as enjoyable, and I probably wouldn't have let myself go like I did with Ash.

Janessa left me thankful for an experience, like I'd taken a class that helped me with finals. Ashley. *Good Lord, Ashley.* Ashley left me craving more of her touch, her kisses. She has the most tantalizing mouth, like it was made just for me. I don't want to hide our relationship, but I don't know how to escape the guilty feelings that come along with it, either.

I sip my coffee, watching a sailboat make its way across the ocean in the distance and wishing there were a guidebook for my life. *How to Crawl Out From Under My Parents' Expectations & Leave Guilt Behind.*

"Another beautiful morning in Harborside." Tristan pats my shoulder as he eases into the chair beside me. He runs his hand down his face and scratches his bare chest, then stretches his long, muscular arms and yawns. He does the same thing every morning, like a cat.

"Is there anything but? Even the rainy mornings are beautiful when you're looking out at the water." When my parents were alive, we came to Harborside for the summers, and usually during school breaks, too. I remember when we met Tristan. Wyatt and I were at the beach with our parents. It was a sweltering afternoon, and Wyatt and I were boogie boarding. Tristan was standing on the shore watching us with one hand on his hip and the other shielding his eyes from the sun, just like my dad used to do. I rode a wave all the way in and couldn't jump off fast enough, or turn hard enough, and I plowed right into him. We couldn't have been more than seven or eight, but he scrambled to his feet and reached for me before tending to the bloody cuts on his leg from where he was dragged against a ridge of sharp shells. Harborside has always been our home away from home, with friends like Tristan and Jesse, Brooke, Brandon, and Charley, but this summer it's become the only home I want.

"You can say that again. Where's Ashley? I assumed she was staying over." He kicks his bare feet onto a chair and reaches for my coffee, arches a brow, waits for my nod, then takes a sip.

My stomach dips at the mention of Ashley, and for a minute I wonder if he knows what we did. Ashley's spent the night before and I never got nervous the way I am now. *This is so stupid.* Even if he did know, of all people, the last person I should be uncomfortable around is Tristan.

"She went home last night."

He pushes my coffee cup across the table.

"Want to talk about the thing we're not talking about?" Tristan smiles, but he doesn't look at me.

I cross my arms on the table and rest my forehead on them. "I hate you."

I feel his hand on my arm. Tristan acts like another protective, caring brother, only he's got a gentler way about him than Wyatt. Wyatt comes to my defense like a bull. Tristan is more like a Transformer. He glides in all sexy and sleek and morphs to aggressive when there's no other alternative. I love that about him.

"Hon, I only have an assumption, and it's a very poor one, based on limited info, since you keep your feelings pretty close to your chest."

I turn my head and rest my cheek on my arms, peering at him out of one open eye. "What's your assumption?"

He crosses his arms and doles out a warm smile. "That you're just realizing you dig girls. Or more specifically, Ashley."

I turn again, resting my forehead on my arms so I can't see

his face, and I groan.

"Why are we groaning?"

Brandon.

I hear the chair on my other side drag across the deck and sense Brandon sitting beside me. I peek at him as he crosses his arms over his chest.

"Not my trouble to tell," Tristan answers.

I sit up straight and sigh. "I feel like I'm on *The Ellen De-Generes Show.*"

Brandon's straight dark hair is standing on end. He's wearing one of his signature black tees and a pair of jeans. He leans back and narrows his dark eyes. "Ah, we're groaning about the argument last night?"

I feel my cheeks heat up. "Did *everyone* hear us?"

"Nope." Brandon eyes my coffee, and I nod. He finishes it in one gulp. "Oh, that's nasty. French vanilla? You should have warned me."

"You didn't give me time. And you owe me a refill."

"I'm on it. As soon as you tell me what the big deal is. So you hooked up with Ash?" He shrugs, like this isn't a revelation.

How can it not be news to anyone but me?

"You *know* I hooked up with Ashley?"

Brandon shrugs again. "It was an educated guess. Until now."

Oh God. I could deny it, but I don't *want* to deny it. "So you knew I was into girls this whole time and you never said anything?"

"Definitely not. You said you were dating some dude at college, so I thought you were straight." Brandon leans across the table and hollers inside the house, "Army, bring out a pot of coffee?"

"Sure," Wyatt calls from the kitchen.

I mull over what he's said, and even though Brandon is bisexual, it doesn't mean he'd assume I was. "So why would you assume I hooked up with her?"

Brandon throws an arm over the back of his chair and stretches his long legs out to the side. "I've seen the way you look at her, and there isn't anything *straight* about those looks. So I assumed you swing both ways." Brandon levels a stare at Tristan. "The way it *should* be."

Tristan rolls his eyes. He's used to Brandon's brash comments. Tristan doesn't hide the fact that he's gay, but he doesn't flaunt his sexuality the way Brandon does. Brandon openly eyes girls and guys like they were put on this earth solely for his taking. He hits on whomever he pleases, and if they turn him down, he simply moves on to the next, while Tristan is all about his heart. He's selective about the men he goes out with, but he opens himself up too quickly—and gets hurt too often.

"I definitely *do not* swing both ways." I have to fess up to my closest friends and tell them how I have been hiding my sexual identity. It's embarrassing, and I feel horrible for keeping it from them, but really, I had no choice. My parents watched us like hawks, and if they had gotten wind of me being interested in girls, God only knows what they would have done.

Someone else might try to lie her way out of coming out to her friends, but I've spent enough time lying. I'm trying to shed my lying coat of armor, not figure out how to live within its confines for even longer.

Wyatt comes out from the kitchen with one arm around Cassidy and a pot of coffee in his other hand, which he sets on the table.

"You okay, Dee?" He sits across from me, and Cassidy sits

on his lap and circles his neck with her arms.

No, but I'm trying. "Yeah. Fine."

Tristan gets up and retrieves one of our deck chairs from the beach, where we moved them last night before the party.

He sets the chair next to Wyatt. "Here you go, Cass."

Wyatt tightens his grip on her. "She's fine where she is."

Cassidy gathers her long brown hair over one shoulder and kisses Wyatt's forehead. "One day he'll get sick of me. Thanks, Tristan."

"Never." Wyatt nuzzles against her neck.

Jealousy claws up my spine. I want what they have. I want to wake up with Ashley and touch her when I feel like it, without guilt or worry or any goddamn bad feeling at all.

It's never going to be that easy for me.

What I want and what I'm capable of giving are two different things.

"Aren't you the one who tells me to keep it behind closed doors?" Brandon asks as he fills my coffee cup.

"*We're* not having a ménage on the couch." Wyatt's tone stops Brandon from saying anything more. His voice softens when he addresses me. "Everything go okay with Ashley last night?"

"Yeah." I answer, remembering how Ashley opened her arms to me even after she knew I'd been with Janessa and knowing I might not be able to reciprocate publicly for who knows how long.

Yet.

This is my new plan. I'm convincing myself that I'll figure out a way to move past everything that's holding me back.

"Dee, we have to figure out when we're going back to Connecticut," Wyatt reminds me. We decided to sell our house in

Connecticut since we both want to stay in Harborside. I think he's bringing it up now to take the pressure off of me coming clean with everyone. He's always watching out for me, even when I don't think he is. "Aunt Lara is packing up most of Mom's and Dad's stuff, but I asked her not to do their bedroom, like you wanted. The real estate agent said we should get it on the market before winter."

"I think the weekend after next is good," I answer.

"Okay. What are we going to do about the Taproom?"

"Why don't you stay and take care of the bar while I go back home, and then I'll manage it while you go another time?"

Wyatt shakes his head. "No way. I can't let you go back alone. You don't know how you're going to react to being there."

I press my lips together to keep my annoyance from coming out. Normally I'd just say okay, but lately I've been feeling too restricted, *too* taken care of.

"I'm not a kid, Wyatt. I'll be fine."

"Dee…" His eyes turn serious again.

"I know it's going to be hard, Wy, but I can handle it." I watch as doubt fills his eyes, and it stirs anger—and worry—in my gut, because I have no idea if I'll be fine. I've never had to handle anything like this on my own. Heck, I've never had to handle much on my own. But if I'm ever going to break free of this guilt, I have to try.

"The grief counselor says we should try to envision a future where memories of Mom and Dad don't pull me under. This is a start. I'll be fine."

"But—"

Cassidy touches his arm and shakes her head. I'm thankful when he relents.

"Okay, now that that's settled." Brandon's eyes shift between me and Wyatt. "So, Delilah, let me get this straight. You're a lesbian?"

Wyatt grabs his arm so hard I'm sure he'll leave a bruise.

"Back off." Wyatt's eyes narrow.

"Wyatt." Cassidy touches his arm, and he loosens his grip.

"It's okay, Wyatt. I have to do this at some point, and I know I'm not exactly comfortable saying this in front of strangers, so...I might as well say it where I can. It's a start." I meet Brandon's expectant gaze and push past the twisting in my stomach.

"Yes. I am. I'm..." Why is it so hard for me to say *I'm a lesbian*? I hate that it's hard, but the word gets stuck in my throat. It kills me that I'm finally with Ash, and even dead, my parents are stealing the joy of it.

Tristan covers my hand with his. "Baby steps. Finding your comfort zone isn't a race. It's a slow progression of coming into your true self, and no one can set that pace but you."

"Fuck baby steps. Own it, Delilah. Be loud and proud." Brandon pats his chest.

"Loud and proud isn't for everyone." Tristan glares at Brandon, then turns softer eyes toward me. "This is a first step for you, and I'm proud of you."

Wyatt eyes Brandon with a silent warning to back off. Brandon holds his hands up in surrender.

"I need to tell you guys something." I swallow the fear that's prickling my limbs and threatening to steal my voice. "I'm not proud of the way I've lived my life so far, but it's what I had to do. You guys knew my parents. You knew their views on this." I pause, because when I think back, I *don't* remember my parents ever looking at Brandon or Tristan the way they looked at me when I came out to them on graduation day.

"Your parents?" Tristan releases my hand and looks at Wyatt.

"They weren't exactly pro same-sex relationships," Wyatt explains.

"They never said anything to me." Tristan sits back and crosses his arms. His biceps flex and his brows knit together.

"How do you know, Wyatt? Because I'm with Tristan on this," Brandon says with a serious tone. "They never said anything to me either, or made me feel out of place, and hey, I don't exactly hide my lifestyle."

Wyatt tried to talk to me about Mom and Dad several times this summer, but I haven't wanted to. When we first got here, my emotions were too raw and I was too scared about how we were going to learn to live without them to even think about my feelings in *that* department. But over the last few weeks, my feelings for Ashley have grown, and I want to get past this.

"They were pretty verbal with me and Dee," Wyatt explains. "I always thought it was weird that they could treat you guys fine, when back home they made no bones about what they believed was right and wrong. Dee—"

I hold up my hand to silence him. "I'll tell them." Wyatt likes to take care of me, and I love that he does, but if I'm going to figure this out, I have to learn to deal with these things on my own. I hope that starting here, among our friends, will make it easier to face the rest of the world.

"I hid my sexuality from everyone and denied it to myself. I'm not proud of it, but I hid it from you guys, from my parents, from Wyatt and Cassidy. Well, until Wyatt confronted me a few years ago and I finally told him the truth." Wyatt holds my gaze, and I read a hundred things in his eyes. That he's there for me, that I don't need to explain anything. That he'll take care of it, which only makes me want to stand up and do it on my own even more.

"I did date a guy in college," I admit. "But it was just to fit in and to be able to go to parties without being hit on."

"Aw, Delilah. Plenty of gay people hook up with straight people to fit in. Don't be so hard on yourself." Tristan touches my arm again.

"If what you're saying about your parents is true, it's people like that who cause their kids to commit suicide and feel ashamed of themselves." Brandon sips my coffee. "Been there, done that. Well, not the suicidal part."

"Hey, our parents aren't here to defend themselves," Wyatt says in a serious voice. "Believe me, Brandon, if anyone wants to give my parents hell, it's me. But that's my place, not yours, so be respectful."

Brandon turned a serious and respectful gaze to Wyatt. "Sorry, man."

"I know lots of people do that, Tristan, but I'm not sure how to get past it, and I want to. I desperately want to." The hurt in Ashley's eyes crashes back in like a wave breaking in my chest.

Cassidy moves from Wyatt's lap and pulls up the empty chair next to me. She sits down and leans in close. Cassidy grew up around the corner from us in Connecticut. Her parents were never around, so she spent lots of time at our house, and until meeting Ashley, Cassidy was my closest female friend.

"Delilah, I'm sure that right now it seems like you have two choices—come out to everyone or live a secret life. But it's really not that black-and-white. Have you talked to Ashley about this?"

I nod, thankful that she understands, too. "She knows, and she still wants to be with me."

Cassidy looks at Wyatt and smiles, then looks at me again. "Then it doesn't matter what anyone else thinks. Just do what comes naturally."

"Sometimes doing what comes naturally is the hardest thing on earth."

CHAPTER SEVEN

Ashley

THIS HAS BEEN the longest day of my life. Learning to surf is about a million times harder than I thought it was going to be, and I had a terrible time trying to concentrate on anything other than Delilah. Drake was patient as a saint, but every time he held on to my board to steady me, I wished he was Delilah. When he cheered me on, I wanted it to be her who was proud of me. And I knew she would be. I kept looking up at the dunes, where she and I have been meeting in the early mornings, hoping she'd appear.

And then there is the war that's been raging between my head and my heart. I promised myself I wouldn't get involved with anyone who wasn't *out*. I've been down this road. I know how painful it is, and yet here I am, doing it again.

Oh, Delilah, what am I going to do?

Luckily, the surf shop was superbusy today, so I didn't have much downtime to brood or count down the hours until I'd see Delilah again. After work I stopped at the Harborside General Store to pick up a few things, like Delilah's favorite crackers and hot chocolate.

I check the clock. She's going to be here any minute. She

had to work until ten, and it's almost ten fifteen. She's been to my apartment a million times, but tonight I'm extra nervous. I've already washed and changed my sheets, run the vacuum, showered, and put on the prettiest underwear and bra that I own under one of my regular tops and shorts, so I don't look too eager. It's been a long time since I cared about any of these things, and even though I know Delilah won't care if my apartment is messy or my underwear doesn't match my bra, I can't help the fluttering in my chest or the anticipation that's been building since she first returned my text this morning and asked if she could see me tonight.

Can she? I couldn't even believe it was a question.

Doesn't she know she owns me?

From the moment I saw her, she's been weaseling her way into my heart. She's the only person who could ever break through the walls I built around my heart after Sandy.

I turn on my iTunes playlist, which has been full of Delilah's favorite bands since we first met: Paramore, 5 Seconds of Summer, Imagine Dragons, and a handful of others. My apartment is on the second floor and faces the ocean. It's not very spacious, but I like having my own place, and the view of the ocean reminds me of Delilah's house, which makes me feel closer to her. I dance around the room lighting candles, then dim the lights. My living room feels romantic with the candles flickering in the breeze coming through the balcony doors and music playing softly in the background.

A knock on the door sends my stomach into a whirlwind. Suddenly the room feels like I'm trying too hard. I run around blowing out the candles, waving my hands around, trying to get the scent of sulfur out of the room.

Crap. Why did I do that?

She knocks again, and I flick on the lights, feeling like an idiot. There's no disguising the scent of extinguished candles.

I breathe deeply, once, twice, three times. I'm never nervous like this, and it makes me even more nervous because it's such an unfamiliar feeling.

I reach for the doorknob, then hesitate, giving myself a get-your-head-on-straight talk.

I'm not going to kiss her first thing. This is all new to her. She needs time to adjust.

I'm going to be cool about it so I don't scare her off.

No. Kissing.

Until she wants to.

One more deep breath and I open the door.

Delilah smiles.

She smiles.

I can't get enough of Delilah's smiles, and it melts all my good intentions.

As she steps into the room, I slip my hand behind her neck—her neck, that's another part of her that I can't get enough of—and I press my lips to hers.

So much for keeping it cool.

Finally, after hours of feeling like I was holding my breath to get from one minute to the next, I can breathe. And she kisses me back. I love how she kisses me back, like she's been as desperate for me as I've been for her. The door clicks softly behind her, and I back her against the wall, fisting my hand in her hair. Her hands are all over me, on my waist, my ribs, my ass. I love when she grabs my ass like I'm hers.

I *am* hers.

I know I'm already in way too deep to walk away if she can't be open about our relationship. I know this as I lift her shirt over her head and toss it aside. I know this as she does the same to mine, then kisses the crest of my breast, making my knees weaken. We're kissing, panting, begging, moaning, as we strip away each other's clothes right there in the foyer.

"Where have you been all my life?" I say against her lips as I unsnap her shorts and tug them down her beautiful hips.

"Waiting for you."

Her perfect answer spurs me on.

How can she do that with three little words?

She's wearing her favorite boots, and this makes me happy, because it means she feels confident. I love *confident Delilah* as much as I love *shy Delilah, uncertain Delilah, sexy Delilah,* and *sleepy Delilah.* But tonight of all nights, I'm thankful that *confident Delilah* is here, kissing me in my foyer wearing nothing but a light blue thong and those boots.

"Jesus, you're sexier than hell." I rake my eyes down her body, and her cheeks flush, but she returns the heat-inducing leer, dragging her eyes down my nearly naked body, save for my own pink panties and bra. The hunger in her eyes sets me in motion again.

She tries to toe off her boots, and I crouch to help her. I take them off and set them aside, then place one hand on the back of each of her legs and kiss my way up her right calf to her thigh, where I linger. I kiss the inside of her thigh and trail featherlight kisses up and over her muscles. She fists her hand in my hair, and when I lift my eyes, I catch her staring down at me, biting her lower lip. Her cheeks are flushed, and her long blond hair hangs loose and tousled over her peaked nipples. She's too stunning for words, and for a beat it's all I can do to stare at her. I force myself to my feet and nudge her legs apart with my knees, grip her hips, and hold her against the wall as I bring my mouth to her neck and kiss her lightly.

A breeze sweeps through the living room from the open balcony doors, and I feel her shiver as she presses her hips to mine.

"I want to taste you," I whisper against her cheek.

She stops breathing for a second. I've embarrassed her, and I fear she'll retreat.

"No." I freeze, but before I can react, she adds, "Let *me* taste *you*."

I'm not sure how I remain standing or how my legs carry me as she leads me into the living room. With shaky hands she unclasps my bra and watches it fall to the floor. She glances over my shoulder at the sheers blowing in the wind.

"Can people see inside?" Her voice is shaky, too.

"Not with the lights out. We can go to the bedroom."

She shakes her head and crosses the room, turns off the lights, then returns to me.

"I love the way you look right here." She settles a shaky hand on my hip. "With the breeze brushing your hair and the moonlight coming in through the curtains."

I love artistic Delilah, too.

She touches the sides of my underwear with her fingertips and looks me in the eye. "I apologize ahead of time if I suck at this. I've never done it before."

Now I'm the one shaking. I just fell a little harder for her. She's telling me she didn't do this with Janessa. *This is ours.* I'm her first. I seal my lips over hers and kiss her as she lowers me to the couch. I've thought about what Delilah's body would feel like beneath me, on top of me, beside me, a million times, but nothing compares to this first time of feeling the weight of her on me as we kiss. Her hips press to mine, and her hands slide beneath my back and she holds me close. My legs naturally wrap around her. I'd climb inside her if I could. I want to be her everything. I want to be the breath she breathes, the words she says, the blood that pumps through her heart.

She rises up on her palms and looks down at me. Her hair curtains our faces, creating our own private world.

"You're playing my favorite songs."

I nod, because my heart is beating so hard it's swallowed my voice. She smiles and kisses my collarbone, my shoulder. She runs one fingertip down the center of my body so lightly that it tickles and excites me at once. How can one fingertip send so much heat through my body? She follows that finger with her tongue, stopping every few seconds to lavish my heated flesh with an openmouthed kiss. Every time I feel her mouth settle over my skin, it sends a shiver of anticipation right through me. When she gets to my underwear, she kisses each of my hips and splays her hands on my thighs as she runs her tongue along the crease beside my sex. First up one side, then the other.

My body is on fire.

She looks at me through her lashes, then closes her eyes and runs her tongue between my legs. I'm so wet that I can feel the heat of her tongue through the damp material, and it's about the most erotic sensation I've ever felt. She does it again, and I close my eyes. She repeats it again, and again, and just when I think I'll tear a hole in my couch cushion with my fingernails if she doesn't put her tongue on *me*, she pulls down my underwear. The breeze sweeps across my wet skin as she tosses them to the ground and comes back up so we're eye to eye. She claims me with a deep, possessive kiss that takes me by surprise and draws me further in to her. I'm pulling at her thong, pressing my hips to her thigh, about to crawl out of my skin.

She smiles against my lips, and her eyes go as dark as the center of the ocean. My heart's beating so hard my chest feels like it's going to explode. She takes my breast in her mouth and drives me out of my freaking mind.

"Delilah," I plead.

She sucks and licks and moves to my other breast, giving it the same lavish attention as the first as her fingers trail south.

Yes, yes, yes.

I'm already so close to the edge I know it won't take long, but she parts me and teases me with one finger. Languid, torturous strokes that make my insides feel like they're clawing their way out.

"More. I need more." I push her shoulders, urging her down. I know I probably shouldn't rush her, but I can't help it. When her lips curve up in a coy smile and she shifts lower with greater speed than I've ever seen her move, I know she doesn't mind.

And then her mouth is on me and—*yes, yes, yes*—she totally knows what to do. I writhe beneath her, moaning and pleading and making noises I've never heard myself make. She uses her mouth, her tongue, her teeth, and her hand. *Oh God, her hand.* My thighs flex and my toes curl under. Pinpricks explode up my limbs and my body bucks and thrusts uncontrollably. She holds my hips down as she strokes and teases, prolonging my climax until I'm sure I'll die right here on the couch.

"Delil—"

She moves up in record time and captures my plea in her mouth. I taste myself, but the taste of her mouth overpowers it, and I reach between her legs. She's so wet, so ready. She rocks against my hand, and I know she's as close as I was when she took me. I push my hand inside her thong and take her right over the edge, swallowing her moans and taking every shudder of her body as a plea for more. My muscles are fatigued, but after the glorious attention she's just given my body, I want to give her the same pleasure. I wrap my arm around her and shift her beneath me, then make quick work of ridding her sleek, hot body of that pesky thong. I want to kiss her breasts—I love her breasts—but I'm too anxious to get to the rest of her, and she's pressing on my shoulders. Urging me lower. She doesn't need to urge. I'm there, and there's no place else I'd rather be. I spread her thighs and don't even try to slow my desire. I take her like it's a race and I'm the winner, and when my name comes off her lips and her body rocks with pleasure, I take her in my arms and hold her like I'm never going to let her go. And hope I never have to.

CHAPTER EIGHT

Delilah

"I DEFINITELY DID not come over here expecting to attack you." Ashley and I are lying on the couch beneath a blanket she grabbed from her bedroom. There's a breeze whisking over our damp skin. We're facing each other, and I'm glad she's got an arm around me, holding my body against hers, because I'm so relaxed that my limbs feel like spaghetti.

Ashley smiles and kisses the tip of my nose. I love lying in her arms. It feels so right.

"I thought *I* was the one who attacked *you*. I was about to apologize."

"Oh good. Then it was a mutual mauling."

We both laugh.

The music is still playing, and as our pulses calm, she brushes my hair from my shoulder and presses her lips to mine.

"I'm glad you came over." She kisses me again. "I missed you today."

"I couldn't stop thinking about you, either. I was so worried that you'd wake up this morning and decide I wasn't worth the headache."

Her eyes narrow, and as a breeze sails through the room, she pulls the blanket up over my arm.

"You're worth waiting for, Delilah. But I'm not good at keeping my emotions hidden, and I've already had to hide them for the past two months." She sits up, and the energy between us shifts and cools. "Let's get dressed and sit on the balcony."

As we retrieve our clothes from the floor, I watch her carefully, unsure if I've said something that caused her to separate so quickly. She steps into her shorts and smiles over at me, but it feels forced.

"Did I just say something that upset you?"

She walks slowly toward me as she pulls her shirt over her head. Then she gathers me in her arms and touches her forehead to mine.

"No, you didn't upset me. It's hard for me, Dee. But I can deal with it. I just want to talk for a while, make sure we're both in the same place."

She rubs her hands down my arms, warming me from the breeze. "Let me get you a sweatshirt." She presses her lips to mine, then disappears into her bedroom while I retrieve my shorts from the foyer.

I like being in Ashley's apartment because it's *hers*. I can feel her presence in every room through her taste in furniture—comfortable and not showy, with pastel colors and wooden accents. She painted several of the pictures hanging on the walls. I recognize the one of the pier that she painted during the first few weeks after we met. On the wall outside her kitchen there are three small paintings. A scene of the shoreline, a painting of a boat, and another of the dunes. The one of the dunes wasn't there last week when we were here watching movies.

She hands me a sweatshirt.

"Thank you." I inhale as I pull it over my head. It smells

like her, and I'm already planning to take it home with me. I watch her as she walks into the kitchen, evaluating every step, every glance, and hoping she's not going to change her mind about me being worth waiting for.

"Do you want something to drink?"

"Sure. Hot chocolate?"

"I love that you're not a big drinker." She pulls me closer by the pockets of the sweatshirt and kisses me again. "I like you way too much, Delilah Armstrong."

Delilah Armstrong.

She makes my name sound special, and she probably has no clue that she's just helped alleviate my worry.

"I'm going to take that as a golden nugget, and when you get mad at me for something, I'm going to pull it out and say, *Remember that day you said you liked me way too much?*"

She laughs as she heats up the water.

"When did you paint this picture of the dunes?"

She shrugs. "I've been working on it the mornings that we don't meet and sometimes in the evenings. Do you like it?"

"I love it. It amazes me that you can make every blade of grass look as though it's moving with the wind."

"You do the same thing with hair when you sketch," she points out as she fixes our hot chocolate.

"Yeah, but that's not using a paintbrush. I have much more control with a pencil."

"Come on, let's sit outside and argue about control." She takes my hand and squeezes it with the tease, then leads me onto the balcony, where we sit on mismatched chairs and listen to the sounds of the ocean, the noises of people in the distance.

The mugs we're drinking from are made of pottery, and they don't match, either. I like that Ashley's taste is eclectic more than conservative. My beach house was decorated by my parents, and I think it would be nice to have my own place. I love living with Wyatt and Cassidy, and Tristan and Brandon, but I've never lived on my own, and I think that I should.

Baby steps.

I steal a glance at Ashley and catch her staring at me. She smiles, but she doesn't look away. Everything about her intrigues me. I blush just knowing she's staring at me, and she's not at all embarrassed.

"Have you had many girlfriends?" I'm not sure where the question comes from, but once it's out, I want to know her answer.

"Enough." She sips her hot chocolate, holding my gaze.

"Enough? Girlfriends aren't like ice cream cake." I make my voice an octave higher and mock sarcasm. "I think I've had enough, thank you. Oh, no, not yet. I need a little more."

She laughs and looks out at the water. "No, they're not, are they? I said *enough* because I've had enough girlfriends to know how special you are."

"Aw, Ash." I reach for her hand, and she brings it to her lips and kisses it. She's so much more romantic than any guy has ever been with me. I have the urge to ask her all the things we've never talked about. I want to know as much as I can about her.

"Have you ever been in love?"

"No, but I thought I was headed there once."

She's still holding my hand, and I wait for her to say more. When she doesn't, I push a little.

"What happened?"

She releases my hand and looks down at her mug. When she looks up again, she scoots her chair over so she's facing me, and our knees touch. She looks right at me, and it makes me nervous, like she's going to tell me something bad.

"I want to tell you the truth, but you have to promise me you won't assume the worst, because…well, because that will be easy to do, given what I'm about to say."

My stomach lurches.

"Maybe you shouldn't tell me."

She smiled, still holding my gaze. "I want to."

I swallow my fear and nod. "Okay."

"I dated a girl named Sandy for a few months, and I thought we were happy together, but like you, she hadn't come out yet. She kept telling me she was going to but she wasn't ready, so I didn't push her. We only saw each other at my place, never hers. And I started putting things together, like how she only saw me before ten at night and never on the weekends. We had a class together, but in public she didn't acknowledge me as anything other than a friend, so it was awkward in that class and around our friends."

She pauses, sips her hot chocolate, while I'm clinging to every second. I feel like she's describing me. *She hadn't come out yet…In public she didn't acknowledge me as anything other than a friend.* I can't help but wonder what she's doing with me.

"Anyway, after a while I couldn't take hiding our relationship anymore. I told her I needed more, and she wasn't willing, so I ended the relationship."

Ended the relationship.

No. No, no, no.

"I was heartbroken, and she…Well, she acted like it didn't matter. Like I didn't matter. I found out shortly afterward that she had a boyfriend and was living with him in an apartment near campus. I wasn't the first girl she'd had a fling with." She looks away and says softly, "She used me. I was falling for her, and she was using me."

"Ashley, I'm so sorry. Do you ever hear from her?"

She nods. "Sometimes she'll send a random text, but I usually don't respond."

She leans back in her chair and pulls her knees up to her chest, then wraps her arms around them. "I promised myself that I would never again date someone who wasn't *out* or pretend in public not to have feelings for someone I cared about."

She lifts one shoulder almost imperceptibly. "And then came you."

"Ashley..." I'm staring at her, but she's not looking at me, and when she does, it's with a pained look in her eyes.

"I asked you not to jump to conclusions."

"Ash. How can I not? Why would you take a chance on me? I mean, you know I'm not seeing anyone else, but I don't know how long it will take me to be comfortable in public. It could be tomorrow, but it could be weeks." I don't say, *or months*, which is what worries me most, because I don't really know how to get past the hurdles I'm facing.

"I *tried* not to like you, and every time I tried to stop thinking about you, I only thought of you more. I already feel more for you than I have ever felt for anyone else. I don't know how long I'll be okay resisting you in public. I don't even know if I'm okay hiding it for a *day*, much less longer, but I want to try to make this work." She sets her feet back on the ground and reaches for my hand.

I can't think. I can't talk.

She doesn't know if she'll be okay for a day? Where does that leave us?

She moves closer, telling me we'll figure it out, but she

doesn't know everything, so how can she say that? She doesn't know the pieces of guilt that are lodged deep within my psyche, spearing me every time I have certain thoughts or feelings. She doesn't know the thing that might make it impossible for me to ever feel comfortable with public displays of affection. She doesn't know that when I told my parents I was a lesbian and they gave me *that* look—the look that nearly brought me to my knees—I wished they didn't exist.

And hours later…they didn't.

CHAPTER NINE

Ashley

AT SIX THIRTY this morning the sky was gray and the air was damp and cold. It looked like rain was moving in, and the waves were rolling in with it. I was out in the frigid water, trying to learn to surf, when I spotted Delilah up on the dunes, bundled up in my sweatshirt, which she *accidentally on purpose* wore home last night. I didn't care that I wiped out a zillion times, or that by the time I was done I was as frozen as a Popsicle. Delilah was here. She came on her own to watch me. She stayed for a long time, but I didn't wave to her because I didn't know if she wanted me to know she was watching or not. She didn't mention coming to watch when she left last night. Then again, I got the feeling there was a lot she wasn't telling me.

I know I freaked her out when I told her why I broke up with Sandy, but I don't want to give her false hope. I know myself well enough to realize how tenuous my ability to be patient really is—*or was*—before meeting her. It took me a long time to finally end things with Sandy. Probably too long, and it took me only half a second to decide I'd never keep a relationship secret again.

Until Delilah.

I didn't want her to leave last night. I wanted to wake up with her in my arms. I wanted to have coffee out on the balcony and laugh about how bad I am at surfing. I wanted to *ask* her to come and watch me.

It turns out I didn't need to.

That kept a smile on my face all day. Now it's seven thirty and I'm shoving clothes for tomorrow into my backpack. I grab my toothbrush and take one last look in the mirror. I'm meeting Delilah at the Taproom at eight. We're having drinks with Wyatt and Cassidy, and then we're spending the night at Delilah's house. This will be the first night we've spent together since we became girlfriends, and I'm nervous and excited. I didn't question why she didn't want to stay at my place even though I was a little surprised that she wanted to sleep where there were other people in the house. I'd have thought she would want more privacy, but I don't mind staying within Delilah's comfort zones. I have a feeling I'm going to be learning what they are for a while yet.

I'm not much of a dress-up kind of girl, but I'm wearing a cute tribal-design miniskirt that fits like a glove with a loose-fitting, sheer, silky white tank top and a lace bra beneath it. It's kind of mean, given that we're going to be in public and knowing how much she loves seeing me dressed like this, but hey, sometimes a girl's gotta pull out all the stops. I like seeing the look in Delilah's eyes when she first sees me in a miniskirt. Her eyes go wide and her lips curl up in appreciation. I know she's unaware of how seductive she looks when she drags her eyes down my body like she's an addict and I'm her favorite drug. My entire body heats up, as if she's just touched every inch of my flesh. I wasn't ever sure if she meant to look at me that way, but now that I know I'm reading the look right, I want to see it even more.

I'm not going to push her to show affection toward me in public, but I'm only human. I *want* her to want me, and I want her to want me enough to open up and tell me why she clammed up last night when I reassured her and said we'd figure things out.

I sensed her building a protective wall around herself. Maybe not a big one, and maybe not one that will be up all the time, but she definitely went into self-preservation mode. I guess I don't blame her.

Hopefully she'll be no better at keeping up her walls than I was at keeping up mine.

I want to tear down all of her walls, but I have a feeling she needs to come to this decision on her own. I was fifteen when I told my mom I liked girls. She didn't try to change my mind and she didn't ask me if I was *sure*. She wrapped me in her arms and told that she loved me. She didn't say that she loved me *despite* my sexual preference. She didn't say she loved me despite anything. She simply said, "I love you."

When I came out to my father, he looked at me for a long time. His bushy eyebrows knitted together and he crossed his arms over his round belly and narrowed his serious dark eyes. My father's a businessman, and I felt as though he were analyzing me, taking apart the pieces of me that he understood and trying to right them against the pieces of me that he didn't understand. It was the longest ten minutes of my life. Finally, he unfolded his arms, waved a hand at me, and said, "I'm just trying to figure something out."

I tried to reassure him. "You didn't do anything wrong, Dad. This isn't some big failure on your part."

He got angry, pressed his full lips into a firm line, and spoke in the fatherly tone that always gets my attention, and when he pointed at me, I knew I was in for harsh words. I never expected that they would be the most supportive harsh words I could ever hope for.

"Now, you listen to me, young lady. I don't think I did something wrong, and don't you ever let anyone tell you you're doing something wrong either. I'm sitting here thinking about how your mother and I did something right. This can't be easy for you, stepping out into the world where people are ass backward and judge based on their own cockamamy beliefs. I'm proud of you, baby girl. When you love someone, you don't tell them *who* to love—you support who they are." He folded me into his arms, and I knew that whatever I faced in my life, I'd always have their support.

My parents' reactions taught me a very important lesson. *Acceptance* and *tolerance* are two totally different things. I want Delilah to feel accepted, not tolerated. But Delilah has to want that, too. And that isn't something a person can force on someone else.

All I can do is hope that I mean as much to her as she does to me.

Delilah

AFTER WORK I went home and took a really cold shower, hoping it would help temper my anticipation of seeing Ashley. After last night, I'm not sure how I'll react being close to her when we're having drinks tonight. Before going to her house last night I told myself I was going to take things slow. Slow,

slow, slow. Then I saw her, and all bets were off. I didn't *need* slow, and I definitely didn't *want* slow.

The walk to the Taproom is only a few blocks, and it gives me time to think, which is good and bad. There's a lot of foot traffic on Main Street. Summer brings tourists, and tourists love to meander through the shops in the evenings. There's a line out the door at Pepe's Pizza. A group of kids are sitting on the curb with an open pizza box as they scarf down pizza and laugh about who can take the biggest bite. Habit draws my eyes to Endless Summer Surf Shop. I'm looking for Ashley even though I know she's off work. The shop is lit up like it's midafternoon. Bikes are lined up in the bike rack, and guys in board shorts and girls in bikini tops and skimpy shorts are talking out front. I feel ten years older than them, although I'm sure I'm about their age. Losing your parents will do that to a person. Suddenly I'm working a more-than-full-time job, and the fate of an entire business is in mine and Wyatt's hands. I don't mind working at the Taproom. I actually really enjoy the work and dealing with the customers and the staff, but some days the responsibility definitely weighs on me.

As I cross the parking lot and the beach comes into view, I am reminded of watching Ashley learning to surf this morning. I didn't go just because I missed her, which I did. I went to see how my body would react to seeing her. It was a test. If I could see her and not feel like my heart was going to climb out of my throat to get to her, I knew I'd be okay. Then I could go out with her tonight and not want to rip her clothes off right there in the Taproom. But it was an epic failure. The minute I saw her, I lost all ability to think about anything else. My pulse sped up, my palms got warm, and just seeing her in her bikini turned me on so much I had to leave.

I. Had. To. Leave.

Leave.

As in, come home and take my *first* cold shower of the day. I thought only guys took cold showers, but apparently it's about the only thing that takes the edge off of naughty thoughts. My body reacts to her in ways I'm not used to. By the time I got in the shower, I was wet. *Down there.* Wet. Not just damp, but totally turned on from thinking about what we'd done last night.

It's sick.

Depraved.

Gloriously depraved.

I smile to myself, fiddling with my silver bangles. Tonight I put on several silver rings, too. Wanting to dress nicer is new to me. I'm such a comfort girl, and all of a sudden I want to look *hot.* Scorching, I-can't-resist-you hot. I want to look so hot that *Ashley* has to take two cold showers.

Only I don't want her to take a cold shower.

I want to feel her heat.

Uh-oh.

Now I'm turned on again.

Gaaaaahhhhh!

I look for her car as I walk through the lot, and when I spot it parked by the pier, my pulse quickens again. I pull out my phone and text her.

Are you inside?

She responds quickly. *Yes. Where are you?*

I step onto the pier and walk toward the Taproom, debating how to answer. I want to buy a few minutes to try to calm myself down. The pier is crowded with people eating ice cream from Scoops, an ice cream shop located at the end of the boardwalk. Others are walking along the pier and talking, looking out at the water as if they're window-shopping. I know that feeling. The pier is usually so serene and calming, but tonight, by the time I reach the Taproom, my nerves are buzzing like a swarm of bees in my belly, and I'm hoping and praying that I can keep my hands and lips to myself. I take a minute to breathe deeply before responding to Ashley's text. *Be there in one sec.*

It was Wyatt's idea for me and Ashley to meet him and Cassidy for drinks tonight. He thought that if I went out with people I trusted the first time I was out in public with Ashley as her girlfriend, it would be easier for me to be open with my feelings. It's worth a try. I want to be able to hold her hand and not be afraid of being a spectacle, and in my mind I know that I shouldn't even worry about it, because at least in our circle of friends, no one really cares. But I do worry, thanks to my parents. I want nothing more than to walk right through the door and kiss Ashley on her beautiful lips. I want to hold her hand and cuddle up against her like Cassidy does with Wyatt. I want to *be* her girlfriend.

I run a nervous hand down my dress, pull my shoulders back, and give myself a pep talk before opening the door.

The noise of the crowded room fills my ears.

Tristan waves from behind the bar as I step inside. He points to a table in the back.

I can do this.

I can kiss her.

I want to kiss her.

I follow Tristan's lead, passing tables and booths filled with patrons. Brandon's band is already set up in the back of the bar, and there are a handful of people milling about. Brandon lifts his chin in my direction and smiles. I smile, but can't seem to lift my hand to wave. I'm so nervous my chest burns. Wyatt and Cassidy are in a booth, facing me. Wyatt's eyes widen as I approach the table. I smile, or at least I think I do. I can't see Ashley, but I see her long, sexy leg slide out of the booth, and then her smokin'-hot body follows as she steps in front of me. She flips her long blond hair over her shoulder and pins me in place with a seductive stare, followed by a quick lift of her brows. *Ohmygod, she's so hot.* Her skirt hugs her curves and stops midthigh. I've tasted those thighs, and holy smokes, I can see her bra right through her shirt. It's lacy and pink, and the memory of her softness on my palms makes me curl my fingers up.

Stupid cold shower didn't do squat.

"Hi," I manage.

She reaches for my hand, and her eyes take a slow stroll down my body, making my mouth go dry. She leans forward, and my eyes quickly dart around the bar. *No, no, no.* I feel like there's a spotlight on us. I close my eyes for a second, and when she kisses my cheek instead of my lips, I'm ashamed to be relieved.

"You look delicious," she whispers.

Delicious.

How am I supposed to think when she looks like sex personified and says things like that? Her eyes fill with mischief as she leads me to the booth, obviously pleased with the way she's left me feeling like a dog in heat.

"Wow, Dee. You look great." Wyatt drapes an arm over Cassidy's shoulder. "I'm sitting with the three hottest babes in the place. Lucky me."

Ash slides into the booth and I sit beside her. She presses her thigh to mine. Our dresses are so short that we're skin to skin. *Hot skin to hot skin.*

I need to distract myself, or Wyatt and Cassidy will see all the dirty things going through my mind, like remembering what Ashley looked like naked beneath me and the way she cried my name as she came apart against my mouth.

Stopitstopitstopit.

I need a distraction...

I search for something to talk about, and my eyes bounce over Brandon and Brent playing in the band, then land on Cassidy, who is whispering something to Wyatt.

"Cassidy, how's the party planning going?" *Good. Safe subject.*

"Great. Brooke and I got hired for another big event in a few weeks." Cassidy picks up her camera from the seat. "Can I get a picture of the two of you?"

"Definitely." Ashley puts an arm over my shoulder and places her hand on my thigh. Her hand sears against my skin. I'm sure it's going to leave a scar.

I feel my cheeks heat up, and it's all I can do to keep my eyes from darting around the room to see who's watching.

"Will you take one of me and Wyatt?" Cassidy asks.

I lean forward to take the camera, hoping Ash will move her arm from behind my shoulder because I feel guilt creeping in and I want to keep it at bay. I hate feeling like my parents are staring down at me. I don't want to feel like anyone is staring at me. I just want to enjoy the evening with Ashley like we used to, but I know those days are gone. I can't look at her without wanting to kiss her. I feel like it's tattooed on my forehead.

She moves her arm but places her hand on my thigh again. Her thumb moves in a slow circular motion beneath the edge of my dress. I close my eyes behind the camera lens, enjoying the tingling sensation it's sending through my body.

"Dee, take the picture," Wyatt snaps.

"Sorry." Oh my God, I'm turning into a sex addict. I take the picture and hand him the camera, desperately needing to put some room between me and Ashley. I feel like the room is closing in on me. I wonder how my parents had the power to manipulate my thinking. Once I accepted that they had died, I really thought I'd just be able to move on and be myself. Part of me was, shamefully, relieved to have the freedom to finally act on my feelings. But there's nothing easy about any of this. Guilt sinks into me with every dirty thought, with every clean thought, too. Just wanting to hold Ashley's hand in public makes me remember my parents' disturbed look from graduation day.

Right here, right now, I vow that if I ever have kids, I will never, ever make them feel bad about who they are.

Never.

That's flippin' great for *my* future children, but not for me. I still feel the need to put space between me and Ashley. I look around the room. Livi and Rusty are both swamped with customers, which gives me the perfect escape.

"Drinks. We need drinks. I'll go order them from Tristan. What do you guys want?"

Wyatt stands. "I'll get them. Relax. You just got here."

I stand anyway. "We'll both go. You can't carry four drinks."

"I'll have whatever you're having," Ashley says with a smirk that tells me she knows exactly what effect she's having on me, and she's enjoying it way too much.

"Something fruity," Cassidy answers.

"You've got it, babe." Wyatt leans down and kisses her.

I long to kiss Ash, and I can tell the way she's watching them that she's wishing I would, too.

I feel a heavy hand on my shoulder before I hear Jesse's voice. "Delly. Wow. You look hot."

I turn, and he embraces me. I hate that my first thought is wondering whether he saw Ashley's hand on my thigh.

"Hi, Jesse. Thank you." I fidget with the edge of my dress as he looks over my shoulder at Ashley.

"Ash. How's it going?"

"Really, really good, Jesse." Her voice slides over my skin like liquid heat.

I need to get out of here before I climb into that booth and make out with my girlfriend.

Whoa. My girlfriend.

The fictitious spotlight is beaming at me again. I half expect someone to point at me and yell, *Lesbian! She's a lesbian!*

Holy shit. I'm a loser, and totally fucked-up.

"I'm going up to get drinks. Want one?" I ask as fast as I can.

Jesse shakes his head. "I'm heading down to Brooke's to help her out with moving some boxes. I just came by to tell you that Tim's getting out of rehab soon. He did really well, and I thought you'd want to know." *Uncle Tim...*My eyes shoot to Wyatt, who looks away for a beat. I don't think Jesse knows that Wyatt's visited Tim a few times since he went into rehab. I know by the clenching of Wyatt's jaw what he's thinking. He's trying to figure out how to protect us from getting tied up in Tim's mess again without pushing away my father's best friend completely. Wyatt's got a big heart and he's smart. I know he'll figure out the right thing to do, and I trust his judgment. It's not like we were personally tied up in Tim's gambling. He stole money from the Taproom, but now that we own the bar, it no longer feels like he stole from our parents. It feels like he stole from us. It's definitely more personal.

Wyatt nods. "I know. I've been in touch with him."

"You're a good man, Wyatt." Jesse puts his arm around Wyatt and lowers his voice. "But don't be stupid. Don't hire him back."

"No chance of that."

I steal a glance at Ash. She runs her tongue across her lower lip, and in that moment I wish I wasn't embarrassed, because I'd slide right in beside her and claim that taunting mouth of hers with a kiss so passionate Wyatt would tell us to get a room. Since that's not about to happen, I decide to give her a little torture of my own. My tie-dyed tank dress is loose and flowing. I lean down close, knowing she can see right down the neckline. Her eyes widen and fill with lust when she notices that I'm not wearing a bra.

I put my mouth beside her ear and whisper, "Paybacks are hell."

"You guys are too cute together," Cassidy says. "You look like you want to claw each other's clothes off, and it's really hot."

Holy shit. I bolt upright. "I...No...Really?" I hightail it up to the bar to get the drinks, but not before noticing that Ash has a big, cheesy grin on her face and there's a curious look on Jesse's.

"Hey, hon. What'll it be?"

Tristan leans on the bar, waiting for me to answer him, but my mind is stuck on *You guys look like you want to claw each other's clothes off...* That's exactly how I feel, which means I'm transparent as hell, and that rattles me to my core.

I look up at Tristan, and my mind goes completely blank. I can't remember what drinks anyone wanted, and Wyatt is still talking with Jesse.

"Um...whatever Cassidy and Ash usually order, I guess. And I need a blue margarita please. Superstrong."

Tristan raises his brows. "Uh-oh. One of those nights? I was hoping this double date would ease your discomfort with the whole...you know what."

I climb onto a barstool and lower my voice. "Yeah, well, it turns out that now that I've kissed her, apparently I can't be around her without wanting to kiss her again. And again. And again."

Tristan laughs.

I try to focus on the song the band is playing, but my eyes keep drifting toward the booth.

Tristan taps my shoulder. "Baby steps, remember? This is a good thing."

"No. It's not. Because doing those things here will only make me feel guilty as hell, and then I get all teary-eyed and weird." I watch him mix our drinks, and when he brings them to me, I down the margarita and get a wicked brain freeze. I close my eyes and wince.

"Shit, shit, shit."

"Slow down, girlie." Tristan shakes his head.

When the pain eases, I push the glass across the bar to him.

"Better?" he asks.

"A little." At least now I can hear the music instead of just the battle between want, need, and embarrassment that's warring in my head.

Tristan takes the glass and makes another. "You're finally

the one making the rules, Delilah."

I feel Wyatt's hand land on my shoulder. He leans in close. "You and your girlfriend are getting eyed by every guy in here."

I drop my head between my shoulders. "Great."

"It's a compliment, Dee. You guys look hot."

"Together? Because Cassidy said we look like we want to rip each other's clothes off." I meet Wyatt's gaze, and he's got a serious look in his eyes.

"No. Not like that at all. Jesus, Cass said that?" He glances over his shoulder at the table. "I don't know what she sees, but from my perspective, you're just two hot girls out having a drink. Don't sweat it, and don't worry—I'm giving the evil eye to the gawkers."

I roll my eyes. He always watches out for me. I wish I could say it's gotten worse since our parents died, but it hasn't. This is who Wyatt has always been. He's almost two full minutes older than me, and he thinks that gives him the title of supreme protector. He'll probably always be overly protective, and in some ways it's the best feeling in the world knowing he'll always stand up for me, but I know it also makes it way too easy for me to *let* him do it.

We return to the table with the drinks and fall into a conversation about music, bands, and movies. Ashley's had her hand on my thigh under the table the whole time we've been talking, and while it stole my ability to concentrate at first, now it feels familiar and nice. I slip my hand beneath the table and lace my fingers with hers. My eyes dart to the dance floor and the people at the nearby tables, but no one seems to notice, and I'm relieved.

"I almost forgot. This weekend my little brother is going to be in his first lead role in a play." Ashley squeezes my hand. "I'd love it if you'd come home with me and meet my family, go see his play."

"Meet your family?" Butterflies flutter in my stomach again.

"Yeah, you'll love them."

"Meet your family."

Wyatt nudges my toe under the table as if to signal that I'm being an idiot, which I am. If we had never kissed, I wouldn't think twice about accepting the invitation. Now it carries the fear of wondering if her parents will act like mine would if I had brought a girlfriend home.

I want this to work. I want to be with Ashley. I have to try.

"Sure, okay. If you're sure your family won't mind."

Ashley squeezes my hand again. "They won't. I can't wait for you to meet them."

"I didn't even know you had a little brother." Cassidy's sitting beneath my brother's arm, pressed up against his side.

"I do. Kenny's seven. He wasn't exactly planned." Ashley sips her drink and shifts her eyes to me. "Dee, want to dance?"

We've danced together a million times, but never as a couple. I push past the nervous feeling in my stomach.

We're just two friends dancing. I can do this. Baby steps.

I unlace our fingers and move out of the booth and toward the crowded dance floor. I try not to think about how much I want to touch her, or kiss her, and I dance as we always have— only this time it feels like we're in a zone all our own as our hips move in tandem and our bodies move with a different type of familiarity. The kind of familiar, seductive movements that occur only between two people who have experienced moments of intense passion.

Ashley holds my gaze as her hand brushes mine, and she steps in closer, stealing all the air from the room. She's so sexy I swear it takes all my focus *not* to touch her. The music slows and she moves her shoulders and hips as she slithers her body down mine, our thighs skimming, like a scene straight out of *Dirty Dancing*. Her eyes are still locked on mine as she dances her way back up. Need rushes through me, and my body stills. I'm trying to move. Anything. My hips, my arms, my shoulders, but I'm a statue. My entire body's aflame. I feel as if I'm in a spotlight again and scan the other people, all dancing without giving us a second glance, and I realize it's the heat of *her* gaze that makes me feel like I'm the only one in the room.

I can't stand it one more second. I can't resist her. I don't know how I find the courage to reach for her hand and drag her toward the ladies' room. I need to touch her, to kiss her, to let her feel what's going on inside me. I push into the tight bathroom and seal my lips over hers, kissing her like this second, this kiss, is all we have. It's sloppy and wet and deep and hot and I never want it to end. I know she needs air, and I give her mine. She grabs my face and pries our lips apart, eyes wide as she searches my face.

"You held my hand."

I can't respond. I want her lips on mine again.

Ashley, Ashley, Ashley.

"Delilah, you *held* my hand on the way to the bathroom."

I nod, or maybe I don't. I can't tell, because she's repeating herself, so it makes me wonder if I moved at all.

She kisses me slowly and tenderly, and I melt against her. Then she touches my cheek with her hand and whispers, "Thank you."

CHAPTER TEN

Ashley

WAKING UP WRAPPED around Delilah is so much better than I'd ever dreamed. All those nights we'd spent sleeping in the same room after parties had given me plenty of time to conjure up what it would be like to actually sleep with her body against mine. But nothing compares to this, or to falling asleep with her in my arms, knowing she's mine. I was overwhelmed when she took my hand last night in the bar. I know it was a huge step for her, even though we could have easily looked like two friends simply going to the ladies' room together. It's a common enough occurrence that it wouldn't raise any eyebrows, but Delilah has been so sensitive to how others see us that for her it was a major deal. And I'd be lying if I said it wasn't for me, too.

We spent the night at her place as we'd planned, and this morning, as much as I wanted to join her in the shower, I didn't. I'm so grateful she's taking these steps, no matter how big or small. I didn't want to add any pressure. I think we were both testing boundaries last night. She looked sexier than hell—not that she doesn't always, but last night? In that dress? I think she was testing her own boundaries, while I was testing ours as a couple.

I've decided to let her lead. No more pushing her limits. I know she's trying to figure out how to live a lifestyle she's had to pretend she didn't want, and I want to be there for her and help her through the hard times and the good times. I have faith in Delilah, and when we kiss—*Lordy, Lordy, when we kiss*—I can feel that she's falling for me just like I'm falling for her.

I watch her walking through the kitchen from my seat on the deck, where I'm having coffee with Tristan. My stomach gets all fluttery. My stomach never gets fluttery. At least it never used to. Delilah's watching me, too, and she's smiling as she comes through the door. She touches my shoulder as she sits beside me. Even that small gesture, touching me in a way that speaks volumes about how she feels about me, is a big deal. I reach up and cover her hand with mine.

"Hey," she says in a shy voice.

Reading Delilah can be confusing. Her touch and the shy voice conflict, but I'm trying not to question the conflicting messages, because if I find them confusing, chances are that Delilah finds them even more so.

"Good morning." I eye her shorts and billowing top. I know she has no idea how sexy she looks. Her hair falls over her shoulders, and the scent of her lilac shampoo fills my lungs. "I love your outfit."

"You do?"

She looks down and touches the edges of her lacy white boho chic top. It's one of those shirts with spaghetti straps, cut-out shoulders, and three-quarter sleeves that fall halfway down her arms. She's wearing my favorite pair of her cutoffs, the dark blue ones with thick fringe at the bottom, and several colorful bangles circle her wrist. She looks amazing.

I peer down at her feet, secretly hoping to see her boots, and sure enough, she's wearing them unlaced with frilly white socks. So freaking cute I can't help but break my own rule about letting her lead and kiss her cheek.

"You look amazing."

"God, why can't I find a guy like you?" Tristan leans back with a sigh.

Delilah's cheeks pink up, and I move away, giving her space. She reaches over and laces her fingers with mine. My heart skips a beat, and I swear it takes all my strength not to jump up and down and scream, *Yay! She's mine! She's mine!* I clear my throat to suppress the cheesy smile that's fighting to part my lips and hope the one I allow is not enough to make her retreat.

I don't mind walking on eggshells for a little while.

"You will, Tristan," Delilah assures him.

"Not anytime soon. I'm giving up on guys for a while."

Tristan's comment draws her attention. "Giving up on guys? Why?"

Tristan flicks an invisible piece of lint from his white tank top and looks out over the water. "After Ian I don't really trust my instincts. I think I need to take a step back."

"You need to play the field and not care," Brandon says as he comes out from the kitchen and stands beside Tristan. He does a pelvic thrust and raises his brows in quick succession. "You know what I say about getting over a guy."

Tristan shakes his head. "I have no desire to get *over* or *under* another guy right now, thank you very much. Get your package out of my face."

Brandon sinks into the chair beside Tristan and eyes mine and Delilah's linked hands. "Tristan, you should have been a lesbian."

Tristan closes his eyes for a beat and shakes his head. "Do I even want to ask?"

"Seriously, dude." He nods at me and Delilah. "Chicks make out and suddenly they're in love and moving in together. We're not like that. Guys are about sex. Girls are about relationships."

Uh-oh. This is one of those eggshell moments. He's right. Women tend to move much faster toward relationships than men. I watch Delilah for signs of discomfort at his reference of moving in together. She's playing with the fringe on her shorts.

"No shit, but I like dick, not vag." Tristan slides an apologetic look to us. "Sorry. I have to speak his language or else he'll ramble on and on for an hour."

Delilah shifts uncomfortably in her chair. She leans in closer to me and whispers, "He's right. Brandon will keep pushing him."

There's nothing Brandon can say that shocks me anymore. Beneath his brash exterior is a big, loving heart. I still remember the day he set those almond-shaped dark eyes on me after I broke up with Sandy. He saw I was hurting and said, *Not everyone is a prick. Come back with me to Harborside. You'll love my friends.* I don't know if Brandon saw something in me that would click with Delilah, or if he meant his friends in general, but he was right. I needed this group of warm and wonderful friends, and Delilah? Well, I can't imagine my life without her.

Brandon shrugs. "Whatever, dude. It is what it is."

"There *are* monogamous guys out there. Brandon just doesn't look for them." I smirk at Brandon, and he smirks right back.

"I'm not giving up for good—just taking a hiatus. No hookups. No searching for Mr. Right." Tristan's eyes warm as they glide over me and Delilah. "But I'm happy that you two found each other."

Delilah blushes again and drops her eyes, but her smile tells me that she is, too.

CHAPTER ELEVEN

Delilah

ASHLEY AND I spent Tuesday night at her place. This time I actually made it through most of the evening without tearing her clothes off. It wasn't easy, but I love spending time with her and I don't want her to think that I only like her for sex.

Boy, is that a weird thought.

Me using someone for sex?

Me. The lesbian virgin until just a few days ago?

Weird. Definitely weird. But not as weird as knowing that the entire time she was getting ready for work this morning, I couldn't take my eyes off of her. She moves so confidently and gracefully at the same time. She's like the perfect woman.

My perfect woman.

Our toothbrushes hang in the holder side by side. Our hairbrushes and elastic hairbands sit on the dresser. My clothes are on the chair in the corner of her room, tucked beneath her hoodie and shorts. Seeing our stuff comingling has definitely had an impact on me. It makes me want to be comfortable outside of our homes with her, too. It makes me want to try harder.

I've been thinking about what Brandon said about girls and

relationships and guys and sex, and although I think there is some truth to it, I also think he has it a little skewed. Girls are about sex *and* relationships. Finding the one person in this world who understands me the way Ashley does, who is patient with my insecurities and *also* turns me on the way she does? I know our relationship is a rare gift, and I know I'll never tire of being with her, emotionally or physically.

Before leaving her apartment for the day, I run down to my Jeep and get the gift I bought for her yesterday. I had to have Brent give it to Brandon to bring to me so she wouldn't find out, but it was worth the sneaking around. I make the bed and gather my things. We're staying here again tonight, so I leave my bag on the chair in the corner, then write a note in the card I brought and set the gift in the center of the mattress.

As I climb into my Jeep I see a white paper stuck beneath the windshield wiper. I look around and don't see any NO PARKING signs. With a heavy sigh I get out and snag it from the windshield.

Ashley's handwriting makes me smile, but her words cut straight to my heart.

D, I miss you already. Xo, A

CHAPTER TWELVE

Ashley

IT'S THURSDAY. I hate Thursdays. I never used to hate them, but ever since Delilah fooled around with Janessa, Thursday has become my least favorite day of the week. I woke up feeling jealous and insecure an hour ago, and I'm lying here trying to hide it, but Delilah and I have become so in tune with each other that I know when she wakes up she'll feel it rolling off of me. She looks so peaceful sleeping beside me. I don't want to ruin her day with my own insecurities, so I slip from my bed, tiptoe into the bathroom, and turn on the shower.

I step beneath the spray and close my eyes, hoping it'll help clear my mind. The warm water soothes the tension that has my shoulders riding practically beneath my ears. I look down at the shampoo bottles, and my heart squeezes with the sight of Delilah's shampoo, her scented body wash, and her pink razor. How can these little everyday items hold so much meaning? I pick up her shampoo and open the cap, inhaling the scent. I feel myself smile even though it only sort of smells like Delilah. Her skin has a scent apart from all of these manufactured aromas that is purely her own.

Thinking about Delilah brings me back to it being Thursday and Delilah attending group counseling tonight with Janessa. I've been able to put the image of Janessa touching her out of my mind for the past week, but now that it's Thursday, it creeps right back in. Janessa is gorgeous, and I know she and Delilah are friends. I've noticed when she gets a text from Janessa she's careful not to react too strongly in front of me, although she never hides the texts or waits to answer them, and I appreciate that. I probably shouldn't be jealous, given that I've been with other girls before I was with Delilah, and she doesn't even ask about them. Well, other than Sandy, but I kind of offered her up, and Delilah never asked about the intimate side of our relationship.

I know Delilah needs the group sessions, but I just don't know how to get past this. She seems to gain something from them even when she says she doesn't. Every day she gets a little more confident. When she first moved here, on the heels of her parents' deaths, she was pretty withdrawn. I think moving back into the house with Wyatt after staying with Brooke was a big step in her moving forward and healing. When she moved to Brooke's she told me that Wyatt reminded her too much of her father, which made it hard for her to stay at the beach house. I know his fight at the Taproom also fed into her reasons for leaving, but knowing she was able to move back and push past the similarities between Wyatt and her father is huge.

I've also noticed a difference in the way she handles herself. She moves with more confidence around the Taproom. I know her counseling sessions have a lot to do with her progress, and I'd never ask her to choose between the sessions and me. That would be totally unfair. But that doesn't mean it didn't cross my mind this morning when thoughts of her kissing Janessa were sailing through my mind.

My eyes fill with tears knowing that today my stomach will twist into worse knots than it already has, and I'll be nervous the whole time she's there. It's selfish. I know how she feels about me. She surprised me with a wet suit for goodness' sakes, and left it on my bed with a card that said, *I wish I were always with you to keep you warm.* She cares about me a lot. I can feel it every time we're close. She said she saw how cold I was the other morning and she couldn't stand to see me shivering. She was actually mad at the guys for not giving up their own wet suits. She's so cute. I think there's a protective side to her, similar to Wyatt's, but she's buried every feeling so deeply that she probably doesn't even realize it's in there somewhere.

I can't wait to discover more about who she really is. I want to know everything about her, and I want her to know everything about me.

The shower curtain opens and Delilah peeks in. She's told me that she's never showered with anyone before, and this is another one of her baby steps. That's what she calls them, even though I know they're gigantic steps, and I'm so proud of her for trying that tears sting my eyes again as I reach for her hand.

I *never* cry, and Delilah brings tears to my eyes by stepping into the shower? I'm in deep trouble.

She crosses her arms over her chest and looks at me with a sweet, embarrassed wrinkle of her brow. I kiss the worry lines away as I back her under the warm water and fold her into my arms. I feel her apprehension ease as the rigidity in her limbs dissolves and she becomes soft and pliable once again.

My Delilah.

I'm falling for you, Delilah.

Your vulnerabilities and your insecurities and your strength to try to push through them. I'm falling for your sweet lips that are pressing against my shoulder and your gentle caress as you stroke my back. I'm falling for your voice, whispering in my ear.

"Do you mind that I'm in here?" Delilah asks so tentatively. I'm surprised she can't feel in my touch how much I want to be with her.

"No. I always want you with me."

I'm falling for the way you make me feel full and whole and like a girly girl and a lover and your best friend. I'm falling for the way you're turning my body so I'm beneath the warm spray, too.

I close my eyes and pull her close without telling her any of these things, even though keeping them inside is like trying to keep a lid on boiling water. I don't tell her because it's Thursday, and she needs Thursdays, even if they scare the shit out of me.

CHAPTER THIRTEEN

Delilah

WHEN I DRIVE Ashley to the beach to meet Drake for her surfing lesson, it makes me feel even more like we're a couple. It's a small thing, driving her to her lesson, but it feels like another level of commitment, another level of opening my closet door and sticking my toe out. Testing the waters. Granted, there aren't many people here yet, but there will be soon.

I'm glad Ashley doesn't mind if I tag along. I like watching her, and I feel better knowing that she has her wet suit to wear. I was working when she got home and found it on the bed. She called me when she opened it, and I could hear her sniffling over the phone. I'm not sure if she knew I could hear her, but I did. Ash is so strong all the time that hearing those emotions took me by surprise. Just like this morning when I joined her in the shower. I could tell that she was upset when I first joined her, even though she told me she was fine. I felt her holding something back. But she never pushes me, so I didn't press her about what it was. I assume she'll tell me when she's ready.

I brought my sketch pad so I can draw while Ashley works with Drake, but I can't concentrate on anything except watching her. I bury my feet in the sand, set my sketch pad aside, and bury my hands in her sweatshirt pockets. I've claimed this sweatshirt as my own. Not that she cares. I think she'd let me borrow anything, just like I'd let her.

Drake's really patient with her as Ash wipes out a dozen times or more, and he's right there to help her out. I'm glad, because even though she can totally handle herself, having him there keeps me from wanting to run into the surf to help her myself. All these unfamiliar emotions keep tumbling forward, like *wanting* to be the one to help her in the water and not being able to get enough of her when we're alone. I always thought couples were kidding about that overwhelming desire to ravage each other. I couldn't imagine it. Now it's hard not to.

She's so cute, and she keeps glancing over at me and laughing. I'm sitting a good distance away because I didn't want to distract her, but I think I am. Her laughter is better than the sound of the ocean or the gulls, or any other sound I've ever heard. I know I'm not going to sketch a darn thing, and part of me wonders if my sketching was filling a gap in my life for all these years. I love to sketch, but having a sketch pad and pencil used to be like extra limbs, always with me, at the ready. Now they often feel like accessories that don't match my moods.

My phone vibrates with a text, and I dig it out of my bag. *Janessa.*

Oh, shit. Janessa.

No wonder Ash was upset this morning. It's Thursday. I didn't put two and two together. Over the past week Janessa has texted me on and off with pictures of Jackie and just friendly stuff, touching base. She's been totally supportive of me and Ashley, and I don't want to end our friendship just because we made out once. It wasn't even like really making out. It was more like she provided physical CliffsNotes. I had friends in college who dated guys and then dated their best friends, and sometimes they'd even date another one of their friends and still remain close to all of them. I don't want to make Ashley uncomfortable, but I think once she gets to know Janessa, she'll like her, too.

I read her message.

Coffee after the session tonight?

I look over at Ashley and hope I'm not making a mistake as I respond.

Sure. Mind if Ash comes?

My heartbeat speeds up.

Not at all. Where? Dean will pick me up with the kids afterward. My car's in the shop.

I breathe a little easier. I'm about to take a really big baby step, and it scares me, but as I watch Ashley and think about the risk she's taking for me—by allowing me the time and space to learn how to deal with our relationship in public, even though she'd promised herself never to be in this position again—I know she's worth it.

I'll have Ash meet us at Brooke's Bytes.

Ashley

DELILAH AND I carry our stuff to the Jeep after my surfing lesson, laughing as we wave goodbye to Drake.

"I swear it's like I have two left feet on that board." We secure the board into the back of the Jeep. The morning is warming up, and even though it's early, young families are already arriving at the beach, carrying enough paraphernalia for an army. I reach for Delilah's hand, and her eyes dart around the lot, landing on a couple heading in our direction.

I don't say anything as she pulls her hand out of reach. I tuck away my hurt feelings and remind myself she's worth it. She climbs into the drivers' seat, and I take a deep breath before climbing into the passenger seat.

"Janessa texted about tonight."

Ugh. "Oh?" I hate that my voice sounds strained.

She pulls out of the parking lot as if she hasn't just given me a double whammy. "She asked if I wanted to meet for coffee after group tonight."

"Mm." It's all I can manage. What does she expect me to say? *Great? Have fun?* Sorry. I'm patient, and I'm understanding, but they've been down and dirty with each other. The last thing I want to think about is the two of them alone somewhere.

She stops at a red light and reaches for my hand. "Will you meet us at Brooke's?"

Her voice is so hopeful that it's hard to stay upset with her for not taking my hand in the parking lot. And then...I realize what she's just asked.

"Brooke's? Why would you go where everyone knows you when you're so careful about people knowing about us?"

She raises her eyebrows and her lips curve up in a nervous smile. It's not until she traps that plump lower lip of hers with her teeth that I realize what she's doing.

She's trying.

Well, I'll be damned. My eyes well with tears again as I nod, and she throws her arms around my neck and hugs me.

The car behind us honks and we both laugh, but inside my heart is singing.

CHAPTER FOURTEEN

Delilah

AS I WALK up the front steps to the YMCA, I remember the first time I went to group counseling with Brooke. Despite Brooke telling me that we would sit in a circle with other people who had lost loved ones and discuss the trouble we were having working through our losses, I still didn't really know what to expect. Nothing can prepare you for the look on people's faces when they share their stories of longing to see someone they love or the overwhelming sadness that envelopes you as you watch pain turn their hands to fists and pull tears from their eyes. Nothing could have prepared me for the moments of grief that I would experience over the first few months after my parents died. And certainly nothing could have prepared me for the way their deaths impacted my ability—or inability—to *come out*.

I really need to find a better way to think about this than coming out, because I hate how that phrase makes me feel. I mull that over for a few minutes as I settle into my seat. I'm the only one in the room and it's quiet. The linoleum floor makes the room feel cold when there's no one else in it.

Coming out.

Admitting I'm a lesbian.

Being myself.

Nothing feels right. How about *none of anyone's damn business?*

I swear I can think like a confident person when it comes to this stuff, but thinking and acting are two different things.

"Hey there, Delilah," Janessa says as she comes through the door and takes the seat beside me. She tucks her hair behind her ear and pushes her purse beneath her chair. She's wearing a tank top and shorts, and as she settles into her seat, she sighs loudly.

"What a day. Jackie and I spent the afternoon making sand castles. I've never built so many in one day." She arches a brow and smiles. "I wonder if there are surrogate castle builders. I'll have to look into that."

We both laugh.

I like being with Janessa, and I still don't feel funny around her—and she obviously doesn't feel weird around me. For the first time since coming to group, I notice I'm holding my head higher. I have a little better handle on who I am, and it feels really good.

Mark and Cathy come into the room holding hands. Their shoulders are rounded forward and there's no mistaking the red rims around Cathy's eyes. I wonder if she's upset over the daughter they lost or something unrelated, and then I realize that everything in their life is probably connected to her death in some way. No words can come close to taking away their pain. *It'll be okay* is something people say when they don't know what else to say. Or *give it time.* I wonder if they ever want to respond with, *No, it won't,* or *All the time in the world won't bring our daughter back.* I can't imagine losing a child, and I can't imagine how they make it through each day.

"How are things with Ashley?" Janessa whispers.

"Amazing. But also nerve-racking. I'm not very good at the whole PDA thing. It still makes me feel funny."

She nods as if she understands, but before she can respond, Michael and Meredith enter the room and take the seats across from us.

"Good evening, ladies." Meredith folds her hands in her lap. She looks like a librarian in her long skirt and button-down blouse. "Mark, Cathy. It's nice to see you."

Mark smiles, but I can tell it's forced by the pinched lines around the edges of his mouth. They lost their daughter to leukemia some months before I began attending the sessions. Sometimes they seem like they're doing well, moving forward. Then there are times like tonight, when their tired eyes and boneless postures speak of sleepless nights and longing for a daughter they'll never hold again.

Janessa leans in close and whispers, "You need to acknowledge her in public as soon as you're comfortable."

It takes me a minute to realize she's talking about Ashley.

"I know." I watch Meredith as she rights her purse beside her chair.

"You'll hurt her feelings, and that's hard to overcome." Janessa holds my gaze and nods, as if to say, *Trust me.*

Mark's voice calls both of our attention. "Meredith, I think Cathy and I have fallen back into a cycle of guilt and bargaining, and we're not sure how to break free from it. We feel guilty that our daughter died, when we would have gladly given our lives instead, and even though we know that's not a reasonable bargain to wish for, we can't stop. And then we feel guilty for not being able to stop." Mark clasps both hands around Cathy's. Cathy nods in confirmation. "Is there anything you can suggest to help us through this?"

I try to pay attention, to think past what Janessa said, but I know she's right. I see the hurt in Ashley's eyes every time I pull out of her reach. I wish I could have told my parents years ago and just dealt with the fallout. I think it would have made things much easier now.

"Mark, Cathy, as you know, stages of guilt aren't always singular, and they don't follow regular patterns. For some people, bargaining and guilt go hand in hand, and for others, they skip over one of those stages altogether. Everyone's grief is different."

Meredith's voice pulls me from my thoughts. Her eyes are empathetic and her tone is warm and understanding. "It's very common for a person to feel as though they've gotten past the hardest stages of grieving only to find out that their legs are knocked out from under them a few weeks or months later. Was there something that started this cycle? A birthday? An anniversary?"

A first girlfriend.

Mark and Cathy exchange a knowing glance. Cathy nods, and Mark answers for both of them. "We went out with our friends and they were talking about their daughter starting college in the fall. As you know, our Mara would have been attending college this fall, too."

"And how did that make you feel?" Meredith leans forward as she asks this.

I think it's a cruel and unnecessary question. Of course they're feeling sad and angry. Why does she want them to reiterate it? I glance at Janessa, wondering if she's thinking the same thing, but she's looking at them expectantly as well.

"At first I was happy for them. That they get to see their

daughter go off to college. Then it made me upset, of course," Cathy explains. "And then I was just angry. I was mad that they'd bring that up when they knew we lost Mara." Tears stream down her cheeks, and Mark pulls her against him and whispers something, then kisses her temple.

"That's perfectly understandable, Cathy. And I think you know what I'm going to say next." Meredith pauses as her words settle in.

I don't know what she's going to say. I shift in my seat, uncomfortable with the sadness in the room.

Cathy nods. Mark nods. Janessa and Michael nod, and I feel lost.

"You lost your daughter, and that's a horrific loss for you and Mark."

"Yes," Cathy agrees, patting her tears with a tissue. "And if I could have been the one who was sick, I would have. I would have died twice over to save Mara."

Mark pulls her closer, his own eyes tearing now.

"I know you would have. But the world is full of families who *didn't* lose their children." Meredith pauses again.

My stomach clenches. Just like after my parents died. I couldn't understand how the whole world functioned normally around me when everything I knew had been turned upside down.

Cathy and Mark nod.

"Remember when we talked about finding ways to accept our losses so we can move forward? That's not an easy thing to do. For some people it means avoiding certain friends from before they lost their loved ones. Others choose to talk to their friends and let them know the topics that are still too raw to deal with. Sometimes friends will shy away, and that's another type of loss that isn't easy to get past." Meredith wrinkles her brow.

"Meredith, may I say something?" Janessa asks.

I'm surprised. She rarely contributes.

"Yes, please." Meredith nods.

"When I lost my older sister, I was pretty young. For the longest time, I held on to the grief. I thought that if I didn't, I would forget her, or let her down. And she had always been there for me, so even though she was gone, I didn't want to let her down."

I reach for Janessa's hand and squeeze it. I knew she'd lost a family member, but I didn't realize it was her older sister. How could I not have asked? I've been so closed off, worrying about my own grief, my own sexuality, that I never opened my eyes long enough to offer support to her. I've been a terrible friend.

Janessa covers my hand with hers and manages to smile at me before turning back to Mark and Cathy and continuing her story. "One day my mom told me that I was focusing on losing her and forgetting all the good times we had. She said that I was putting an unfair burden on my sister. At first I didn't understand that. I was a teenager when she committed suicide, and I didn't feel like I was putting a burden on her."

My stomach careens south. *Suicide? Oh, Janessa. I'm so sorry.*

"It took a while for me to understand what she meant. I was so focused on not forgetting her that she became a legacy of pain instead of being remembered as the supportive, fun, loving big sister that she was." Janessa takes a deep breath and blows it out slowly. "It's been years since she died, and the loss is still there. Sort of like a scar. Every once in a while I get a wave of sadness, but I've learned to move past it by drawing on the good memories. I can't exactly keep myself from being friends with anyone who might mention their sister." She pauses for a moment.

"I realized that by trying to hold on to that pain, I *was* trying to please my sister. My mom was right." Janessa shakes her head. "It sounds strange, but I thought that if I kept that pain, I'd make up for the reasons she killed herself. It wasn't until recently that I realized I could learn from her death and help other people in her situation not feel so alone."

"That's a big discovery, and it's also a common coping mechanism. Using your grief to help others can be cathartic," Meredith says.

"Like you do." The words come without thought. Meredith lost her husband ten years ago, and I know she's been running these meetings for the past few years.

"Yes, like I do." Meredith smiles at me.

"My thoughts are no longer centered on how unfair it is that I lost my sister." Janessa pulls her shoulders back and releases my hand. "I realized how hurtful those thoughts were. Now when I'm confronted with similar situations, I draw upon the good memories, and it's like...*Yeah, I had a sister.* She was funny and protective, and sometimes she was a big pain in the butt. And she loved green ice cream. Any flavor as long as it was green." Janessa smiles. "It feels good to remember the good times."

The rest of the hour we talk about bargaining and letting go, moving past the guilt of wanting to live our lives to please the people we've lost. Or at least that's what I hear, because it's what I realize I'm doing with my parents.

After the meeting, Janessa and I walk toward the boardwalk. The glow of lights on the boardwalk is pretty in the distance, like halos from stars that are too close to earth. Janessa hasn't said a word since we left the YMCA. Her eyes are trained on the ground and her hands hang loosely by her sides. I have never seen her this disengaged, and I know she must be thinking about her sister.

"That was an intense meeting," I say quietly, letting her know I'm here if she wants to talk. There's so much I want to say, but I'm feeling her out, seeing if she's okay with talking after revealing so much.

"Yeah."

"I'm sorry about your sister."

She loops her arm into mine. "Do you mind if I do this? I'm not hitting on you, and I respect your relationship with Ash. I just need a little support."

"No. It's fine." And it is. I've been right where she is. I have Ashley, Wyatt, Cassidy, Tristan, Jesse, and even Brandon, to support me. I wonder who Janessa has besides her brother. "Do you mind if I ask why your sister committed suicide?"

She shakes her head. "She was attending a really conservative college up north. She was also a lesbian, but she never came out, and one day her roommate found her in bed with a girl who happened to be the girlfriend of one of the football players."

"Ouch."

"Yeah. She couldn't take the bullying. She left me a voicemail before she did it, but I was thirteen. I had no idea what it meant. Talk about carrying guilt." Janessa looks away. Her voice gets thin. "She said, no matter what, live the life I'm meant to live. She said…" Her breath hitches and she stops walking.

"I'm sorry, Janessa." I pull her into my arms, trying to comfort and keep my own tears at bay.

"She said that she loved me and to always remember that. She said…" She draws in a fast breath. "She said I was someone special and that…" Another hitched breath. "That I should tell my parents she loved them."

"I'm so sorry."

"Her name was Jacqueline. Jackie."

My heart cracks open and tears spill down my cheeks.

She draws back and holds my shoulders. Remarkably, she's smiling despite her tears. She reaches up and wipes my tears.

Wipes *my* tears. She lost her sister and she's wiping *my* tears.

"It's okay, really." She sniffles and wipes her own tears. "Come on. Let's go meet your girlfriend before she worries that we got lost."

I'm floored that she can move past this so quickly, while I'm still scrambling to pick up the pieces of my heart for *her* loss.

Thinking about Ashley makes my stomach clench for an entirely different reason.

"Um…About Ash. She's a little uncomfortable about all of this, but I really enjoy our friendship, and I—"

"Don't worry," she interrupts. "I get it. It would be weird if she wasn't jealous, but I'll explain to her about my sister. She'll understand."

"Your sister? What does your sister have to do with this?"

"She's the reason I reached out to you. You were struggling so much, and it was obvious that you're carrying a ton of guilt about your parents, and you were hiding your feelings for Ashley."

"Wait. Did you think I was suicidal?" I stop walking again.

"No. Not at all. I just…I liked you from the moment we met a few weeks ago. As a friend, so don't get weirded out. You remind me of my sister, and when I saw how conflicted you were, I wanted you to feel safe and…"

"Confident. I remember." As her words sink in, I gather courage to ask what I've been trying not to think about. "Have you offered that for many others?"

She shakes her head. "No. Just you. When I said I wanted to help people in her situation, I didn't mean by offering my body to them. I meant by talking, letting them know they're not alone."

"Oh…"

"I know you wonder why I offered myself to you, and it just felt right, Delilah. It's not like I go around sleeping with people I hardly know. I'm not a one-night-stand kind of person. You were so…tortured. Floundering. I felt close to you and wanted to help."

I assume that her feeling the desire to help me was very much like my acceptance of her offer. It felt right and doesn't need to be dissected.

"Thank you, Janessa. You really did help me more than you can ever know."

"I think I know," she says softly.

We walk in silence for the remainder of the way. The din of tourists grows louder as we turn down a residential side street and cut through an alley to the boardwalk. We weave through the throng of tourists heading toward Brooke's Bytes. The smell of French fries grows thicker as we pass Fried Critters, a walk-up fast-food restaurant.

"Mm, that makes me hungry," I say to break the silence.

"Really? I figured you for an ice cream girl." Janessa's tone is lighter, and I notice she's standing taller and her face isn't as pinched as it was when we left counseling.

"Oh, I'm definitely an ice cream girl, a pizza girl, a French fry girl." I laugh. "I'm not a picky eater at all. My mom used to tell me that I'd weigh six hundred pounds when I grew up with the way I ate."

Janessa's eyes shift to me, watching, assessing.

"It doesn't feel weird to talk about my mom," I say so quietly I wonder if she can hear it. "It feels good to remember."

She touches my shoulder. "Good, Delilah. That's good."

We pass the arcade, greeted with the *ping*s and *ding*s of the games, and I spot Ashley leaning on the railing in front of Brooke's Bytes. My heartbeat speeds up, and I feel myself smiling. She must sense my eyes on her, because she turns and searches for a second before finding me. Her lips curve up, and she takes a step in our direction. Her eyes shift to Janessa, and her smile falters, but she forces it to return. Well, mostly, anyway.

She's trying.

Ashley

I CONSIDER MYSELF a pretty good judge of character, despite the way I misjudged Sandy. There are certain things we have to forgive ourselves for. Otherwise we'd never learn and grow or move forward on any level. I forgive myself for Sandy because, let's face it, if a person wants to deceive someone badly enough, they will make it happen. Sandy was well versed in the act of deceiving, and I was well practiced in the ability to trust. I'd never been with anyone I didn't trust. Sandy broke that in me, and until Delilah, I feared my ability to trust was broken for good. But I never felt like I couldn't trust Delilah. Even after I found out about her night with Janessa, I still trusted her.

She's never tried to hide anything from me. Well, except I can tell she's keeping some things about her parents close to her chest, but that's a whole different ball game. Those aren't lies. Those are pieces of herself that she's just not ready to share yet.

"Hi." Delilah comes close but doesn't reach for my hand, which is hurtful, especially since she's with Janessa, but I get it, so I don't say anything.

"Hi. Sorry if we made you wait," she says. "Ash, you remember Janessa."

"Yeah, hi." God, she's pretty. I glance at Delilah, whose eyes are on me.

On me.

Thank you.

I'm an idiot for worrying.

Janessa leans in and hugs me, and I manage to make it completely awkward, with one hand dangling by my side and the other kind of patting her on the back.

"Hi, Ashley. I'm so glad you're here. Delilah talks about you nonstop."

I have no idea if she's telling me the truth or trying to make me feel better because she can tell that I'm battling feeling like a third wheel around them, but her comment makes me feel better.

We go into Brooke's Bytes, and Brooke whips by us carrying a tray of food.

"Hey, girls! Take a seat. I'll be right there." Brooke's dark hair is tied back in a low ponytail. She's wearing a bright blue apron with BROOKE'S BYTES across the chest.

We sit at a table by the wall and Delilah still doesn't take my hand, but her knee presses against mine. It might seem silly, but that's enough for now. It's something. And I know for her, it's a lot.

After we're settled in, Brooke comes to take our orders.

"Girls' night out after counseling. I like it." Brooke smiles, nods. She pats Delilah's shoulder. "What can I get you?"

"Coke for me, thanks," Janessa says.

"I'll have a Sprite."

Delilah looks at me, then up at Brooke. "I'll have a Sprite too, thanks, Brooke."

"You've got it. Hey, that was a great party for Brandon the other night, wasn't it?" Brooke's eyes run between me and Delilah, and I wonder if she heard us arguing.

"Yeah, it was," Delilah answers. "Thanks for putting it together."

Brooke waves her off. "*Pfft.* What good is a party-planning business if I can't plan a party for friends? I'll grab your drinks and be right back."

Brooke serves our drinks and glances over a few times while we make small talk about my learning to surf. When we first arrived I was sure that I'd want to make up an excuse and leave early because I couldn't imagine being near Janessa and Delilah together. I thought I'd sense their attraction to each other—or at least Janessa's attraction toward Delilah. I anticipated a really uncomfortable evening. But as our discussion moves to Delilah's boots, what it's like to work at the surf shop, and Janessa's daughter, Jackie, I feel much more at ease. Janessa isn't eyeing Delilah or vying for her attention. In fact, she doesn't look uncomfortable at all, until she begins telling me about her sister.

And I see her through new eyes.

Her eyes glass over as she tells me about her sister's suicide and how she still attends the grief-counseling meetings from time to time when things get hard.

"Sometimes being with Jackie is hard, because she reminds me so much of my sister. The way one of her eyes is a little squintier when she smiles and the way she moves her mouth like she's chewing when she's deep in thought. When I start to miss her too much, I go back to counseling so I don't get depressed and make things hard for my daughter."

Janessa tucks her hair behind her ear and drops her eyes.

How can I not soften toward her? She takes a deep breath and explains why she reached out to Delilah, and maybe it shouldn't, but it makes me feel better. I still don't know how she could be close to Delilah like she was and not look at her like she's hungry to do it again. But then again, I don't understand how *anyone* can know Delilah and not fall hopelessly in love with her. She's sweet and smart, caring, and so hot I can't keep my hands off her. But I guess if love wasn't about a unique connection between two people that goes above and beyond sexual attraction, then we'd all be fighting over each other.

"So, that's my big dark secret." Janessa sits back, and when Delilah reaches over and squeezes her hand, I know it's out of friendship and nothing more, because after she releases her hand, she reaches beneath the table and takes mine.

And holds on tight.

The bell above the door chimes, and we turn to see a tall, muscular guy with a little dark-haired boy propped on one thick forearm and a little girl on the other. His eyes meet Janessa's and he flashes a warm smile.

"Mommy!" The little girl's eyes widen. Her arms shoot straight out toward Janessa, and the man crouches and lets the excited little girl down.

Janessa slides off her chair and scoops her into her arms. "How's my princess?" She kisses her cheek.

Delilah's told me about Jackie, and in Janessa's arms, it's easy to see the resemblance between mother and daughter.

"We had ice cream." Jackie rubs her stomach and licks her lips.

Janessa looks at the handsome guy. "Uncle Dean's the best uncle ever, huh?"

Jackie nods, then waves to me and Delilah. "Is those your friends?"

"Yes. These are my friends Delilah and Ashley."

Jackie leans forward and touches our heads with her little hands. "You have pretty yellow hair."

Delilah and I both laugh.

"Thank you, and you have pretty brown hair," Delilah says.

Delilah stands to greet Dean.

"Hi, I'm Delilah. I've heard a lot about you."

"You too, Delilah." He glances at me, sharing another smile that reaches his dark eyes. "And you must be Ashley."

Delilah and I exchange a confused glance. "Yes. Nice to meet you."

"I noticed you holding hands when I walked in, and Janessa told me you were a couple." He glances at Janessa, who's busy exchanging Eskimo kisses with Jackie.

Delilah's cheeks pink up. I can't help but smile. It feels good knowing that Janessa told him Delilah and I were together. Now I like her even more.

"And who's this handsome boy?" Delilah touches the little boy's shoe.

"This is Drew, my little man." Drew hides his face in Dean's neck. "He's tired and a little shy."

"He's adorable." I remember Delilah telling me that Janessa's brother had a son Jackie liked to have slumber parties with.

"Thanks," Dean says. "Well, sis, we'd better get going and put these guys to bed."

Janessa reaches for her purse, and Delilah hands it to her. Janessa opens it and fishes for her wallet.

"I've got this one," I offer. I step back so I'm shoulder to shoulder with Delilah. She may not be ready to hold hands, but a little comfort goes a long way.

"Thank you, Ashley." Janessa looks at Delilah and narrows her eyes. "Don't forget what I told you."

Delilah hooks a finger around one of mine and nods.

I just fell a little harder.

Delilah drops my finger before we leave, but not before Brooke sees us and flashes a warm smile. I think Delilah has blushed more times tonight than the whole time I've known her. We walk out of town toward her house, where we've chosen to stay tonight, and although we're not walking hand in hand, Delilah is close enough that I don't feel a distance.

"Thanks for meeting us tonight," Delilah says.

"Thanks for inviting me. I *really* wanted to hate Janessa."

Delilah laughs. "I guess I don't blame you. I want to hate Sandy."

"Be my guest. Hate her. But I can't hate Janessa. Now I get why she offered you what she did. I can't imagine losing a sibling."

We turn down her street and she reaches for my hand. I have to work hard to stifle my grin and hide my elation at her gesture, but I know she can feel positive energy coming off of me because her eyes keep darting to me and she's got a wide grin on her lips, too. Working through Delilah's insecurities makes me feel like I'm back in high school, holding hands for the first time ever.

"Do you mind if I ask you what Janessa was talking about when she said to remember what she said?"

Delilah remains silent for a few minutes, and when we reach her driveway, she turns to face me.

"You can always ask me anything. She told me to acknowledge you in public, or I'd hurt your feelings." Her eyes get serious. "I don't want to hurt your feelings, Ash. I'm trying."

I step closer. It's dark and there's no one outside, so I'm pretty sure she won't mind, but I don't touch her, even though I'd like to gather her in my arms and tell her how wonderful she is.

"I know you are, and I appreciate all of your efforts. The way you held my hand under the table. The way you linked one finger with mine. The way you look at me."

She gazes into my eyes for a long while. Her eyes shift right and then left. Her brows knit together, and she releases my hand and places her hands on my cheeks. My heart is pounding so hard I'm afraid I'm going to pass out. She closes her eyes and presses her lips to mine.

It's a quick kiss.

A sweet kiss.

A kiss that lasts only three seconds at most.

It's a kiss that makes the earth shift beneath me.

CHAPTER FIFTEEN

Ashley

THE RAIN THAT threatened earlier in the week passed us by, leaving sticky days in its wake. Friday greets us with mugginess that rivals the worst of them. Delilah finishes packing a bag for the weekend, and when Wyatt walks out of his room and sees her carrying it, he takes it from her. Delilah rolls her eyes. I know she loves how Wyatt is always there for her, but I have noticed recently that she has been getting a little irritated when he tries to help her with things.

"You'll be back Saturday evening?" He's wearing a tank top and cargo shorts and has a serious look in his green eyes.

"Yeah. I made sure the Taproom was fully staffed, and I programmed Ash's number and her parents' address into your phone."

He slides that serious look to me. "No drinking and driving."

I roll my eyes, but catch myself midroll when I remember that their parents were killed by a drunk driver. "I promise, Wyatt. I'll take excellent care of her."

I reach for Delilah's hand, and she takes it willingly. Of course she does. We're in the privacy of her house. I long for her

153

to feel this comfortable in public.

"We'll be fine, Wy. I'll text you when we get there so you don't worry."

"Cassidy will kill me if I don't remind you to take pictures of Kenny's play. You know how much she loves kids." Not only does she love kids, but she loves plays and loves looking at pictures of everyone's families. I have a feeling that if—when— they get married, Cassidy will want kids right away. Wyatt motions for us to go down the stairs first. Always the gentleman.

"I'm a photo fool when it comes to Kenny. I'll take more than she'll want to see."

"Have you met my girlfriend?" Wyatt teases. Cassidy takes all the pictures for hers and Brooke's party-planning business. She almost always has a camera in her hands, and when she's home, she's tweaking pictures on one of her many computer programs.

I go into the kitchen to make us coffee, and Tristan hands me two to-go cups.

"Already made them, hon."

"Thanks, Tristan. You didn't have to do that."

"I knew you guys would be anxious to get on the road and beat the traffic." Tristan puts an arm around me. "Text and let me know you get there safely."

"Wyatt beat you to it, but I will—don't worry." I love that they've all accepted me into their close-knit group. I cross the hardwood floor toward Delilah and hand her a cup of coffee. "Compliments of Tristan."

"Thanks, Tris," she says.

He bows.

"Oh, I forgot my shampoo. Hold on." She hurries upstairs.

Wyatt drapes an arm over my shoulder—what is it with the

guys in this house and arms? He guides me toward the far side of the room and lowers his voice.

"Are your parents cool with you and Delilah? Because I know you're excited about your new relationship, but this is a big step for her, meeting your parents and—"

I press my finger to his lips. "I've got this, Wyatt. I would never put Delilah in an uncomfortable position. Yes, my parents are comfortable, and I've already told them that she's my girlfriend, but she's not exactly comfortable with public displays of affection. They know everything they need to know about us and about her. They're good people, Wyatt. I'm a good person. I won't let her get hurt on my watch."

He nods. "Thank you. This is the first time she's traveled since…"

I hadn't taken *that* into consideration. "I'll be extra aware. I promise. I know you love her, and I know you worry. I do, too."

He nods again, but I can see it's a struggle for him to trust me—or probably anyone—with taking Delilah away from Harborside.

"She really likes you, Ashley."

"I know."

"But she's still dealing with a lot of stuff."

"She knows."

We both spin around at the sound of Delilah's voice.

"Dee…"

"She knows I'm dealing with stuff, Wy. You don't need to warn her like I'm a volcano about to blow." She puts a hand on her hip and holds his stare.

"I don't think you're a volcano. I'm more worried that—"

"That you're a fragile little butterfly whose going to get

blown away with the first gust of wind," Cassidy says as she comes up behind him and reaches for his hand. "He means well. Really, he does."

Delilah rolls her eyes. "I know you do, Wyatt, but I'm not a fragile butterfly. I'm not a volcano. I'm just a girl who lost her parents and fell for another girl."

When she wraps her arm around my shoulder, it's one arm I'm happy to snuggle into—and I am floored to hear determination and confidence in her voice. But when she kisses me smack on the lips, my eyes widen and I can't help but laugh a little. It's so...rebellious. And I like it. A lot.

She settles a smirk on those luscious lips of hers and wiggles her shoulders at her brother.

"I've got this, Wy."

"Yeah, I guess you do." He pulls her away from me and into his arms and squeezes her so hard she complains. "But I'm always going to be your big brother, and I'm always going to worry. So you can act all tough and kiss as many girls as you like—"

"Hey! No, she cannot." I level him with a harsh stare.

Wyatt's voice remains serious. "Okay, you can act all tough and kiss *Ashley* as many times as you want, but it won't stop me from worrying."

"Fair enough. You worry, but tell Cassidy about it, not me. Let me live under the guise of being a grown-up." She takes my hand and pulls me toward the door. "Come on, Ash. Let's go by your place and get your stuff."

As soon as we're in the Jeep, she cranks the radio. "Are there any open apartments at your complex?"

"What? Why?"

"Because I think it's time for me to start cutting the umbilical cord."

She backs out of the driveway, and I have no idea if she's kidding or not, but I just added *growing up Delilah* to my list of the Delilahs I love.

Delilah

THE DRIVE TO Ashley's parents' house is so fun that I forget I'm nervous about meeting them. We sing too loudly and off-key and talk about everything from our favorite foods—*Ash's is sushi, mine's brownies with cream cheese frosting*—our favorite shoes—*Any of Ash's sandals, my leather boots*. We stop for snacks and joke about how we'll weigh eight hundred pounds by the time we get there if we keep eating M&M's and Starburst. This is the most fun I've had in years. Ashley is so easy to be around, and when we went into the rest stop to get snacks, she didn't get upset when I didn't hold her hand, and I loved the way she smiled when I hooked my finger in her belt loop instead. I know it's silly. I mean, what's the difference between a belt loop and a finger? I have no clue, but it made me feel less like my parents were glaring down at me from above. And I'll take it for what it's worth.

I may never be ready to leap, but like Tristan said, this is a slow progression of coming into my true self, and I'm so thankful that Ashley's with me as I try to find my way free of my insecurities.

Ashley's parents' neighborhood is totally different from our community in Connecticut. The houses are smaller and the cars out front are older, not as flashy. Even the yards look more like they're lived in than the manicured lawns around ours. All of that makes this area feel homier and less stuffy, but the thing that strikes me with the greatest impact is the number of parents and children that are outside, a rarity in our neighborhood. Women are talking on front porches, watching children playing in the yards. Two teenage girls are sitting in the grass in the side yard of a house across the street. I can't remember ever seeing neighbors socializing on our street in Connecticut, unless you count Halloween, when kids went door to door begging for candy. Only our neighbors' candy was bagged in sparkly little bags and tied with ribbons.

A black car pulls into the driveway next door, and a guy jumps out and waves to Ashley.

"Hey, Ash!" He jogs up the sidewalk toward the Jeep.

"That's Bolton. We went to school together." Ashley climbs from the car, and Bolton, who's at least as tall as Wyatt, with blond hair and bright blue eyes, picks her up and spins her around. "God, look at you." He sets her back down on the ground. "You're gorgeous."

Seeing Bolton reminds me of Wyatt. I text him before I forget, and let him know we've arrived safely.

Ashley slaps Bolton's stomach. "And you've turned into a rock star. You're all muscles and manly."

"I've always been muscles and manly. You just never noticed." Bolton waves to me as I step from the Jeep. "Hey. I'm Bolton."

"This is my girlfriend, Delilah."

I hadn't considered how it would feel to be *introduced* as her girlfriend. It feels good *and* embarrassing. I watch Bolton's face for a reaction, but his smile broadens, revealing dimples that could rival Mario Lopez's.

Bolton comes around the Jeep and hugs me. Tight. "You've

got the best girlfriend around. I'd date Ash in a heartbeat if she liked guys."

Okay, now it feels good. Really good.

"Let me help you guys bring your stuff inside. Are you here for Kenny's play?"

"How'd you know?" I ask.

"Kenny's leading lady is my sister Patricia. You should see the two of them practicing. I swear they're not seven. They're teenagers." He reaches into the back of the Jeep and grabs our bags. "So, how'd you two meet? Where'd you go to school? Do you live in Harborside, too?"

"Don't give her the third degree." Ashley grabs my arm and holds me back from following him. She lowers her voice. "I don't want you to be uncomfortable, so I won't hold your hand or anything inside, but just don't take it as me not *wanting* to. Okay?"

She's just won the best-girlfriend-of-the-century award.

"Okay. Thank you."

"Come on," Bolton hollers. "The minute I open the door, Kenny's going to barrel out. Are you ready?"

"He's right." Ashley glances at the house, then back at me. "Kenny also has no filter. He'll embarrass you. I apologize ahead of time."

"He's seven. How embarrassing can he get?"

Ashley touches my arm but doesn't hold it as we walk toward the house. "Way more than you can imagine. He doesn't slow down to think before he speaks. Maybe he'll be sidetracked with Bolton. He adores him."

The front door swings open and a lanky blond boy barrels into Bolton and wraps his spindly arms around him.

"Bolton! You're back! Are you coming to the play? Patricia

and I have to hug and I think it stinks. I don't want to hug her, but she said sometimes I have to do things I don't want to."

"Hey, buddy. I wouldn't miss it for the world, and one day you'll be glad you got to hug Patricia. You'll see it won't stink. Trust me on that."

Kenny laughs. "You're so weird." He pries himself from Bolton, and his eyes widen, his mouth drops open, and he sprints toward us. "Ash! You're home! You're home!" He jumps into her arms, and the force of his body sends Ashley stumbling back. She laughs and hugs him tight.

"Hey, little buddy. Wow, you're so tall." She sets his feet on the ground, and he's chin height. I have no idea if that's tall for a seven-year-old, but he's beaming, so I assume he likes hearing it.

"I know. Dad says I'm going to be tall like him." He looks at me and squints, then looks back at Ashley. "Is that your girlfriend? Mom said you're bringing your girlfriend home and that I shouldn't say anything about it. She said it's okay for girls to be girlfriend and girlfriend and boys to be boyfriend and boyfriend. I think it's okay since Mom said it's okay. Is that her? Is she your girlfriend?"

I can't help but laugh. I like Kenny's lack of filter. It actually eases the tension that had made my legs feel like steel rods bolted to the ground. Ashley looks at me and smiles, shrugs, then mouths, *Sorry.* I let her know it's okay by answering him.

"Yes, I'm Delilah. I've heard a lot about you." I haven't really, but I know he'll like hearing that.

"You have? Did Ashley tell you that I can run faster than her? And that I can whip her butt in any video game on the planet?" He walks between me and Ash as we go inside.

"Hey, buddy, why don't you help me with these bags?"

Bolton looks over his shoulder and smiles.

Ash mouths, *Thank you,* as Kenny sprints toward him.

"You okay?" she asks me quietly.

"Yeah. He's great. They both are, Bolton and Kenny."

"Really?" She wrinkles her brow. "Thank you. I adore them both, but I know Kenny's a little much for most people. If he wears you out, just let me know and I'll distract him."

"He's fine. Really. He actually makes it less stressful for me, and Bolton? How could you not have told me about him? He seems like a really good friend."

"He is. We spent lots of time together growing up, but since we left for college, we only see each other a few times a year. Sometimes we text or call, but not much."

"Well, you should definitely keep in touch with him. He seems really nice."

She tilts her head and smiles again, then touches my fingers with two of her own. "Thank you, Dee. I stopped reaching out because Sandy felt threatened by him. I'm glad to know that you don't mind."

"Threatened? By him?" Then I remember that Sandy was seeing a guy. "Oh, right. She liked guys so she thought you might as well?"

"Something like that."

"Well, if we can be friends with Janessa, why not with Bolton? I like that he didn't bat an eye when you said I was your girlfriend." I lean in close and whisper, "Which I loved hearing, by the way, even though I was embarrassed at first."

"I didn't mean to embarrass you. My family knows, as Kenny so eloquently revealed. Let's go inside. My mom is dying to meet you." She releases my fingers. I want so much to hold them again, but I know I'd drop them the minute we see her family.

Ashley's parents live in a split-foyer home. Bolton is still holding the door open for us as we climb the steps.

He's smiling and watching me pretty intently. When I walk past him, he leans in close and whispers, "If you need an escape, just scratch your nose."

I laugh, but I secretly worry about why I might need an escape.

Kenny is dragging Ashley's bag downstairs. Bolton's still holding mine as he closes the door behind us. The house smells like Thanksgiving, warm and foody, even though it's only August. We're standing in the foyer. To our right are two sets of stairs, one that leads up and one that leads down. I can hear a television playing downstairs. I'm not used to split-levels. Our house in Connecticut is a Colonial with tall ceilings and a center staircase. This is much cozier.

"Is that my baby girl?" Ashley's mother comes out of the kitchen to our left and folds Ashley into her arms.

"Hi, Mom." Ashley rolls her eyes over her mother's shoulder, but her smile says she loves the attention.

I get a pang of longing deep in my chest. It's been months since I hugged my mother, and I'll never be able to hug her again. I've been so entrenched in battling the look my parents gave me when I came out to them that I've stopped seeing the warmer looks, stopped feeling the love they doled out so readily. How could I have pushed that aside?

Ashley's mother steps back and holds Ash's shoulders. Her hair is the same dirty blond as Ashley's, her eyes the same warm brown as she assesses her daughter. When she smiles, it's easy to see what Ashley will look like when she's older. "Are you eating enough? You look thin."

Do all moms worry about that? My mom said something similar when she first saw me on graduation day.

"Mom." Ashley's voice is thick with annoyance, but it's contradicted by her smile.

How often did I sound the same way toward my mom? I wish I could take each and every time back. I push those thoughts away, determined not to let my parents' absence get in the way of our visit.

Ashley puts her hand on my lower back as her mother shifts a friendly gaze my way.

"And you must be Delilah." She touches her cheeks and her eyes widen. "My word, you are even prettier than I imagined." Before I can thank her, she pulls me against her and hugs me much longer than I anticipated.

"I'm so glad you're here. Ash has told me so much about you." She takes my hand and calls down the stairs, "Paulie? The girls are here," then leads me across the hardwood floor and into a cozy living room with a small piano set against the wall to the left. Above the piano hangs a large frame of orange fabric that looks like burlap. Haphazardly pinned to it at cockeyed angles are several photos of Ashley and Kenny and their parents. Ashley as a baby holding a bottle, as a toddler walking in the grass. She was a pudgy baby with almost white-blond hair, and so cute it makes me smile. The arrangement is vastly different from the carefully placed frames in our house. It's more appealing to me, this homier arrangement. I imagine her mother changing the pictures from time to time, adding more, standing before them smiling, sighing, and reveling in memories of Kenny on his bicycle or her and her husband sitting on the front porch.

There's a couch against the wall to our right and a love seat beneath a big window on the wall opposite us. A small dining room is off the living room, tucked behind the kitchen, with sliding glass doors that lead out to a deck. I know Ashley grew up in this house, and I imagine her toddling across the room, running into her mother's arms, and opening Christmas gifts by a big, decorated tree.

"Dad."

I turn at the wondrous tone of Ashley's voice as she falls into her father's open arms. He's a heavyset man, and he closes his eyes as he hugs her.

"I missed you, pumpkin."

"I missed you, too, Dad." Ash reaches for me again. "Dad, this is Delilah."

I like that she respects me enough not to cling to me in a way that would make me feel uncomfortable in front of her parents but still touches me enough that I feel special.

He smiles down at me. Even though he's about the same height as Bolton, who's standing behind us, he looks much bigger. It might be his sheer breadth, or maybe the way he's opening his arms to me, as he did for Ashley, but as I walk forward and accept his embrace, I feel like I'm hugging a gigantic teddy bear.

"Welcome to our home, sweetheart."

"Thank you, Mr. Carver."

"Call me Paul, please." He reaches a hand out to Bolton.

"How's it going, son?" Bolton takes his hand, and Paul pulls him into a hug, too.

"You okay?" Ashley whispers as her mother sits on the couch.

"Perfectly. How could I not be? Your family is wonderful." I've been here only for a few minutes, and already I feel like I walked through a portal that instantly made me part of their family. Being here makes me long for my parents, but it also amplifies how different my parents' reaction would have been if I had brought Ashley home and introduced her as my *girlfriend*. I imagine my parents as flustered, hot messes the moment they laid eyes on us holding hands. Their disapproving looks might even have gotten lost in their inability to find something appropriate to say. I force myself to push that away, but it's not as easy as I hoped it would be. I focus on Kenny bounding down the stairs. That helps.

Kenny plows into Bolton. "Are you staying? Want to see what I built in Minecraft?"

"Yeah, sure." Bolton turns to Paul. "You guys mind if I stick around a few minutes with Kenny?"

"What kind of question is that? Of course you can stay." Ashley's mom waves a hand as if he's being ridiculous. "Stay for dinner if you want."

"Thanks, Mrs. C, but I can't. My mom is planning a big family dinner. Ash, if you and Delilah want to hang out later, text me."

"We will." Ashley watches her mother spring up to her feet and rush into the kitchen. "Mom, do you need help?"

Bolton and Kenny head upstairs.

"Oh, no." Her mom waves another dismissive hand. "I'm just making a few things for later. Go ahead and show Delilah around. We'll catch up when you girls are ready. Dinner's not until five, so you have oodles of time to do your own thing."

"Come on. I'll show you my room." Ashley leads me downstairs. "This is the rec room, or my dad's man cave."

The rec room, like the rest of the house, feels warm and inviting. There are two comfortably worn couches, a wide coffee table with *ESPN* and *Good Housekeeping* magazines on it, as well as a Nintendo 3DS, which I assume is Kenny's. Ashley reaches for my hand, searching my eyes for approval first before taking it.

I take it and we walk down a narrow hallway. She presses her hand on a closed door as we pass. "This is the basement, but it's full of junk." She points to the open door across from it. "My dad's office." We walk a little farther and she points to a laundry room, and across from that another small room. "My mom's domain."

I peek in and there's a sewing machine, a rocking chair, and several bookshelves. At the far side of the narrow room is a door leading outside.

At the end of the hall Ashley waves a hand to the open door. "This is my bedroom." I peer inside and note the white dresser and queen-sized bed with a matching white headboard. Two bookcases filled with books and knickknacks sit off to the left. There are posters of bands on the walls, as if the bedroom hasn't changed since she was a teenager. Ashley pulls me into the room, then pushes the door almost-but-not-quite closed, and whispers, "Can I just give you a little kiss? For making it through meeting my parents?"

"You don't have to ask." I lean forward, and the second our lips press together, butterflies take flight in my stomach. She kisses me quickly, as promised, and I crave a longer, deeper kiss, but I'm still a little nervous, so I resist the urge to pull her back for more.

There's a light knock at the door, and I stumble away from Ash as Bolton opens the door.

"Sorry to interrupt." He runs his eyes between us.

"Come on in." Ashley's cheeks are flushed, and I know I'm

beet-red.

"I just got a text from Carly. She and a few of the old gang are going to Marco's tonight. You guys want to go?"

Ashley turns to me. "Marco's is a dance club. We went to high school with Carly."

"You'll like the gang, Delilah. They're pretty much like me and Ash, and Marco's is a great place if you like to dance." He moves his hips and flashes a bright white smile.

I love to dance, but I'm nervous about how to act around Ashley's friends. I remember how hard it was to keep my hands off her at the Taproom, but I can't miss the hope in Ashley's eyes, and it does sound fun.

"Sure. I'll go." I can hardly believe I agreed, but when Ash throws her arms around my neck and hugs me, I'm glad I did.

"Thank you! You'll love them." She unravels herself from the embrace. "Sorry. I was just—"

"It's okay." I drop my gaze, but I realize that I don't feel uncomfortable around Bolton.

"Cool. So...ride over together? Leave around eight?" Bolton points over his shoulder with his thumb. "I've gotta get home before my mom sends out a search squad. I just arrived when you guys did."

"Sounds good." Ashley's gaze hasn't left mine since she hugged me. After Bolton says goodbye, she exhales a loud breath and flops down on her fluffy white comforter.

"You sure you don't mind? I didn't mean to hug you like that."

"It sounds fun, and I like Bolton. He makes me feel comfortable. I don't know how I'll be around a *gang* of strangers, but..."

She laughs. "They're hardly a *gang*. Just two or three others, depending on who shows up. They're really nice, and they know I like sexy blond chicks, so…" She twirls her finger in her hair and lowers her chin, giving me a playful look.

"And here I was thinking you were going to make this easy for me. You can't look at me like that tonight. And no miniskirts, either. How about you wear body armor and keep your eyes averted the whole time?"

"No promises…" Ashley stands and pulls me to my feet.

"So…Where am I staying?" I look around, and it dawns on me that I didn't see another bedroom down here.

"What do you mean? Here with me, of course."

"Here? What about your parents?"

"Dee. They know we're a couple." Her eyes go serious. "Oh God. I didn't think you'd mind. I mean, my parents expected us to stay together. They know we've been staying together at Harborside."

I draw in a deep breath and sink back down to the bed, unsure of how I feel. "They already assume we're staying in your room together and they still welcomed me so warmly."

"Why wouldn't they?"

I look up at her, and her eyes widen as understanding dawns on her. She sits beside me again.

"Oh, Dee. I'm sorry. I guess I assumed too much. I thought you'd want to stay with me. My parents have never had an issue with my sexuality, and I've never brought a girlfriend home before, so when they heard I was bringing you, they were more than thrilled." She looks around the room and wrinkles her brow, thinking.

"You haven't brought any other girlfriends home with you?"

"Nope. They knew a girl I went out with in high school, but it's not like she stayed over or anything."

"Aw, Ash. That makes me feel really special."

"Well, duh. You are really special." She reaches for my hand. "But if it makes you uncomfortable, I can sleep in my dad's office. The couch pulls out to a bed."

"No." I shake my head and squeeze her hand to borrow some of her strength. "I'm okay. I don't want to hide from your parents. They're obviously not like my parents, and they seem supportive of you. Of us. What about Kenny?"

"My mom and I already discussed Kenny."

I cover my face with my hands. "Oh my God. Really?"

"Yes, really." She pulls my hands down. "He probably won't notice, or he'll just think we're having a sleepover. My mom doesn't think it's an issue at all."

"Okay, but I'm not fooling around with your parents right upstairs."

She rolls her eyes. "Whatever floats your boat, but you know you can't keep your hands off of this…" She stands up, holds her hands above her head, and sways her hips seductively, then laughs.

I don't laugh, because she's got that right.

CHAPTER SIXTEEN

Ashley

I THINK IT'S safe to say that my family is the best around, even Kenny and his boisterous personality and unfiltered comments. We're almost done with dinner and my mom and dad have both acted as if nothing out of the ordinary is happening at our dinner table, when in fact it's the first and only time I've had a girlfriend over. Delilah has laughed and smiled and talked like she's hanging out with old friends, and that's more than I could have hoped for.

"Dinner was wonderful, Mrs. Carver. Thank you."

Mom waves again. "It was nothing, but thank you. I'm glad you liked it."

"Are you guys going out with Bolton tonight? He said you might go. Carly's going, too. I love Carly. She's so funny with all that hair. She looks like Carrothead." Kenny stops only to inhale, and I cut him off.

"Carrot Top, and how do you even know Carrot Top?" I ask.

"The Internet. Duh." He wipes his face on his sleeve.

"Napkin," Mom reminds him.

"Why? I just wiped my mouth. Can I be excused?" He's up

on his feet before she can answer.

"You have twenty minutes before your dress rehearsal," she calls after him as he heads for the stairs. "Brush your teeth and hair and wash your hands, please." She turns her attention back to us. "Are you going out with Bolton? It'll be nice to see your friends again."

I glance at Delilah to see if she's changed her mind and she nods, smiles.

"Yeah, I guess we are." I say it like it's no big deal, but it's another *very* big deal.

Mom reaches her hand toward Delilah and presses it to the table beside Delilah's.

"Delilah, honey. Ashley told us about your parents. I'm so very sorry, and I just want you to know, I'm here." She looks up at Dad, then back at Delilah. "We're here. If you and—your brother, right? Wyatt?" She doesn't wait for her to answer, and I'm not sure Delilah could respond if she wanted to. She looks like her throat has thickened. She's swallowing hard, over and over. "If you need anything at all, just let us know. Or if you want to talk. I'm a great listener."

"Thank you." Delilah reaches for my hand under the table.

She laces our fingers together, and when she shifts her eyes to mine, they're damp, but her lips curve into a slight smile. I'm sure she's missing her mom.

We help my mom clear the table, and I pull Delilah aside and ask again if she's okay.

"Yeah. Your mom is so sweet."

Mom comes out of the kitchen to retrieve more dishes, and Delilah carries the glasses in behind her. My father pulls me aside while they're in the kitchen.

"She seems really lovely, pumpkin, and she looks at you like you're heaven and earth combined." He hugs me close.

I love that he can see the way she always makes me feel. I pick up a few plates and carry them into the kitchen, stopping at the entranceway when I hear Delilah thanking my mother.

"I really appreciate what you said."

"Oh, sweetheart. I meant it." My mother wipes her hands on a towel and turns, leaning her hip against the sink so she can face Delilah. "You don't have to worry about anything while you're here with us. You two seem happy together, and we couldn't ask for anything more." She pulls Delilah into a hug and spots me standing in the doorway, and smiles.

I set the dishes on the counter and Delilah reaches for my hand.

Reaches.

For.

My.

Hand.

Wow.

Mom looks at the clock. "Oh dear. We have to take Kenny or he'll be late for his rehearsal. Ash, you have your key to get in tonight?"

"Yeah."

"Okay." She hugs me, then hugs Delilah like it's the most natural thing in the world. "I'm so glad you're both here, but I've got to scoot." She calls for Kenny and my dad as she leaves the kitchen.

Delilah's face lights up with excitement. "I love your mom. She's so...real!" Her entire demeanor has changed. She's as relaxed as she is in her house at Harborside.

"I know. I'm lucky, aren't I?"

"Your dad, too. He's like a big teddy bear."

"He pretty much raved about you, too." I step closer, expecting her to step back, and when she doesn't, I reach up and tuck a wayward strand of hair behind her ear.

"He did?" I can hear the appreciation in her voice.

"Yes, he did. I'm glad you came with me. I know it's not easy, and I know how difficult tonight will be for you, so I just want you to know that I appreciate it. All of it. I appreciate you."

She touches her forehead to mine but doesn't say a word. She doesn't have to. Just like my dad saw her emotions, I feel them in everything she does.

CHAPTER SEVENTEEN

Delilah

MARCO'S IS NOTHING like any club I've ever been to. It's located in a warehouse, with a concrete floor and enormous screens hanging from the ceiling showing the band. There are no booths or other places to sit, only tall round-topped tables for setting drinks on while standing. Colorful spotlights illuminate the dance floor, which is basically the entire center of the warehouse. We're standing at one of the round tables, and it's so loud that it drowns out my nervousness.

I offered to be the designated driver, primarily so that it would be easier for me to keep from dragging Ashley into the bathroom to make out, although I think my wanting to kiss her has less to do with alcohol and everything to do with Ashley. The way her eyes get dark and sensual when she looks at me and the way she checks on me, brushes her hand against my lower back, whispers in my ear.

Everything about her makes me want to be closer, even in public.

Bolton leans between us. "You guys want a drink?" He's wearing a navy T-shirt that clings to his muscular pecs and a pair of low-slung jeans. I've noticed several girls checking him out.

"I'm good, thanks," I answer.

"Just a soda for me," Ashley says.

"You can drink, Ash. I'm driving."

"Nah. I don't really want to." She moves closer to me as her friend Carly squeezes between her and Bolton.

Kenny was right. Carly's hair is similar to Carrot Top's. It's darker red, with corkscrew curls that spring out in every direction. It's cut above her shoulders and bounces as she sways to the music. Ashley and I ended up wearing miniskirts and blousy tanks, and I guess it was the right choice, because Carly's wearing a minidress. She didn't blink an eye when Ashley introduced me as her girlfriend—Ash had asked me on the way over if it was okay to do so. Ashley is being so careful to ensure that I'm comfortable. I feel ashamed about feeling funny about us in public. Ashley says she understands, but Janessa's advice continually sails through my mind, so I'm trying hard to push past my own insecurities.

"I'll take whatever you're having, Bolt," Carly says.

"Cool. Be right back."

We watch as Bolton moves through the crowd toward the bar along the far wall. Girls turn and watch him from behind as he walks past, and he seems like he doesn't even notice, just continues his beeline toward the bar.

"How long have you guys been dating?" Carly asks.

"Not long," Ash says.

"But we've known each other two months, so it feels longer," I add, and hook one finger with Ashley's. She smiles up at me. I love that my touch means so much to her.

"You seem like you've been dating a really long time. Come on. Let's dance." She grabs our hands and pulls us into the crowd.

Ashley dances close to me, although it's too crowded to put any real space between us. Carly's a good dancer and makes us laugh when she does funky moves. When the music slows, Carly puts a hand on each of our shoulders and turns us toward each other.

"Okay, lover girls. Your turn. I'm outta here." Carly walks off the dance floor, and for a second Ash and I stare at each other.

Ashley's hair frames her face. Her head's tilted gently to the side, and she arches a brow. I can't stop myself from glancing around the dance floor. No one is paying any attention to us, and somewhere in my head I hear myself whisper, *And so what if they were?*

I step closer and place her hand on my hip. Then I wrap my arms around her neck and rest my head on her shoulder. I feel her heartbeat speed up as we begin to move in perfect rhythm. I close my eyes, trying to ignore the nerves prickling along my skin. Getting lost in Ashley is easy, but pushing away the look in my parents' eyes when I told them I was a lesbian isn't. But I'm still trying.

I try.

And try.

And try.

And little by little, as Ashley's perfume fills my senses and the chatter of the other people on the dance floor fades away, I sink into the moment. There's only me and Ash. Her hands on my back, holding me close, her heart beating strong and stable against mine. When the song picks up its beat again, Ashley keeps me close.

"Just for another second? Please?" she asks.

I tighten my grip around her neck. One day this will be old hat to us. One day she'll be able to take my hand and walk out on a dance floor without encountering my hesitation. But right this second, I'm thankful for this brief respite from the discomfort that's been tethering my heart for so many years.

An hour or so later we all pile into my Jeep, Ashley in the passenger seat, Bolton and Carly in the back. Carly sits pressed against Bolton's side, tucked beneath his arm. She's got a drunken smile on her lips, and if I didn't know they weren't dating, I'd wonder, because of the way Bolton holds her protectively and rests his cheek on the top of her head.

"You okay, Car?" he asks.

She nods. "I had a great time. Ash, I wish you came home more often."

Ashley turns in her seat so she can see Carly. "Maybe we'll try to."

We'll. She says it so easily and with such confidence, like we're a given, that the word wraps around me like an embrace.

When we reach Ashley's house, Bolton hugs us both. "See you guys at the play tomorrow?"

"Definitely," Ashley answers. "Thanks for the invite tonight."

"Are you kidding? It's great to see you." He hugs her again. "And, Dee, I hope you had a good time."

"I did. I had a great time, thanks." I watch him walk down to his house, and when Ashley reaches for my hand, I don't do a quick sweep of the area. I take it and hold on tight. "I love your friends."

"I'm glad. They're all pretty cool," she says as we walk up the front steps.

"Bolton reminds me of Wyatt. He even called me Dee."

"I call you Dee sometimes." She unlocks the door and pushes it open.

"But you're my girlfriend. Almost everyone else calls me Delilah except Wyatt." We walk inside and take off our shoes as quietly as we can.

"Let's get some ice water before we go downstairs." Ash takes my hand again. We walk into the kitchen, where we find a note from her mom and a bottle of Motrin.

Girls, drink lots of water and take two of these if you drank too much. Kenny will be up early! Xo, Mom.

"Your mom is the best."

"Do you miss your mom?" Ashley fills a glass of ice water and sets it on the table.

"Yeah, but she wasn't accepting like your mom, so I know it could never have been like this at my house. But I still miss her."

She takes me in her arms and kisses me lightly. "I'm sorry, Dee," she whispers.

"I thought I heard you come in." Her mother comes into the kitchen wearing a short robe, tied at the waist, and slippers.

I step out of Ashley's arms and mumble an apology.

Her mother laughs, a softer version of Ashley's sweet laugh. "Oh, sweetheart. Are you kidding? You're sorry for showing affection to my daughter? Please." She swats at the air. "I'd be more worried if you didn't."

"You're not bothered by us? Not at all?" I don't know where the courage to ask this comes from, but as she fills a glass with juice, then settles into a seat at the table, I'm not embarrassed to ask.

She pulls out the chair beside her and pats it. I sit, and Ashley sits on my other side.

"Delilah, I'm sure there are lots of people who will look at you girls sideways, just as there are still people out there who take issue with interracial relationships. I can't change them." She presses her lips into a firm line. "I wish I could, but…well…I can't. But as far as Ash's father and I are concerned, if you're lucky enough to experience love in this mixed-up world, then you're lucky. Ashley's the same person as the little girl I held in my arms and nursed. The same girl who was Annie in the spring play in elementary school and drew a beach on her walls using markers when she was Kenny's age. All I've ever wanted was for my baby to be happy. You make her happy, and that's good enough for me."

She leans forward and takes me in her arms as tears fall down my cheeks. I'm not sure why I'm crying, if it's because I envy Ashley for her mother's support, or I miss my mom, or if I'm just so thankful to be accepted that it pulls me under. Or maybe I'm crying because finally—*God, finally*—I can breathe without the weight of my parents' stare hovering over me. If even for a few seconds.

She draws away and hands me a napkin. "I didn't mean to make you sad."

I shake my head and wipe my tears as Ashley reaches for me. "You didn't make her sad, Mom. You made her happy."

That night when we crawl into Ashley's childhood bed, I reach for her and I love her without holding anything back. And I hope and pray that in the morning I still feel this confident and this free—because I know I'll feel more for Ashley than I do right now, just as I have every day since our first kiss. And she deserves to be loved without the memory of my parents stealing one second of it away.

CHAPTER EIGHTEEN

Delilah

THE NEXT MORNING I'm sitting on Ashley's bed looking at her photo album while she showers. The bedroom door flies open and Kenny leaps onto the mattress and scrambles up next to me. He leans his chin in his palm, and I wonder how he can go from moving so fast to being almost perfectly still. I'm glad I've already showered and dressed. I make a mental note to remember to always get up early when we're here. I can just imagine how awkward it would be if he ran in when we were still in bed together.

"Whatchya doing?" His hair is askew, and his breath smells like sugary cereal.

I look from him to the album. "Looking at your sister's pictures."

"She was a dork back then." He points to a picture of Ashley when she must have been about his age, with two long pigtails, wearing a pink shirt and matching shorts.

"She was cute." I bump him with my shoulder.

"You only think that because she's your girlfriend and you have to. When I have a girlfriend, I'm not going to think she was pretty when she was a dork. But I guess dorks can be pretty, too. Ashley was a pretty dork. Do you like to play Minecraft?"

I need a lot of coffee to keep up with this kid.

"I haven't ever played, but I'm not much of a video game person."

He frowns at that and shakes his head. "That means you're a dork, too."

"Ah, so a dork is someone who doesn't play video games? Good to know."

"I guess. Sort of. But you can be an ugly dork. But you're not. You're a pretty dork. Do you kiss Ashley? Do you kiss her a lot? I know you hold her hand because my mom said that you guys hold hands sometimes. I don't care that you hold her hand. I like to hold her hand, too. She's a good hand-holder."

Coffee. Coffee. Coffee.

His mother appears in the doorway. She is dressed in a pair of jeans and a blouse and is carrying two cups of coffee. She hands me one and sets the other on the dresser.

"I thought you girls would need these. Ash said you take cream and sugar. I hope that's okay."

"Wow, yes, thank you. You didn't have to do this." My own mother didn't deliver coffee to my bedroom.

"We need to keep our guests fueled to keep up with this little powerhouse." She reaches a hand out for Kenny.

He groans as he climbs off the bed. "Wait." He turns back toward me, and I hold my breath. I don't know what to expect, but after the questions he fired at me a few minutes ago, I'm a little worried that he might ask me again if I kiss Ashley, and I'm not sure how Ashley and her mother would want me to answer that. Although I get the feeling that in this house, honesty goes a long way.

Lucky Ashley.

"Make it quick, Kenny," his mother says with a stern voice and a smile. How do parents achieve that? "You still need to bathe and practice your lines."

"Will I see you *after* the play?" he asks.

"Yes, definitely. We're leaving today, but you'll definitely see us before we go."

"Good." He walks away, holding his mother's hand. "I had to make sure I liked her."

"And? Do you?" his mother asks.

"Nope. I love her, just like Ashley does."

My jaw drops open as Ashley steps out of the bathroom and sees me staring at the door.

You love me?

Ashley hurries over to the door, listening as Kenny's voice— "Do you think they kiss?"—fades down the hall.

I bury my face in my hands, embarrassed that Kenny is asking his mother about us kissing and mortified that a seven-year-old feels comfortable talking about us kissing when I'm such a chickenshit in public. I don't hear her mother's response.

"Told you he has no filter."

I love her, just like Ashley does. That little boy overwhelms me, in a good way. He loves me even though I want to kiss his sister and my own parents couldn't seem to.

Ashley and I have a few hours to kill, so we go for a drive and she shows me the elementary, middle, and high schools she attended. We get out at the high school and walk around the brick building just to kill time.

"What was it like being *out* in high school?" I know she won't mind that I ask. Ash is like an open book, unlike me, whose true self has been kept under lock and key forever.

She shrugs. "At first it was a little weird. Some people

looked at me funny or avoided me for a while, but there were other gay and lesbian kids at school. And I had Bolton. He never acted funny around me. Now that I think about it, he is kind of like Wyatt. He would never let anyone say anything bad, and if anyone looked at me funny, he gave them hell. But I think even if he hadn't been there, it would have been like anything else in life. After a few weeks it was no big deal. And I had my parents' support. I think that made everything easier."

She stops walking and looks at me. "I'm sorry you didn't have that, Dee. I wish you did, and not just so our relationship could be easier, but for yourself. So you weren't so conflicted for all those years. I can't imagine how hard that was for you."

"Thanks, Ash. I wish I did, too, but if there's one thing I learned in counseling, it's that I have to figure out how to move forward, because I can't change the past. Talking to your mom last night helped. She helped me to remember how much I loved hugging my mom and hearing her voice."

"Well, I'm glad it helped, but if it's too hard being here, just tell me."

"No. It's just the opposite. I like it here. I loved my mom and dad, even though they were strict and even though their views were different from mine. I just...I guess it's easy to forget the good when I'm wrapped up in the bad."

We're walking again, and I don't even realize I've reached for Ashley's hand until our fingers connect. I wait for the rush of worry to swell in my chest, but it's so faint I barely feel it, making it easier to push away.

"I'm glad you invited me. Thank you."

"Me too. I think going home next weekend will be good for you, to gain some closure. Do you want me to go with you?"

"I always want you with me, but this is...I don't know. I

think I have to do it by myself. Is that rude?"

"No. I understand. And if you need me, I'm only a phone call away."

"Why are you so supportive of me?" I ask as we cross the parking lot toward the car.

"Why wouldn't I be?" she says lightly. "I love you."

I reach for the car to stabilize myself.

"You *love* me?" I whisper. I heard Kenny say it, but I didn't think it was real. Ashley never said those words to me before.

Ashley steps closer and presses her finger against my lips. "I don't need you to say it back. I just need you to know how I feel."

You love me.

The words are still tying a pretty little bow around my heart as she continues speaking.

"I've been falling for you every second since the moment we met, and I've been trying to hold it back because I didn't want to scare you off, but…"

"Scare me off? You're so careful with me and protective of me."

"Seeing you with my family and being with you…" She shrugs again. "I don't want to hold it back anymore, even if I can't show you in public. I love you."

"Ash."

She shakes her head. "Please, don't say it now. I know how you feel about me. I feel it every time you kiss me. But please don't tell me until you can say it without worry of who hears you, because as much as I want your love, I want it free and clear of all the rest of the stuff we have to work through. I want to know that when you tell me you love me—whether it's next week or next year—that you would be just as confident saying it into a microphone as you would whispering it in my ear."

CHAPTER NINETEEN

Ashley

NEARLY EVERY SEAT in the small community theater is filled. Kenny looks adorable onstage, and Delilah and I take tons of pictures. My parents are positively glowing with pride when Kenny stands center stage and says his lines perfectly. At the end of the play, when Kenny and Patricia hug, he squeezes her with all his might, and the whole audience *aww*s.

When Kenny releases Patricia, she bends at the waist to catch her breath—I guess he really did hug her with all his might. Kenny walks to the edge of the stage and searches the audience.

"What's he doing?" my mom whispers.

My dad shrugs. "It's Kenny. Who knows?"

Kenny puts his hands beside his mouth and yells, "I did it, Bolton! I hugged her and it didn't stink!"

The audience roars with laughter. My mother covers her eyes and shakes her head, but she's laughing, too.

My father rises to his feet and yells, "That's my boy," which leads to a standing ovation, to which Kenny bows about a dozen times.

Delilah gets pictures of the whole thing.

She stands beside me as we clap and presses her leg against mine. Ever since I told her that I loved her, she's been stealing glances at me, like she's trying to figure me out. I haven't told her again, because she knows how I feel, and there's no need to overwhelm her. I guess it was kind of selfish of me to say it out loud when she's already dealing with so much, but when I'm with her, I feel so much. It was really hard to hold back. And I want her to know that I love her when she goes home to Connecticut. I have a feeling it's going to be much harder than she anticipates, but I respect her need to do it alone.

Delilah takes pictures of Kenny and my parents and Kenny and Patricia. She takes pictures of Bolton and the kids and my parents, me, and the kids. She takes so many pictures that I lose track of who's in them.

"Can I see your phone?" Kenny holds out his hand to Delilah.

"Sure. Do you want me to show you how to take a picture?" She crouches beside him and he shakes his head.

"No. I want pictures with you in them." He hands her phone to our father. "Dad, will you take pictures of me and Delilah? Then me and Delilah and Ashley. Then me and Delilah and Ashley and Patricia and Bolton. Then me and—"

"I get it, Kenny." My father motions for us all to get together.

Kenny takes my hand and places it in Delilah's. Her eyes cut to me.

"Mom said if Delilah didn't mind, I could hold her hand, too. Do you mind, Delilah?" He turns his big brown eyes up to her.

She tightens her grip on him. "Nope. I don't mind at all. In fact, I like holding two of my favorite people's hands. It makes me feel special."

Two hours later we drive away, waving to my parents, Kenny, and Bolton all the way down the street until they disappear from sight. Delilah picks up her phone at a stoplight and navigates to the pictures before handing it to me. I stare at the picture of Delilah holding mine and Kenny's hands for a long time. When the phone sits idle for too long, the screen turns black. I press the button to unlock it and notice that Delilah has already made that photo her background image.

I think her baby steps just got a little bigger.

CHAPTER TWENTY

Delilah

AFTER SPENDING TIME with Ashley's family and Bolton, a few things become very clear to me.

I got ripped off in the parental-support department.

Ashley loves me.

I'm nowhere near ready to have children, although I love Kenny to pieces.

Ashley loves me.

The way Wyatt watches over me isn't a bad thing, even if it feels stifling at times.

Ashley. Loves. Me.

It's Tuesday afternoon, three days since our trip. Three days since Ash told me she loves me, which has made it hard for me to think about anything else. Three days since I spent time with what is probably the most supportive family on earth. Three days since meeting a kid who made me realize that I'm pigeonholing my relationship with Ashley. I don't know how it happened, but listening to Kenny's unfiltered thoughts was as enlightening as it was overwhelming. One thing he said stuck with me as much as Ashley's *I love you* did.

I'm standing at the stainless-steel counter in the kitchen of the Taproom, eating a grilled-cheese sandwich, as his excited, high-pitched voice whips through my mind for the hundredth time. *She said it's okay for girls to be girlfriend and girlfriend and boys to be boyfriend and boyfriend. I think it's okay since Mom said it's okay.*

Mom said it's okay.

Kenny puts a lot of faith in his mother.

I pull out my phone and look at the pictures from this weekend. Kenny will probably grow up thinking same-sex relationships are acceptable *because his mother said they were.*

"Hey, Dutch?"

Dutch turns with a spatula in one hand and a slab of cheese in the other. His apron is covered with grease, and true to Dutch's typical style, his hair is a curly, tangled mess, but his smile is as bright as the summer sun. "Yo?"

"Best grilled cheese ever. Thank you."

"But of course." He winks.

"What do you think of same-sex relationships?"

"Um, Delilah. Is this a trick question? Because I'm pretty sure you know Tristan and Brandon are gay, and…uh…aren't you and Ashley an item?" He turns, flips a few burgers, then lowers the flame and comes over to the counter. "Something bugging you? Want to talk?"

I shrug. "Yes and no. Why do you think they're okay?"

"Well, because I don't give a shit about who anyone else sleeps with. Whatever makes people happy and all that." His eyes turn serious. "Is someone giving you a hard time? Because I'll take care of them—"

"No. It's nothing like that. I'm just wondering about something. Do you think you're all right with it because your parents were, or did you decide it on your own?" I finish my sandwich, and he takes the plate and tosses it into the sink.

"I don't know. I've never thought about it that much." He moves to the stove and flips the burgers, then looks over his shoulder at me. "I guess we never talked about it much in my house. I don't think my parents have issues with it, but I couldn't say that for sure. So I guess I came to it pretty much on my own." He finishes cooking the burgers, puts them on plates, and sets them on the counter just as Charley comes into the kitchen.

"Hey, Delilah. Thanks, Dutch." She picks up the plates and heads back toward the bar.

"Wait! Charley."

She turns, her ponytail swinging from side to side. "Yeah?"

"Why are you okay with same-sex relationships?"

She looks from me to Dutch with a worried expression on her face. "Um. Because who am I to judge. Why?"

"Did your parents feel that way?" Now this is really bugging me, and I want to know more about how people come to these decisions.

"Sure. My parents don't care if people are gay. Why? What's going on? Is this about you and Ashley? Because I think it's great that you two finally figured out what I knew all along."

"What?" I laugh, because come on...Really? She knew? How could she? I wasn't even one hundred percent certain. Well, I kind of was, but still.

Charley laughs. "Oh my God, Delilah. You two have been like Siamese twins since you met, and you look at each other with sickeningly dreamy eyes."

"They do?" Dutch raised his brows in quick succession. "Hm."

"I gotta take these out to the customers, but yeah, they do."

Charley rolls her eyes. "Guys never notice anything. Maybe I should date girls." She breezes back into the bar.

"Why are you asking all this stuff anyway?" Dutch crosses his big arms and narrows his eyes.

"I'm wondering if most people form their opinions about this stuff based on what they're taught rather than basing it on their own feelings. And I'm starting to understand the impact parents have on their kids."

The impact my parents had on me.

And it's starting to piss me off.

"Well, hell, Delilah. You should have said that. It's no secret that our parents mess us up big-time. It's like their jobs or something. So, sure, most people probably believe whatever their parents teach them. It takes strong people to break the mold, if you know what I mean."

"Yeah, I know exactly what you mean." *And I want to break it. It's just easier said than done.* I stand up and pull my shoulders back as Wyatt comes into the kitchen.

"Hey, Dee. You almost ready to go meet the accountant?" Wyatt goes into the back office and comes out with a folder.

"Sure. What's that?"

"The agreement so we can work with them." He nods toward the door. "Let's go. We'll talk on the way."

In the car I open the folder and read the agreement.

"Don't worry, Dee. If you don't like him, we won't sign the agreement. But his references were solid, and he seemed like a good guy."

"Did he seem smart and honest? That's what I care about more than *a good guy.*"

"Yes, Dee. Smart, honest, and a good guy." Wyatt drives to the accountant's office and parks beside the building. "I promise, if you don't like him, he's not hired. I'd never do anything without your okay. This business is both of ours, not just mine."

I've known all along that Wyatt feels this way, but hearing him say it so earnestly makes me feel good. As much as he's overprotective of me, he's also confident in my abilities to handle important decisions, and that means a lot to me.

Inside the office, a short, stout secretary brings us into Mr. Park's lavish office, where we wait for twenty minutes.

"Not exactly a good impression," I whisper to Wyatt.

"He's busy."

"So are we," I remind him.

"Wow. I guess you're over your quiet stage." He sits back and locks his fingers behind his head as he stretches. "Relax, Dee."

A swarthy-looking man with too much product in his dark hair and a suit that looks more expensive than the BMW he probably drives peeks his head into the room. He flashes a toothy smile. "Wyatt, my man." He nods at me. "You must be Delilah."

"Yes." I stand and extend my hand, and he waves from the doorway.

"I'll be right in." He leaves the door open and begins talking to a woman right outside.

I sink back into my chair, eyeing Wyatt. "Real classy, Wy."

Wyatt shrugs.

The room is beyond silent. There isn't even noise from an air conditioner to drown out Mr. Park's conversation with the woman in the hall.

"Listen, I don't care what that faggot says. We'll take him to court," Mr. Park says in a hushed whisper.

I curl my fingers into fists and stare at Wyatt. Wyatt's brows draw together.

"I know you will, but what should I tell his *partner*?" The woman says *partner* like it's a dirty word.

I grab Wyatt's arm and feel his muscles tense as he rises to his feet.

"I don't care what you tell that queer—"

I beat Wyatt out the door and plant myself between Mr. Park and the primly dressed woman.

"I've got this, Delilah." Wyatt holds a protective arm out in front of me. His hands are fisted, his chest looks like it's been inflated, and his biceps are tight.

"No. *I've* got this." I step closer to Mr. Park and glare at his beady, dark eyes.

"You should be ashamed of yourself."

He laughs. "Excuse me?"

"Do you think it's professional to call someone a *queer* and a *faggot*?"

His smile fades, and his eyes shift over my shoulder to the woman behind me with an incredulous look that quickly morphs into save-my-ass mode as a practiced smile curls his thin lips. "You misheard what I—"

"I only wish I had. Let's go, Wyatt." I'm shaking as Wyatt steps closer to Mr. Park and pins him in place with a threatening stare.

Wyatt stares him down until Mr. Park backs up and looks away. Then Wyatt takes me by the arm and leads me out of the office. This time I'm glad for his help, because my legs aren't working very well. By the time we reach the car, I have tears in my eyes.

"The guy's an asshole. How could I have misjudged him so

badly? I'm sorry, Dee." When he notices I'm crying, he gathers me in his arms. "I'm sorry. I don't even know how to screen for that shit."

"He's an ass, but they're everywhere. Our own parents were like him." I push away from Wyatt and pace the parking lot as I wipe my eyes, feeling like that asshole just called me names. "I hate people. I hate him. I hate Mom and Dad."

"No, you don't, Dee." Wyatt reaches for me and I pull away.

"Yeah. Right now I do. Because of Mom and Dad I'm afraid of people like him, and I'm so sick of being afraid. I'm sick of feeling like I can't be myself. Sick of feeling like I'm being judged."

He takes me in his arms and holds me despite my fighting to push free. He holds me while I sob, and he holds me while I kick the ground and curse and bitch about how much people suck. He holds me until I have no more tears to cry, and then he drapes an arm over my shoulder like it's no big deal and helps me into the car.

"Creek, home, Taproom, or Ashley's?"

I rest my head back and breathe deeply. "Oh, Wyatt. Why do you put up with me? Why does Ashley? Why does anyone? I'm so fucked-up."

"Put up with you? Dee. I love you. You're just about the coolest girl on earth, and I know Mom and Dad messed with your head about your personal life, but look how far you've come. You're stronger than any girl around."

I shake my head. "No. I'm not."

"Yeah, you are. Mom and Dad died less than three months ago. Do you realize how recent that is? And you've taken full charge of the scheduling and running the ordering and all that shit at the bar. You've gotten yourself into counseling, and you're in a great relationship. I don't know anyone else who could have come that far."

I exhale loudly and close my eyes.

"I wished they didn't exist." My admission comes as a whisper, and when Wyatt doesn't respond, I wonder if I even said it. I open my eyes. Wyatt's arms are crossed over the steering wheel as he stares straight ahead.

"I wished they didn't exist," I repeat, louder this time.

He looks at me. "I heard you."

"Do you hate me?" Fear freezes like ice in my chest.

He shakes his head. "Do you know how many times *I* wished they didn't exist, Dee? How many times *I* wished them away?"

"Yeah, but I did it right before we walked for graduation. After I told them I liked girls, when they gave me that look like they were so disappointed in me that they wished *I* didn't exist. I wished it then, and then we walked for graduation, and then..." Tears spill down my cheeks. "After graduation there were pictures, and congratulations, and there was no time to talk about it. I thought we'd talk about it the next day when we went back home. And then..." My breath hitches in my throat. "And then they died, Wy. I wished they didn't exist and then they were gone."

Tears tumble down Wyatt's cheeks. "It's not your fault, Dee." A statement, and he says it like a command. Like there's no room for arguing.

But there is.

In my head there's way too much room.

"Maybe it is. Maybe they crashed because they were too upset with me to concentrate."

"No!" His fist rises, then comes down hard on the dashboard. "No, Dee. The tractor trailer crossed the line, and the driver was drunk. It wasn't Mom and Dad's fault, and it wasn't your fault."

"Maybe Dad was distracted. Maybe he could have gotten out of the way." I cover my face with my hands and sob. "Maybe…"

"No! No! No! I'm not going to let you do this to yourself. Goddamn it, Delilah. You did *not* kill them!" He pulls me across the console and holds me tight. "You did not kill them," he whispers.

He holds me for what feels like a long time, maybe ten minutes, maybe an hour. I'm not sure. We pull ourselves together and drive in silence out to our house. We walk around back and sit on the steps to the deck, just the two of us. Wyatt puts his arm around me and I rest my head on his shoulder. It's been a long time since we were alone.

"I'm sorry about that guy," Wyatt says quietly.

"I know. I'm glad you didn't hit him."

He smiles. "I don't hit anymore—you know that. Besides, he wasn't worth it."

"Yeah. You're right."

We sit for a while longer, comforted by the sounds of the ocean and the cool breeze coming off the water.

"Wy?"

"Yeah?"

"Maybe Mom and Dad felt the way they did because of how they were brought up."

"Makes sense, but it doesn't excuse them."

I nod. "I know I don't *need* their approval, but it still hurts, you know?" Tears stream down my cheeks again. I let them fall, because I feel like they've been buried so deep inside me that I'm just starting to skim the top of the well.

"I know." He kisses my temple. "You don't need anyone's approval, but you know you have my support."

"I know. Thank you."

"I don't know how to get past this, Dee. I wish I had the answers. I know how much you're hurting, and I wish Mom and Dad were here right now, because I'd give them a piece of my mind."

"I know you would." I have no doubt that he'd go head-to-head with our parents on my behalf without giving it a second thought. "Wy?"

"Yeah?"

"Thanks for always being there for me."

He holds me closer.

"But I think I have to move out."

His hand stills on my shoulder. "What? Why?"

"Because my whole life I've been taken care of. Don't get me wrong. I love you for it, and I loved them for it. But I think it's time. Before I settle down in a relationship and move in with someone...I need to have my own space and know I can take care of myself."

"You mean before you move in with Ashley?"

I shrug. "Maybe one day. I'm definitely falling for her."

"She's really cool, Dee. Like you. I'm happy for you both."

Wyatt clasps his hands in front of him and leans his elbows on his thighs. "When are you thinking of moving out? I feel like you just got here after living at Brooke's."

I shrug again. "I'm not sure. I just wanted you to know I'm thinking about it."

"I don't like the idea of you living on your own. Where

would you move?"

"Probably to the same complex as Ashley. It's walking distance from here and from the bar."

He nods, but his hands are rubbing each other over and over, and I know he's uncomfortable with me moving out.

"I'll let you check out the place first, just to be sure you think it's safe."

He cocks his head to the side and smiles. "And let me put a guard outside your door?"

I bump him with my shoulder and laugh. "You aren't losing me. I promise."

He nods. "Yeah, I know."

"And it won't be for a while."

"Okay." His arm comes around my shoulder again, and he rests his head against mine. "I'm proud of you, Dee."

"Why?"

He sighs. "Why? Because of everything. Who you are. How you treat people. The way you've handled the bar. Everything."

"Right back at ya, Wy. What do we do about an accountant?"

He shrugs. "We'll figure it out. Eventually, the right person will come along. Until then I'm doing the books so there's no chance of anyone stealing, and Cass is double-checking my work."

"I haven't seen her much lately."

"I know. Your schedules haven't crossed much, but she was so happy to get the pics you sent of Kenny's play." Wyatt pulls out his phone and scrolls through his contacts. He holds up his phone and shows me my contact info. He's cropped the photo so it's just me and Ash.

"I love that." I show him his contact info in my phone and

the picture of him and Cassidy.

"You're a dork." He laughs.

"Considering we're twins, that doesn't say much for you."

"You gonna be okay next weekend when you go home? Do you want me to come?" Wyatt shakes his head and sends his hair out of his eyes. He hasn't shaved for a few days, and when he smiles, his scruff darkens around his mouth. He reminds me of my father, and for the first time in months, that doesn't make me sad.

I sit up straighter and draw in a deep breath. Each day it gets a little easier to breathe.

"No, thanks. I'll be fine."

"I always knew you would be."

CHAPTER TWENTY-ONE

Ashley

SOMETIMES WHEN I wake up with Delilah in my bed, it takes me a few minutes to remember how new our relationship is, because it feels like she's been beside me forever. I'm keeping a few items of clothing at her place, and she has a handful at mine. Yesterday I bought extra toothbrushes—one for me at her place and another for her here, at my apartment. Delilah's made similar accommodations without as much as a single word about it. She bought my favorite shampoo and body wash for her place, the lotions I like, and she even set out a little pottery bowl for me to put my earrings in at the end of the day. We've moved into this part of the relationship pretty seamlessly, but we're still navigating the hills and valleys of our public relationship. It's Thursday again, which means I've been up for the past half hour thinking about her group session tonight—and Janessa.

I feel like there's a hamster gnawing on my stomach. I trust Delilah, and I don't think I'm feeling jealous, at least not jealousy over her and Janessa getting together or anything like that. I know that she might have coffee with Janessa tonight and she might not invite me, and I'm okay with that. I have no idea what the awful feeling in my stomach is. Maybe it's another kind of jealousy—jealousy over the time they get to spend together.

Delilah shifts beside me and inhales as she stretches her arms out to her sides. The lingerie top she's wearing slips off her shoulder as she leans up on one elbow and looks down at me with sleepy eyes.

"Hi," she says in a groggy voice as she lifts up and settles her hips over mine.

I love that she's gotten comfortable enough with me to take the initiative in bed. Her green eyes narrow, and I know she's in a playful mood. She lowers her lips to my shoulder and uses her teeth to move the silk spaghetti strap down my arm, sending a shiver down my spine.

"What time do you have to be at work to do inventory?" Her voice is husky, her breath hot on my skin as she lowers her mouth to my breast and traces circles around my nipple with her tongue.

"Before…" I suck in a breath when she takes my breast into her mouth and cups it with her hand. "Before…Good Lord…" I close my eyes as fire spreads through my limbs. Delilah moves her hips against me as she lavishes my body with attention. She shifts, straddles my thigh.

Holy hell, she's not wearing underwear. She's hot, wet, and driving me fucking crazy. When did she take off her underwear? She kisses a path down my stomach, leaving a trail of goose bumps.

"Before?" she whispers.

"Before we open," I say as fast as I can, because I know in seconds I'm not going to be able to think, much less speak. Delilah has learned exactly how to touch me to make me come apart in seconds and how to prolong the magnificent, torturous teasing until *she's* ready for me to fall over the edge.

She caresses my breasts with both hands as she kisses my ribs, my stomach, my belly button. Every stroke of her tongue is sinful. I'm writhing, arching, making all sorts of needful noises as she makes my body hum with desire. I reach for her hips and she grabs my wrists and holds them down, then kisses me hard. Deep. Possessive.

I love in-control Delilah.

God, how I love this side of her, but I need to touch her, and I struggle to free my hands. Our lips part and I crane my neck, reaching for them to return. Her lips curve up in a devilish grin.

"A little greedy this morning, are we?"

"Oh my God, Delilah. You're killing me. I *need* to touch you."

She lowers her mouth to the sensitive underside of my forearm and settles her lips over my sensitive skin, sucking, kissing, nibbling her way up to my wrist, then my palm. *Ohmygod.* I never realized how sensitive my palms were, but as her tongue lazily follows the contours, I climb closer to the edge. I stretch my fingers, trying to reach beyond her restraint, and she sucks each finger into her mouth, swirls her tongue around them one by one. My eyes slam shut as I try to regain control, which I know is completely gone.

"Please, Dee…"

She ignores my pleas and moves to my other hand, taking her sweet time as she makes every nerve in my body heighten, makes my skin feel like it's on fire. She needs a license for her tongue. It should be considered a lethal weapon, or come with a warning label at the very least. She takes my hand and lowers it between my legs, pressing it beneath hers as she strokes me.

This is new.

Naughtier than what I'm used to with Delilah.

I'm not a prude and certainly not averse to touching myself, but the fact that she's initiating it makes me nearly lose my mind. I tug down my underwear and kick it off as she guides my hand back between my legs, then releases my other wrist. With my free hand, I tear at her top, and—thank the heavens above—she takes it off. I pull her down and take her breast in my mouth, hungrily teasing, grazing her nipple with my teeth, earning me the sexiest, hottest moan I've ever heard. She sits up and arches her back, still teasing my most sensitive area with her fingers. I waste no time bringing my hand between her legs and plunge two fingers into her. She moans again as I probe and tease, and the sight of her straddling my thigh, one hand between my legs, her head back, lips parted, is almost too much to take.

I try to capture her image in my mind, imagining the strokes of my brush it would take to replicate her beauty. I bring her free hand to my mouth and suck on her fingers. Her eyes open with a look of surprise, and as I place her fingers between her legs, she holds my gaze. She tries to move her hand away and I hold it in place, wondering if she's willing to take the step. If she trusts me enough. My answer comes in the form of her softening gaze and easing of tension in her hand. I release the pressure and she touches herself as I cup the back of her neck and bring her mouth to mine.

"You're so fucking sexy," I say against her lips. "I love you so much."

Our mouths collide, and our hips rock. The need to take her over the edge rushes through me like a tidal wave. I crave feeling her release shuddering through her. I shift her onto her back, and her knees fall open. She's so trusting, so ready for me, as I move lower and make love to her with my mouth and my hands until she spirals over the edge. Her head turns from side to side as her hips buck against my mouth. I hold her to the mattress and take her up to the peak again and again, until her body relaxes limply into the mattress and she pants out my name.

"Ash…"

I fall to the bed beside her, eyes closed, one arm arced over my head, the other across my stomach. I'm not surprised when I feel her hand moving across my hip. She's the most unselfish lover I've ever had and the last one I ever want.

CHAPTER TWENTY-TWO

Delilah

I'M PULLING MY shorts up when Ashley's phone vibrates with a message. She's showering, and I carry her phone into the bathroom and part the shower curtain. My mouth goes dry at the sight of her beneath the shower spray, water streaming over her breasts, falling in thin streams down the curve of her hips and thighs.

She touches my nose with her wet fingertips, bringing my eyes back up to hers. I know I'm blushing after being caught staring at her, but after the way we've just loved each other silly, I don't care.

"Your phone's vibrating."

"So is my body."

"Ash!"

She laughs. "It's so fun to make you blush. Who's texting?"

"I didn't look." I'd never look at her texts without her knowing.

She closes her eyes and goes back to rinsing the shampoo from her hair. "Can you look in case it's work?"

"Sure." I scroll to the text and my stomach tightens. I hold up the phone, hating the shaky sound of my voice. "It's Sandy."

Her expression doesn't change. "What does it say?"

"You want me to read it?"

"No. I want it to read itself." She turns and faces the spray, washes her face.

"I don't want to read her text."

She looks at me like I'm being ridiculous. "Whatever."

I don't want to read it...but I also do. Really, really badly. "Fine, I'll read it." I open the text and read it quickly, wishing I hadn't. My heart feels like it's going to explode at the sight of the thread of texts from Sandy.

"Well?"

"She...She texts you all the time." I scroll up and read some of the messages from the last few weeks.

"Uh-huh. I don't answer."

No, she doesn't *usually* answer her, but she has a few times.

She turns off the water and reaches for a towel. "What is it this time?"

"She's..." I can't look at Ashley, and I'm not sure I can force myself to tell her what the message says.

She takes the phone from my hand and reads it, then sets the phone on the counter and dries off.

"Well? Aren't you going to respond?"

"No." She walks into the bedroom and opens the dresser drawers, then begins dressing.

"She's *out*. She broke up with that guy and—"

Ashley spins around and faces me. Her eyes are narrow and angry, and her face is pinched. "I know, okay? You don't have to reiterate. I read the message."

"Well, does it make you want to go back to her?" I can't help it. I hate that I ask, but it's not like I have the power to stop my heart from pouring out my mouth.

"No, it doesn't make me want to go back to her. It pisses me off. Why would she send me this now? Months after we broke up? If I didn't mean enough to her then, I don't now."

Her phone vibrates again and we both turn in the direction of the bathroom, where she left it on the counter.

"Aren't you going to check it?" Every word is bathed in sarcasm as I settle my hand on my hip, more to stop it from shaking and offer myself a modicum of stability than for any other reason.

She rolls her eyes and storms out of the bedroom. "No."

I grab my backpack and shove my feet into my boots. I don't know why I'm so upset. She's not doing anything wrong, but all those texts from Sandy are niggling at me like a thorn in my shoe.

"Why didn't you tell me that she texts you all the time?"

"I did."

"No, I'm fairly certain you didn't." I cross my arms and stare at her.

"I told you she sends me random texts."

"Random isn't exactly...I don't know how many, but random implies less than how many she's sent. I saw them, Ash. She texts you every few days! And you've texted her back a few times."

"So what? I probably told her to stop texting or something."

"No." I clench my jaw shut, feeling like a nosy bitch for reading her responses.

"No, what?" Ashley leans against the back of the couch.

I can't lie to her. "You didn't tell her not to text you. When she asked how you were, you said you were good, that you were happy."

She shrugs. "So?"

"And when she said she wanted to see you, you said it wasn't a good time."

She turns away, but not before I see something like sadness flash in her eyes.

"You said yourself you were falling for her, and now she's *out*. It's what you wanted." Tears sting my eyes, but I don't give in to them.

"It's not what I want, Delilah."

"Then why would you tell her it wasn't a good time instead of telling her you didn't want to see her? Why didn't you tell her about us?"

"I don't even know the timing of that text."

"It was the day after our first kiss."

She exhales loudly and covers her eyes with her hands, shakes her head. "Dee, it's not what you think. We were so new, and—"

"And I'm still in the fucking closet. I get it. What were you doing, Ash? Hedging your bets? Did you have a deadline? Like if I didn't come out by a certain time, you'd run back to her?"

"No, and that's not fair." She reaches for me.

I pull away. I know I'm overreacting, but it still hurts to see all those texts. It feels like a lie.

"She's texted you a million times, and you never said a word. How would you feel if the tables were turned?"

"I trust you."

"Yeah? Well, trust is more than telling your girlfriend you get random texts. Trust is telling her that you're being pursued. Relentlessly. Even if you're not responding, it feels like the secret was there for a reason."

I turn and open the door.

"Delilah? Where are you going?"

"Home. I need some space."

"Dee. I didn't do anything. I didn't lead her on, and I'm sorry I didn't tell her about us. I will." She runs into the bedroom and I hear her go into the bathroom as I close the apartment door behind me. I know she was going to grab her phone and show me how many times she responded to Sandy, but I don't want to even see her phone.

I spend the next few hours replaying the whole argument in my mind until I've scrutinized every facial expression, every inflection of Ashley's voice *and* mine.

It still hurts, and I feel like a bitch.

I haven't had a girlfriend before, but even when I was fake-dating Frank, a guy I didn't like as more than a friend, we talked about guys who hit on me and girls who hit on him.

By midafternoon Ashley's texted me a dozen times, and I've texted her back with the same message every time. I just need a little time and space to get past this.

Get past this.

I analyze that phrase as I help with waiting tables into the early evening. I have no idea why we're so freaking busy tonight. It's only Thursday.

"Hey, you okay tonight?" Livi sidles up to me, and we both push through the double doors and head for the kitchen to place our customers' orders.

I shrug.

"Worried about going back home this weekend?" Livi asks.

"A little." Maybe that is why I'm so upset over this. *Nope.* I can't even lie to myself about why I'm upset. I feel like Ash lied to me.

We give Dutch our orders, and before walking back into the bar, Livi touches my arm.

"Sometimes what you find out about your parents after they die can have as big of an impact as their death did. You know, secrets and stuff. So take my number in case you want to talk." She scrawls her number on an order pad and slips it into my pocket. "I've been there, so if you want to talk, I'm here for you."

"Thanks." I shove it in my pocket, though I know my parents aren't causing my angst at the moment.

She smiles. "Hey, that's what friends are for, lessening the impact our parents leave behind."

You wouldn't believe the shit they left behind... I'm not sure anything can lessen the impact of what my parents left behind.

On my way to the counseling session, I drive by Ashley's apartment complex. I debate going in to talk to her, but then I remember she's at work, and I have no idea what I'd say. I'm still stuck between feeling like she lied and feeling like a complete idiot for thinking she would.

I turn back toward the YMCA and crank the music. Ashley's iPod is plugged into the stereo—with all my favorite songs on her playlist.

I drive the rest of the way holding back tears.

Ashley

THE DAY FROM hell plowed into the night from hell. I texted Delilah a million times, and I tried calling, but she was at work all day, and I know she can't talk when she's working. She texted me back a number of times, but always with the same message. She's sorry, but she needs space and time.

Brent and I are the last two in the shop, finishing the inventory that should have been done hours ago, but we got so busy that there wasn't time. As it gets later into the season, everyone wants to pick up the end-of-summer sale items. It's great for business, but on a day when everything makes me want to either punch something or cry, the business is the last thing on my mind.

"I think that just about does it." Brent rises to his feet with a groan. "The worst part about inventory is crouching for so long." His hair is pulled back in a ponytail. Brent's big brown eyes are serious, his strong jaw is set tight, and he's looking at me like he's worried. I know it's because I've been a royal bitch all day, barely talking or acknowledging his efforts at small talk. I don't mean to be that way, but it's not like I can help it after what happened this morning with Delilah.

"The worst part about inventory is *doing* the inventory," I say to lighten the mood. Brent smiles, but worry lingers in his eyes. When I first started working at the surf shop, it took me a few weeks to open up to him. He's a friendly guy, and he tried to reach out multiple times, to try to get me to let him in on why I was so moody. Having just broken up with Sandy, I was in no mood to share my romantic woes. But he asked enough times that I finally gave in. We walked along the boardwalk eating ice cream and talking about breakups, not that he had much experience with them. By the end of the evening we'd become friends. He has the same worried look in his eyes now that he did back then. Like he's going to get me to talk whether I like it or not.

Brent pulls me to my feet. "Thanks for your help. I know you weren't in the mood to do inventory for twelve hours."

"I didn't really mind."

We walk up front and go through the normal closing routine of straightening up the shop, sweeping, closing out the register. As I go through the motions, I wonder what Delilah's doing in group. Is she sitting next to Janessa, telling her what happened between us?

"How did you do with Drake?" Brent asked.

I shrug. "He's a good instructor, but I think I need about a dozen more lessons before I'm any good. He said he'd help me as long as I want." *But I'd rather get help from Delilah.*

"Any fun plans for the weekend?" Brent asks as he locks up behind us.

"No. Delilah's going out of town, so…"

He smiles down at me. "So, it's true, then, the rumor about you and Delilah?"

"There's a rumor about us?" Delilah will hate that.

"Well, not like a Harborside rumor or anything. Jesse mentioned it to me. I've known Delilah for a long time. She's a sweet gal."

"Yeah. She is." *And I want my sweet girl back.*

"Where you headed? Wanna grab a soda?" Brent asks.

"A soda? Wow, you're a real party animal tonight." I smile with the tease.

"Yeah, well, when Delilah and Wyatt's parents were killed, it was a wakeup call." We walk a few feet toward the pier. "You game? We can grab a drink at Brooke's."

Going to Brooke's will make me think of Delilah, which will make me sad. "How about we just grab a can from the machine and sit on the beach? We've been in the shop all day."

He furrows his brow. "Okay. Is today's mood caused by trouble in paradise or just a bad mood in general?"

I shrug, but I've worked for Brent since I first came to Harborside, and he knows my moods too well to let me off that easily.

"Okay, so we have girlfriend problems." He slips money into the soda machine and steps aside for me to make a selection. I press a button for Mello Yello, and he gets a Coke. We take our drinks across the boardwalk and sink down into the sand near a night volleyball game. It should probably feel weird sitting with my boss, talking about this kind of stuff, but Brent doesn't feel like a boss. He feels like a big brother, like Wyatt, Jesse, Tristan, and Brandon. I have a lot of *brothers* around here, but I'd trade them all to have Delilah back by my side.

"Whatever it is, I'm sure you and Delilah will figure it out, but it's a good reminder why I don't do the whole girlfriend thing." He chugs his Coke.

"I hope so, but I don't think this is that easy."

He nods, looking out over the water. "Want to talk about it?"

I shrug again. "Yes. No. I have no idea. How's that for indecisive?"

"About as good as it gets, I suppose. If you weren't into her, you wouldn't care, right? So at least you have that part figured out."

"Oh, I'm into her. I'm so into her I don't want to find my way out." I sip my soda and close my eyes as the cold liquid slips down my throat. Liquid. That's what I feel like right now. Like I'm slipping through each minute without any idea of how to become solid again.

"Wow, that's pretty into her. So, have you called her, tried to talk?"

"Mm-hm. She needs space."

"Ouch." He finishes his soda and crushes the can, then sets

it beside him. "Space. That's not a good sign. You must have done something pretty harsh."

"Why do you assume *I* did something?"

The side of his mouth quirks up. "Because she's the one asking for space."

"Oh. Right." We sit in silence for a while. "So, you don't do the whole *girlfriend thing* because it's too hard? That seems lonely." *Relationships are hard, but Delilah's worth whatever it takes.*

"No. Not because it's too hard. I just…don't. There are too many things that can be misconstrued, and when you're a guy, you get blamed for everything, even when you don't do anything."

I know what you mean. "Then maybe you're picking the wrong girls." I can't imagine him doing the wrong things very often. The way he and Jesse watch out for everyone else, it seems like they were brought up doing all the right things.

He shrugs. "Maybe you did, too."

"No. I have no doubt that Delilah is the right girl for me."

He slides me an arched-eyebrow look that reads, *Then why'd you do something wrong?*

"It wasn't what I did. It was what I didn't do."

"Been there, too. It's all the same."

"Well, some girls aren't worth taking those extra steps for, but Delilah is. I was just stupid." I don't really know why I didn't tell Delilah about Sandy's texts. I'd like to believe that I thought so little of them I didn't want her to worry. But the truth is, I think I might have been keeping them as a reminder of what I *didn't* want to repeat. The problem is, I *am* with Delilah, and although she's not anything like Sandy, she isn't *out.* She isn't openly affectionate in public, and *that* was what those reminders were supposed to keep me from repeating.

But all the texts and reminders in the world couldn't make me walk away from Delilah.

"You're not a stupid girl, Ash. I'm not buying it."

I'm not either.

We walk back toward the parking lot. "Where's your car?"

"I walked. Needed the fresh air."

"At seven thirty this morning?" He takes me by the elbow and leads me to his Harley. "Come on. I'll drive you home."

"You don't have to." Although the idea of walking home alone is not at all appealing. I don't live far, but I feel lonely with the fissure that's formed between me and Dee.

"I know." He lifts a helmet from his bike. "Can you tie your hair back?"

I slip an elastic band from my wrist and secure my hair at the nape of my neck. Then he puts the helmet on me and smiles. "Cute."

"Thanks. I feel like one of those bobblehead dolls we sell."

He puts on his helmet and helps me onto the bike, then straddles the bike. "Hold on tight."

Minutes later we're at my apartment complex. I give Brent the helmet and thank him for the ride. He takes off his helmet and holds it under his arm as he reaches for my arm.

"Ashley, I'm sure that Delilah will come around. Just don't shove whatever you did or didn't do to the side. If there's one thing I've learned, it's that owning our mistakes can help us heal. Unless, of course, the reason we made them in the first place was to give ourselves an out. And if that's the case, cut your losses and walk away, because if you wanted out once, you'll want out again."

As his taillights fade into the distance, I know one thing for sure. I *do not* want an out from being with Delilah.

CHAPTER TWENTY-THREE

Delilah

I DRIVE OVER to group, but I don't want to talk about grieving and depression and moving past our pain when another type of pain is sinking its claws into my heart. A pain that feels worse than the lingering pain of losing my parents, and *that* makes me feel guilty, too. I should go back to work and help out, but I can't. I just fucking can't. I turn my Jeep around and drive home, adding another layer of guilt to my already guilt-laden shoulders.

I park in the driveway behind Brandon's motorcycle and head inside, cringing when the door slams behind me.

Brandon sits up from where he's sprawled on the couch with his laptop perched on his stomach.

"Whoa. You okay?" He sets the laptop on the coffee table.

"No." I take the stairs two at a time and stomp into my room. I grab a duffel bag from the closet and pack my stuff—realizing too late that I left my hairbrush at Ashley's. *Damn it.*

I snag my shampoo from the bathroom, and when I come back out Brandon is sitting on my bed, legs crossed at the ankles, hands folded behind his head.

"Skipping group?"

"Yup."

"Been there, done that. Anything I can do to help?" Brandon's parents had put him into a peer counseling group when he was a teenager because they thought he was too…everything. Rebellious, different, uninterested in schoolwork, despite his excellent grades.

"Nope." I toss shorts and tank tops into my bag, then go back to my dresser for underwear. When I open the drawer, I see Ashley's underwear and bra and stare at them for a few seconds while my throat thickens.

"Thought you were leaving tomorrow."

I grab my underwear and slam the drawer shut. "Changed my mind." I stuff it into the bag, throw in a pair of flip-flops, and zip it up.

Brandon sits up as I grab the handles and he clutches my wrist. "Delilah, what's going on?"

"Nothing." *Don't cry. Don't cry. Don't cry.*

He nods at the bag. "This is not nothing. Wyatt will freak if he finds out you're driving home at night."

I shrug and pull my wrist from his grip. "Wyatt can't control everything I do."

Brandon follows me out of the room and down the stairs. "Want me to come with you so you have company in the car?"

I sigh loudly as I stalk out the door. "No. You have a gig this weekend with your band. I'm a big girl. I'll be fine."

"Maybe you should call Wyatt so that he doesn't tear me a new one when I tell him I let you go." Brandon opens the passenger door and takes my bag, throws it in, then closes the door. "You sure you're not too upset to drive?"

"You're a good friend, Brandon. I'm too upset not to drive. I'll call Wyatt in a little while."

"Once you're out of Harborside?"

"A smart friend, too. If you talk to Wyatt, don't let him tell you that you let me do anything. I don't need permission to leave." I climb into the Jeep and put my phone on the passenger seat. The message light is blinking. *Why can't everyone just leave me alone?*

I start the Jeep and scroll through the messages. *Janessa. Wyatt. Ashley.*

Tossing the phone back on the passenger seat, I wave to Brandon and pull out of the driveway. I'm in no mood to answer to anyone, and I know what Ashley's text is going to say. The same thing she's been texting all day. She's sorry. She wasn't thinking. She loves me.

I drive toward the highway with my head swimming in too many thoughts to try to decipher them. Traffic on the highway is light, and I drive for an hour, listening to Ashley's iPod. As I near the site of my parents' accident, I become consumed with thoughts of them.

What were they thinking right before it happened? Were they arguing about me? Were they thinking about how much I disappointed them? Were they wishing that I didn't exist?

My hands begin to shake and I grip the steering wheel tighter and move over to the right lane as I near the point of their accident. I'll never be able to drive by this mile marker and not think of them. The skid marks have faded from the road, and broken glass no longer litters the pavement. They've been swept away like they never even existed. Thousands of people drive by this spot every day. Did any of them see the accident? Hear about it? Does anyone think about the children my parents left behind?

My Jeep veers onto the shoulder as if it has a mind of its

own. I park way off to the side and put on my hazards. I can't take my eyes off the middle of the road where the truck hit them. My father's face appears before me, and it's not the loving face I want to see. The warm eyes I desperately *need* to see right now. It's the disheartened look of disappointment staring back at me, his green eyes hooded and serious. His lips curved down slightly at the edges. Sobs rumble from my lungs, burning my throat as my vision blurs and my tears wash away my father's image.

I bury my face in my hands and close my eyes tight. My fucked-up mind conjures my mother's face with her own disconcerted look.

Stop. Please, please stop.

I stumble out of the car and run into the grass, away from the blurry headlights coming in my direction. My fisted hands press against my eyes, and at first the screams seem like they're miles away, and I wonder who's yelling. Then I realize the pained cries are coming from my lungs. My burning chest. My broken heart as I collapse to my knees and claw at the grass, like I can dig my way out of the pain. Every tear I've ever held back is falling, one chasing the next and the next, with no reprieve on the horizon. I sink back on my heels and my arms fall limply to my sides as I give in to the sadness.

"I'm sorry. I'm so fucking sorry." My words are drowned out by the sounds of the traffic whizzing by.

By the place where my parents lost their lives.

The place where their lives were *stolen* from me and Wyatt.

The place that swallowed my hope of being able to talk to them again. To try to wipe that look of disappointment off their faces.

Fucking hell.

Life sucks.

It's so unfair.

I sit on the side of the road gulping in air, trying to regain control of my breathing.

I can't go back.

I can't fix what happened. I can't change what I said or make them look differently at me.

I can't do a damn thing.

I listen to the fast noises of the traffic. No one stops to see if I'm okay. Wyatt doesn't come racing up behind my Jeep to swoop me into his arms. Ashley doesn't come to my rescue.

There's only me and the fucking pavement that will forever mark my parents' deaths.

Me and the memory of their disapproving looks.

Me and the guilt of knowing they think it's wrong for me to love Ashley.

And I do love her.

I love her so much.

But of course I can't tell her, because my fucking parents have left me buried in guilt so thick I can barely breathe. They left me scared of never being able to love a woman—to love *Ashley* the way she deserves to be loved. The way I want to love her—publicly, without concern over looks and disapproval from others.

They left me a broken girl.

I imagine Wyatt telling me it'll be okay. I can practically feel his arms around me, and I see myself falling into that comfort— and it pisses me off.

I don't want to be that broken girl.

I don't want anyone else to fix me. Not even Wyatt.

I push to my feet and wait until my wobbly legs become

solid again, and then I force myself to walk back to my Jeep with one goal in mind.

Every step, every breath, comes a little stronger, with more determination.

I'm going to heal myself, because no one else can do that for me, and I'll be damned if I'm going to allow my parents' guilt and disapproval to take me under.

I pick up my phone and type a text to Ashley—*I miss you already*—but I don't send it. I can't give her hope for us until I know I can be whole. She told me herself not to tell her I loved her until I could say it loud and proud.

I'm going to try.

CHAPTER TWENTY-FOUR

Ashley

I DON'T WANT to get out of bed. I don't want to shower, and I don't want to go to work, and I don't want to do anything but lie here smelling Delilah's shampoo on my pillow with the phone in my hand while I wait for her to call. She didn't return my texts last night, and even though Brandon called to tell me that she left for Connecticut, I wish she'd call. Wyatt called me too, to ask what the hell was going on. Or rather, *to demand* to know what was going on. There was no use lying. He was worried, and honestly, so was I. Driving to Connecticut by herself in the dark without telling Wyatt, without even mentioning it to me, tells me just how bad our situation is.

There's a knock on my apartment door, and I fly out of bed, hoping it's Delilah. Funny how a sliver of hope can instantly heal a broken heart. I fling open the door and feel like I've been kicked in the gut when it's not Delilah, but Brandon leaning one hand against the doorframe, his head hanging between his shoulders. He lifts his head just enough for me to see his eyes and raises his brows.

"Nice outfit." His voice is craggy and thick.

I don't say anything to defend wearing Delilah's T-shirt and shorts. I simply turn and walk into the living room and flop on the couch, leaving Brandon to follow me in and close the door behind himself.

"What's the lowdown?" He sits beside me in his black jeans and T-shirt, leans his elbows on his thighs, and locks his eyes on the floor.

I shrug, which he obviously can't see, but he must feel the couch move. He cocks his head so he's looking at me out of the corners of his eyes.

"Bullshit."

I get up, walk into the bedroom, and grab my phone, then return to the living room and toss it to him, before sinking onto the couch again.

He eyes me carefully, as if I might get up and do something else, then scrolls through my texts. When he gets to Sandy's, he eyes me again, then proceeds to read them. He doesn't say a word. He doesn't have to. I know how it looks. I watch him scroll through texts to Delilah. I'm not embarrassed by the number of texts I've sent her or what they say. I don't really care who sees them, least of all Brandon. He's never judged me, not once since the day we met.

He leans back, hands me my phone, and drapes his arms over the back of the couch. We sit in silence, me with my feet tucked beneath me, hovering in the corner of the couch, and him sprawled out like he hasn't a care in the world. Only his dark eyes are treading in a pool of worry. Upon closer inspection, I notice that dark circles hang beneath his eyes and his clothes are disheveled and wrinkled. I worry something in his life has gone awry, and I've been too wrapped up in Delilah to notice, but I don't have the energy to ask.

"Wanna go out for coffee?"

I shrug again. I've decided that shrugs can take the place of any answer. It makes it easier to let the other person make the decisions.

"Wanna go for a...*walk*?" *Walk* is full of sarcasm.

I shrug again.

"Strip club?"

I laugh softly, then wipe the smile from my lips. "Don't make me laugh."

"Okay, no laughing. Well, this fucking sucks, doesn't it?"

I nod. Nodding works almost as well as shrugging. Brandon's not much of a talker, but I can tell he's got something he wants to say.

"Go shower. I'll make coffee."

"I don't want to shower." I sound like a petulant child.

"Well, I need to think, so get in the fucking shower." He stands and lopes into the kitchen.

I sigh loudly enough for him to know he's annoying me and head back into the bedroom. I shower and brush my hair, put Delilah's shirt back on with a pair of my shorts, then join Brandon on the couch again.

He nods at a mug of coffee and a plate of burnt toast he's set on the coffee table.

"Never said I could cook. Eat." He nods to the toast and pats the seat beside him.

"Thank you for the coffee." My tone is not very thankful, but I know he'll forgive me. I'm exhausted after not sleeping and worried about what's going down between me and Delilah.

"And the toast."

"That's still up in the air."

We both smile, and I feel a little better.

"What's your plan?" he asks.

I shrug.

He closes his eyes and shakes his head. "You're not me. You're not a fucked-up guy. You're a smart girl who loves Delilah. *Another* smart girl. So…spill."

"How can I *spill* when I have no idea how to get through to her? I've apologized. She won't talk to me."

"She's in Connecticut dealing with her parents' shit."

"I know. Wyatt called me."

"She had a nervous breakdown on the way down there."

"What?" My heart stops.

"I followed her on my motorcycle. She doesn't know I did, but I was worried about her driving with how upset she was. She pulled off the highway and screamed and cried. I parked way down the road and walked close enough so I could watch her but she couldn't see me."

"Brandon, I have to go to her." I stand, and he pulls me back down and shakes his head.

"No. It wasn't a put-me-in-the-loony bin type of breakdown. She stopped at the sight of her parents' accident. She's working through shit."

"What did she do?" The fear in my voice catches both of our attention, and he sets his hand on mine. "How do you know she's okay?"

"I followed her all the way to Connecticut. She got there okay. I called her as she walked inside her house just to be sure everything was copacetic inside the house. Made up some bullshit about needing to know where shit was at the beach house. She bought it. I talked to her for almost ten minutes. She's okay, probably not fine, but she arrived safely."

"Is that why you look like crap?"

He shrugs, closes his eyes, and rests his head back on the couch. "So, are you going to tell me what your plan is, because whatever you did, if it's fixable, I'd say you have a day or two to figure out how to fix it before she comes back."

"I have to see Sandy."

Brandon lifts his head, and his tired eyes spring open. "Why the hell do you have to do that?"

"Closure. She's still in her apartment by the university. Want to come along for old times' sake?"

"Can I sleep first?" He closes his eyes again and kicks his feet up on the coffee table.

I can't believe he drove to Connecticut to make sure Delilah was safe, but then again, *this* is the Brandon I know. The Brandon who led me to her in the first place.

"Yeah, but you'll be more comfortable lying on the couch or in my bed than with your legs on the table."

His breathing is already shallow.

CHAPTER TWENTY-FIVE

Delilah

SOME PEOPLE DON'T believe in ghosts. I never have, but I feel my parents looking down on me so often, I'm not sure what to think. And this morning, as I was thinking about how I chickened out and didn't call Wyatt when I arrived last night, texting him instead, I started to wonder. I didn't answer his call, which came through seconds after I sent the text, and I didn't answer the next four calls from him either. I thought I'd feel my parents around then, for ignoring my brother's call, but I didn't. Then Brandon called and caught me off guard when I was carrying my stuff into the house, so I talked to him. I was glad to have the company as I walked through the empty house. I hadn't thought about how strange it would feel to be in the house after being gone for so long. I'm still not sure if I believe in ghosts or not, but I wonder if objects can *feel* like ghosts, because that's how the house felt last night. Like the ghost of the house I used to live in. From the moment I walked in, it felt different, colder, not like the house I'd grown up in.

Between texts from Cassidy and Tristan, telling me they were here for me, and Janessa's text wondering where in the hell I was, I didn't really have time to be too unsettled by the changes in the house. I didn't respond to Cassidy or Tristan, but I did reply to Janessa, because after the way she lost her sister, I worried that she'd think I committed suicide or something. So I sent a quick reassuring text. *In CT dealing with house stuff.* Jesse's text, which came in later than the others, gave me pause. I hate to worry him almost as much as I hate worrying Wyatt and Ash, but I can't keep leaning on everyone else.

They love me too much.

They want to protect me from *everything*, but *everything's* already upon me, and they are standing in my way.

I need to do this on my own, and I'm not even sure what *this* is, but I'll figure it out.

The hardest part of last night was not getting in touch with Ashley. I was worried that if I let her back in, even that one tiny bit, I'd cave and give up on taking care of the things that I fear might strangle me forever. I can't give up. If I'm ever going to be whole in our relationship, I need to deal with this stuff.

I still don't know if I believe in ghosts or not, but while I was lying on the couch thinking about being loved *too* much and wanting to love Ashley without being mired down by guilt and insecurities, I swear I smelled my mom's perfume. It was as if she'd walked right past me. I'm not crazy, and I didn't see an apparition or speak to her from beyond the grave or anything like that. I just smelled her perfume. I'm sure it was probably just from thinking about her so much last night, but the most surprising thing was that it didn't scare me. Instead I was comforted by her familiar scent, and the tears that followed weren't tears of anger or guilt. They were tears of longing to see her and feeling like she was right there with me at a time when I needed her most.

I don't know how I was brave enough to sleep here last night, but I figure that's a sign that I'm doing something right. When Wyatt and I left here at the beginning of the summer, I practically ran out. I sensed my parents in every room, and every memory snowed me under. And now, in the light of day, I see more clearly why the house felt so different last night. There are cardboard boxes stacked against every wall. Our personal effects that were scattered about and made our house a home have been boxed and labeled by Aunt Lara. I noticed the boxes last night, of course, but I wasn't thinking clearly. I was too upset to put the pieces together.

I walk around the room with my fingers trailing over the boxes and read the labels. *Candles, knickknacks, vases, books, photos.*

Photos. My heart beats a little faster. I stare at the box and start to believe maybe ghosts do exist and they come in the form of photos. I'm not sure I can handle looking into my parents' eyes.

I look around the living room, noticing the faded rectangles on the walls where our family photos once hung. Spaces that would be painted over, the nail holes filled in. Spaces where our smiling faces used to make silent statements about the people who lived in this house. Photographs that reflected a happy family living in a warm and loving home: Me and Wyatt with our faces pressed together when we were seven. My father holding me on his shoulders and Wyatt in his arms when we were three. My mother gazing up at my father on their honeymoon with Niagara Falls raging behind them.

I sink down to my knees and run my trembling fingers over the tape that's sealed those statements in tight and pluck at the edge until it comes loose. I press my hand flat against the sticky ridge, pausing as I debate my vulnerability again. I close my eyes and breathe deeply, knowing I *need* to see them. If I want to have a future I need to be able to face my past. I have a good past. A loving past. I have a childhood filled with good holiday memories and family vacations. I have a past littered with moments of laughter and positive affirmations from my parents. It was a happy past, one probably many people would long for, but within that happy past sat a scared girl.

I must have been around thirteen or fourteen when I realized I was drawn to girls. And it wasn't until I was about fifteen that I began to worry and take my desires seriously. If only I'd had the courage to talk to my parents, to look them in the eyes and face their disappointment when there would still have been a tomorrow to deal with it.

My hands are shaky as I pull the tape up and open my eyes. When the tape reaches the end of the box, the flaps spring up, then nearly close again, sobering me to what I'm about to see.

I scoot away from the box on my knees. I'm not ready. Not yet, because there are pictures in that box of me when I was a teenager, when I was scared and hiding who I was. I don't want to see that girl. That's the past I wish I could deny. I wish never happened.

I push to my feet and walk to the stairs, put one foot on the lowest riser and look over my shoulder at the box. I wish Wyatt were here. He'd take my hand and lead me upstairs, or outside, and he'd tell me everything was okay.

He'd make the pain go away.

Until it returns.

It always returns.

I stare at the box, and anger simmers in my stomach. I don't want Wyatt to help me or to fix this. It's so easy to fall back, so easy to let him lead. I walk over to the box and sink to my knees again, thinking of Ashley. She doesn't need a girlfriend who *needs* someone else to help her through a hard time. She needs an adult, a partner. I want to be that person.

The flaps open easily, and relief washes through me when the first thing I see are crumpled-up pieces of newspaper. I exhale a breath I didn't know I was holding and realize my veil of courage isn't as strong as I'd thought. I press my hand over my racing heart and take a number of deep breaths while deciding whether I'm *sure* I need to do this. I hear Wyatt's voice telling me I don't have to. I see Ashley's warm brown eyes, feel her hand on mine. I don't need to hear her voice, her eyes tell me that she's with me no matter what I decide.

I decide to follow my heart.

Ash has faith in me.

She loves me.

The newspaper comes out easily, and I set it on the floor. Beneath the crumpled papers are the actual photos, individually packaged in Bubble Wrap. Leave it to Aunt Lara to do a perfect packing job. I remove the first wrapped photo and know from the size and shape that it's the one of me and my father. My stomach lurches, and I set it aside. My courage is still finding its feet after its mini vacation.

The next photo is longer, wider.

Me and Wyatt.

I peel off a single piece of clear tape holding the Bubble Wrap in place, and strip away the wrapping, revealing our young, smiling faces. Even as a boy Wyatt wore his hair long, and in the picture it hangs tousled over his eyes, brushing his shoulders. A single tear slides down my cheek. We didn't know then what life had in store for us. I stare into my youthful eyes and try to remember my thoughts—any thoughts—from back then, but I come up blank. I don't remember when the picture was taken, although I remember it being ever-present on our wall. As I stare at our wide, carefree smiles, sadness washes through me. I'm sad for these two children who will lose their parents too early. I'm sad for the parents who hope to see them grow old and never will. As I gaze into my brother's mischievous green eyes, guilt presses in on me. Wyatt's never left me to deal with stuff on my own. He always puts me before himself, and in this moment I realize that even if I don't want him to be here for me now, I know he does, and I've taken the choice away from him. He loves me too much, but who am I to decide that? And who am I to hurt him for loving me?

I reach for my phone and send him a quick text.

Sorry I have been out of touch. I'm here and I'm okay. I love you. Please understand that I need to do this by myself.

No sooner do I set the phone down than it vibrates with his response.

Okay, but I should give you hell for making me worry. Promise me that if you need me, you'll call. If it's too hard, I'll come get you. Okay?

More tears fall down my cheeks.

Promise. ILY.

I don't put the phone down this time, and I smile when it vibrates seconds later with his response. *ILY2.*

Setting my phone down, I know I can handle this. Courage has climbed back on board. I know it will be hard. Who am I kidding? It's going to suck. But as I wrap the picture of us and set it aside, I feel confident.

I take out a few more of the wrapped photos, identifying each one by size and shape, until I come to the last, a very small package. I look at the walls and can't see any telltale signs of what this sized photo might be.

The tape comes right off, and I unwrap the frame a little quicker this time. It's a photograph of our family and Cassidy in Harborside. I recognize the pier and the boardwalk in the background. Wyatt and Cassidy are sitting side by side on the beach, and I'm sitting on a blanket between my parents. My father is looking at me, and my mom is looking at him. I wonder who took this picture, and I wonder what my father's thinking. If he were here, he'd remember. He remembered everything he ever said as if it were etched in his mind. It strikes me that I can't remember the sound of his voice, and I'm momentarily paralyzed.

I close my eyes and try to pull his voice from the depths of my memory, but like an afternoon wind, it slips through my head. *Come on, Dad.* I close my eyes tighter and clench my teeth, remembering what he said to us every night at dinner when we were kids. *How are my little leaders?*

"Come on, Dad!" I say through gritted teeth.

It's no use. His voice doesn't come.

I wipe my tears and set the photo aside. My mother's laugh sails into my mind. It's high-pitched, and breathy at the end. I look around the empty room, and of course I'm alone. I fight the urge to bolt. I know my subconscious is trying to weaken me, and I'm determined *not* to run back to Harborside.

I head for the stairs and decide to box up my room instead. Maybe something up there will stir the memory of my father's voice.

My room feels cold and stale. It doesn't smell like my room anymore. It doesn't smell like anything but emptiness. I open the windows to air it out. Aunt Lara left boxes on the floor beside my bed, labeled, with a roll of tape beside them. *Books, pictures, school stuff, shoes, clothes, notebooks, sketch pads...*

Sketch pads.

I open my desk drawer and take out a pad and a pencil, then sit on my bed. Even though I've just seen a picture of my father, his image doesn't come easily. I wonder if one day I won't be able to remember his face at all. That thought makes me try harder to recall his image. I used to be able to sketch my parents from memory. I did it a hundred times over the years.

My pencil begins to move along the rigid paper as if it has a memory of its own. Shading comes easily as I sketch his rounded cheekbones and angular nose. I shade his wide, full mouth and strong, square jaw, which Wyatt inherited. His features aren't present in my mind, but a while later, with a slight breeze whispering across my skin, the image of my father's face comes into focus.

And the affection in his eyes stills my heart.

CHAPTER TWENTY-SIX

Ashley

"YOU SURE YOU want to do this? I mean, most people just block their exes' numbers and move on." Brandon's reclining in the passenger seat of my car. His feet are propped up on the dash.

"I know they do, but I need to tell her face-to-face. She left me insecure and untrusting, and I hate her for that."

"Whoa. Am I going to see a bitch fight?" Brandon rights his seat and runs his hand through his hair.

"No, you weirdo." I park the car at Sandy's apartment complex. I know she still lives here because in one of her texts she said that when she broke up with her boyfriend, she kept the apartment. Not that I asked. "You coming up or staying here?"

"I'm coming up, because you may not want a bitch fight, but bitches be crazy, so…"

"God, Brandon. That's offensive."

He cocks a brow and climbs from the car. "I'm protecting you."

"Whatever. You're probably hoping we end up tearing each other's clothes off." We walk across the parking lot and into the building.

"If you weren't dating Delilah, I'd totally be into that, but I don't want you to hurt her."

Like most of Brandon's friends, I'm usually exposed to his crass side, but every now and then he comes out with something like that and surprises me.

"Thank you, Brandon."

He shrugs. "Whatever. Don't get all sappy on me."

When we reach her apartment, I draw in a deep breath. Brandon steps aside and waves his hand, as if he's Vanna White showing me a prize. I roll my eyes, then knock on the door. It's almost as loud as my heart hammering against my chest.

A skinny brunette answers the door wearing a pair of tight shorts and a tank top. She eyes us cautiously. "Yes?"

I didn't think this through very well. I wonder if she's Sandy's girlfriend and Sandy's texts to me meant she was willing to cheat on her, too. My stomach gets queasy.

"Um…Is Sandy here?"

"Sure. Hold on." She partially closes the door. "San? There's people here for you."

Sandy opens the door, and it takes a second for my face to register. Her dark hair is piled on top of her head in a messy bun. She's wearing a shirt that says NIKE across her chest and a pair of jeans. Her blue eyes open wide and a genuine smile stretches across her lips.

"Ashley." She opens her arms, and I take a step back, holding out my hand to keep her a good distance away.

I'm surprised by my visceral reaction to seeing her. She's the same pretty girl with the same perfect smile and amazing body, but I see past that to the devious girl who hurt me, and I realize that I don't give a shit if that other girl is her girlfriend or not. If she is, I feel sorry for her.

Her brows knit together and her eyes shift rapidly between me and Brandon. She crosses her arms over her chest and leans her hip against the doorframe.

Goodbye smile.

"So…?"

"I got your texts." *Shit, shit, shit.* I don't have a plan. Oh my God, this sucks. Brandon steps forward. He must feel my discomfort, which means she does, too.

Yup. Her lips curve up in a gratified smile.

Fuck. This.

I draw my shoulders back and look her in the eye. "Don't call me. Don't text me. We're done."

"Yeah, I got that picture when you didn't return my hundred texts."

"Right." *Way to go, dipshit.* What was I thinking when I came here? I want to wipe that smirk off her face. I want her to know that she hurt me and I think she sucks, but I'm not a mean person by nature, so actually telling someone she sucks is not really something I'm very good at.

Damn it. Why can't I be a bitch?

"But if you get it, why do you keep texting?"

She smirked. "Maybe you'll get one when you're down and you'll respond. You texted back a month ago." She shrugs, and it pisses me off even more.

I draw in a deep breath and think of Delilah and how hurt she was that I'd kept the messages from her. It hits me like a brick in the face. *This is all on me. It's my fault Delilah is hurt.* I can't blame Sandy for that. But I can blame her for what she did to me. I'm breathing hard now, angry with myself for stumbling over words, and when they finally come, they fly fast and hard.

"You hurt me, and it was unfair. You can't treat people like they don't matter, or lie to them so they'll play along with your little games."

Brandon steps closer to me, but I'm past needing support. I'm in tell-her-off mode whether I'm good at it or not.

"I trusted you, and you took my trust and walked all over it." Every word comes back at me like a slap.

Oh God, Delilah. I'm so sorry.

"Forget it." I grab Brandon's shirt and drag him down the steps, leaving Sandy to stare after us.

We cross the parking lot and head for the car.

"Um, Ash. I'm not sure you accomplished anything there."

"Yes, I did. I realized that I should be yelling at myself. I took Dee's trust and walked all over it. People do shitty things, Bran, but blaming *my* shitty stuff on them isn't going to fix anything."

I climb into the car and start the engine, then head for Wyatt's house.

"What now?" Brandon leans his arm on the passenger door and rests his head back.

"I'm dropping you off at Wyatt's. You're living there now, right?"

Brandon sits up and gives me a serious stare. "Pretty much, but my bike's at your place, remember?"

"Crap." I turn the car around and drive toward my apartment, speeding up to make a yellow light.

"Where are *you* going after you drop me off?"

"Connecticut."

CHAPTER TWENTY-SEVEN

Delilah

WITH THE IMAGE of my father's warm eyes now fresh in my mind, I close the sketch pad and begin packing up my room. His voice still eludes me, but his eyes have made this process a little easier. I had forgotten how they crinkled at the edges when he smiled and the way he could look at me from across the room and soften his gaze until I felt his support without him ever saying a word.

Baby steps.

My room feels like the room of a younger, more naive girl, not the room of a college graduate who has been living without parents for an entire summer. It feels like someone else's room, and because of that, I don't feel connected to the things in it. I dump drawers into boxes, separate the clothes I want to keep from the ones I can live without, and box those up for charity. I take one last look at the bedroom that once was my sanctuary and try to conjure up appropriate feelings for the moment. Sadness, grief, regret. None of them come.

Relief and anger mingle uncomfortably inside me at my loss of the ability to feel something for the room that was once my private world.

Why the hell can't anything be easy?

You won't appreciate things that come easily.

I sit on my bed with my mouth gaping open. *Holy. Shit.* Those were my father's words. His voice. My eyes shift around the empty room. I listen intently, but no further words of wisdom come. I stand on wobbly legs and begin packing my closet.

After a few minutes I'm past the disbelief—and the relief—and annoyance comes back for a visit as I picture my younger self and nights spent debating my attraction toward women, tamping it down with guilt. I don't want to live in this uncomfortable place anymore. I *refuse* to live in it. I'm done.

So very done.

I walk down the hall toward my parents' room, and like a winter coat falling from my shoulders, the weight of those tormented years lessens. I thought I'd feel worse, not better, as I approached my parents' bedroom. I pull my shoulders back again, as I'd done downstairs, and gaze into their dark room.

It smells the same way the rest of the house does, foreign and cold. I flick on the overhead light and survey the room. Their paisley bedspread is perfectly made, and my father's dresser is stacked with books, as it's always been.

A lazy brain is a dull brain.

I still momentarily from the memory of my father's voice, then shift my eyes to my mother's bare dresser. I walk into the room, wondering if I'll smell my mother's perfume again, but I don't. Nothing strikes me. Not even guilt or longing, and this worries me. Shouldn't I drop to my knees in tears? Shouldn't I feel like I've been hit by a truck? I'm in the room where they slept, where, as a little girl, I'd crawl into their bed in the mornings and cuddle up against my mother's side. She'd snuggle me in close and kiss the top of my head as my father slipped out of the other side of the bed.

I walk to his side of the bed and sit on the edge, again waiting for a sudden impact to steal my ability to move.

Nothing happens.

I'm not sure if this is good or bad.

Does it say something bad about me? Am I losing my ability to care?

I have no answers. I reach over and open his nightstand, feeling mildly like a Peeping Tom. My father was a private person, but I asked Aunt Lara to leave my parents' room for me to pack. This is my last chance to learn about them. As I stare into his meticulously neat drawer at a notepad, two pencils, and four quarters, I know that I won't learn anything more about him from these items. I close the drawer and my shoulders drop. I don't even know what I'm searching for.

I cross the room and open his dresser. Every pair of underwear is neatly folded and color coordinated. Wow. I had no idea he was *this* meticulous. His socks are separated from his underwear by a thin wooden slat. The items in his next drawer are equally as neat and ordered. White undershirts in one stack, beside grays, next to more whites. We learned at a young age that our parents treasured their privacy. I remember opening my father's nightstand drawer when I was little, and he gave me that disapproving look, slanted brows, lips pressed in a thin line. Even then he didn't need words. It never occurred to me to nose around after that. Now curiosity gets the better of me, and I head into his closet and sift through his color-coordinated suits and dress shirts. Benignly patterned ties in grays and blues hang from a wooden tie rack, each perfectly spaced from the next.

The top shelf of my father's closet is lined with shoe boxes. I use the shelf at the back of the closet as a step as I grab the boxes one by one and drop them onto the floor. There are eight boxes, and when I drop the last, I sit among them trying to imagine my father deciding which shoes to keep in boxes and which to put on the two metal shoe racks on the floor. I look at the full racks. My father did like shoes, even more than my mother did. I never thought about that until now.

What man is this neat? Wyatt's shoes are toed off at the door and left where they fall, not set neatly on the mat, the way my father always left his. My father had high expectations of us—and neatness was part of who he was. When Wyatt and I were home, we were extra careful not to leave a mess. I never questioned my father's rules, and now, as I open one of the boxes and find a pair of leather flip-flops, I begin to wonder about his parents. I didn't know my grandparents very well before they passed away, but what kind of meticulous expectations did they have for him to have turned out like this—and why aren't Wyatt and I neat freaks, too?

I put the lid back on the shoe box and set it aside, then lift the lid off the next. Loafers. I repeat the process two more times and come across a pair of white sneakers. I don't remember him ever wearing white sneakers, and these are particularly ugly. I take one out of the box, shaking my head. He should have had my mom help him find sneakers. I put them back in the box and set them aside. Those are *definitely* going in the charity box. I lift the lid off the next box and there are no shoes, only a dark wooden box. I lift it out and run my finger over the edge. It's not fancy, and the simple golden clasp lifts right up when I flick it. I lift the lid and find a stack of folded papers. As I lift them out of the box, I imagine my mother writing my father love letters. They met in high school and dated all through college, even though they attended different schools, marrying shortly after graduation.

With the letters on my lap, I wonder if I'm crossing a line I shouldn't. What if they've written personal stuff that grosses me out? I close my eyes and think of my parents. I can't see them writing about sexy nights and longing for each other. I can only imagine my father detailing long nights of studying and my mother writing about missing him.

I unfold the first piece of loose-leaf paper. The penmanship is neat and familiar. The letters slant slightly to the right, with no curls or swoops. The paper is still dented with my father's determined writing.

It's dated at the top with mine and Wyatt's twenty-second birthday.

Soon they'll graduate. I couldn't be prouder of them. They're smart and steady. Both born leaders.

Three simple lines that bring tears to my eyes. He was proud of us. I don't wonder for more than a second why he's written this to himself, or why he didn't write more. I'm just glad he did.

I read it again and again, then I fold it and set it aside, reading another, dated at the top with our twenty-first birthday.

Rules have changed. College is more parties and sleeping around than I ever thought possible. They're careful and smart. I have faith in them both.

He had faith in us. Why didn't he ever say those words to us? He pushed. He said things like, *Good job on your grades,* which feels very different from *I have faith in you.*

I fold the letter and set it with the first one, then read the next few. He's written similar letters on each of our birthdays.

Our sixteenth birthday...

Driving. My biggest fear. Please keep them safe.

Tears slide down my cheeks. *Please keep them safe.* A prayer. A plea. *For us.* If only he could have sent the same prayer and plea for himself and for Mom.

He loved us so much.

I read a few more and find the one dated on our sixth birthday.

We no longer have two. Now they're three. Cassidy Lowell has become one of us. We're blessed in so many ways. Wyatt has moved into a stronger leadership role, as it should be. Delilah is coming into her own, not a pushover, but happy to let him be the big brother.

Wyatt will be glad that he included Cassidy, but who refers to their six-year-olds as moving into a *leadership role*? I wish I could talk to him. I want to understand him better.

I find the last...well, the first, really—from our first birthday.

They're smart and steady. Wyatt is a born leader. Delilah is a born watcher, but she'll lead one day, too.

My hand drops to my leg and my stomach sinks. A born leader at a year old? *Leader, watcher, steady.* Even in these letters he was sensible, and thought in terms of us being adults, not warm and loving the way people usually gush over babies. I wonder about his upbringing again. Why don't these letters speak of how cute we were, or the milestones we reached? They're all so formal and sort of impersonal—well, except the one about us driving. I remember when we got our licenses. Dad was a nervous wreck. Mom was better, less worried, but my father practically timed us wherever we went, door to door. If we were fifteen minutes late, he'd call. I always thought it was because he worried that we'd lied about where we were going. Now I know he worried whether we'd made it to our destinations alive.

My perfect, demanding father, who made me feel like shit about who I was, worried about our safety. I'm not sure why this strikes me with such a strong impact, but it does. I never thought about *why* he was so overprotective. It just annoyed me that he was.

I rise to my feet and cross the room to my mother's closet. I'm not as respectful of her things, because I'm losing patience, and I want answers. I tear through her closet, top to bottom, pulling clothes off the hangers and everything she's got stacked on the top shelf comes down in a big pile, landing on the floor with several *thumps*. I toss the sweaters aside, searching for a diary, her own box of secrets. Something that will clue me in to the person she was, beyond the caring mother who was always present when we needed her.

Maybe there's some secret in their past that would help me to understand why they were so unyielding in their beliefs. They weren't religious by any stretch of the imagination. The need to understand why they were so adamant consumes me as I face my mother's belongings.

Her closet is full of normal stuff: scarves and clothes, shoes, belts. I glare across the room at my father's closet, and something inside me snaps. I tear open his drawers again and pull them out. They crash to the floor. I toss his clothes on the ground, searching for something more. Anything to explain why he was so against my lifestyle. I feel like a raving lunatic as I throw his stuff around the room, knowing damn well I won't find anything but unable to stop myself.

After coming up empty on my search-and-discovery mission, I run down the stairs to my father's office and tear through his desk, but my aunt's already cleared it out. Every drawer, every shelf is empty. I pace his office, breathing hard and debating where else I might find answers. Finally I pull out my cell phone and call my aunt. She answers on the first ring.

"Aunt Lara?"

"Delilah? Wyatt called and said you're already at the house. I'm coming down tomorrow, unless you need me today?"

"I don't."

"What's wrong? You sound upset. I can go through your parents' room, sweetie. Don't stress over it. I know it's hard to face."

She's so supportive that I feel guilty for dragging her into this.

I'm sick of feeling guilty.

I'm alone in my sea of guilt, and I'm so sick of it I could scream.

"It's…I was going through my father's closet and I…" I don't tell her about the letters. I'm not sure why I feel like those are his private thoughts and I've already done something I shouldn't have, so I cut to the chase and tell her exactly what I want to know. "I want to know why Dad was so against same-sex relationships."

Silence fills the airwaves. I look at the phone to see if we've lost connection.

"Aunt Lara?"

"Yes, I'm here," she says just above a whisper. "It's a little complicated. He wasn't really against them. He was uncomfortable with them."

I pace again. "Why?" The need to understand gnaws at my stomach.

"Delilah, honey. Why don't I come talk to you in person? I can be there in a half hour."

This is bad. I can hear it in her voice. I grab my father's desk to steady myself.

"No. Tell me, please. I can take it. Just…Was it because of me? Did they know before I told them?" She was with them at my graduation. I'm sure if they'd told anyone about my confession, they'd have told her, since she drove home with them.

She's silent again, but I hear her breathing. "No, baby. No, it wasn't because of you."

Tears spring from my eyes and my legs crumple beneath me. I hadn't realized that I was so scared of that being true.

They didn't know before I told them at graduation.

It wasn't because of me.

Even though it's a relief, I can't breathe. I still don't have the answers I need.

"Delilah? Are you there?"

They were prejudiced against gays.

I can't move.

"Delilah, honey. I promise, they didn't know until you told them."

Anger blasts from my lungs. "Then why? Why would my parents be so pigheaded?"

"Dee, calm down. Please. Please, honey. Take a deep breath."

I shoot to my feet and storm into the living room, feeling completely out of control. This isn't new information, but it feels new, like because Aunt Lara doesn't dispute that my father felt that way, it is somehow more real.

"Dee, you're breathing so hard." The cadence of her voice tells me she's on the move. "Please, just sit down and relax. I'm getting into the car." I hear her car door shut and the engine turn over. "I'm coming there. Don't go anywhere."

I'm panting like I've run ten miles. I wonder if it's hard for her to come here after being in the car when my parents were killed. She was right there in the backseat. She heard their screams, and may have heard them take their last breaths. I know she's recovered from her injuries, but it's not the physical scars I'm worried about. I freeze, weighing my selfish need and her suffering, but my need to put this behind me is so big I can't move past it.

"I need to understand." It comes out strangled.

"Delilah…" She says my name so seriously I stop walking. "I'll be there soon. Stay put."

The world spins around me as she continues talking. My head is swimming. I can comprehend only a few words past the blood rushing through my ears.

Our parents were strict…Did the best he could…Loved you…

"Delilah?"

I need answers. Real answers.

"I gotta go."

I grab my car keys and storm out the front door toward my Jeep. I start it up and toss the phone on the passenger seat as I pull out and speed toward the cemetery. I don't remember stopping at stoplights, although I'm sure I did. I don't remember driving through the iron gates or navigating the winding road toward their freshly turned graves. I don't remember getting out of the Jeep and walking to their graves.

But I'm here.

Staring at their headstones.

I read my father's headstone. *Loving husband, father, and friend.*

The word *conditionally* is missing.

Why? Why? Why?

I pace the recently turned earth, too upset to think. "You made me feel like shit. I wasn't a legal case for you to steer in a direction you approved of. You should have looked at me like I was your daughter, not a case to win or lose. You should have been compassionate, for fuck's sake. I hate you for making me feel like shit." I fall to my knees, and tears steal my voice. My chest burns, and my entire body quakes with every forceful sob.

"Why, Dad?" I plead. "Why would you do this to me?"

I look at my mother's grave, but I can't pull the words from my throat. She was also standing beside him, agreeing with the things he said. A silent partner who wasn't always silent. I have a feeling that she doesn't need me to repeat myself. She knows. She's still beside him.

I bury my face in my hands, feeling like my heart has been ripped from my chest again. How can a person's heart be ripped out over and over again? I remain there, overtaken by sadness, for a long while. Tears come and go, and my mind continues to swim.

I rise on shaky legs and stare down at my parents' graves, crossing my arms to try to gain control of my trembling. It doesn't work.

"I don't hate you," I spit out. "I hate what you did. I hate how you made me feel."

Kenny's words come rushing forward. *She said it's okay for girls to be girlfriend and girlfriend and boys to be boyfriend and boyfriend. I think it's okay since Mom said it's okay.*

I sink to my knees again, the hurt overtaking my anger.

"Dad, what did your parents do to you, for you to do this to me?"

"It was pretty bad."

I spin around at the sound of Aunt Lara's voice. She kneels beside me and touches my shoulder. Her other hand wraps around her rib cage. She broke a few ribs in the accident, and I wonder if she feels the pain anew.

"Delilah, your father loved you, honey. He adored you."

"No." I shake my head. "He only loved the perfect parts of me he wanted to love. I saw it in his eyes. Once I told him, he didn't love me for *me*. I ruined it."

"Dee, this is going to be a lot to digest. Do you want to go somewhere to talk?"

I shake my head. "No. I think I should hear it right here in front of him."

She stares at me for a long time, assessing me. I know she's trying to figure out if she can convince me to leave, so I clench my trembling jaw to let her know I'm not going anywhere.

"Okay." She sits beside me and crosses her legs. "You didn't know your grandparents very well, but our parents were super-conservative. If you think your father's rules were strict, you can multiply them by about a million. I don't claim to know much about gay lifestyles, and I don't think my brother did, either. We were from a different generation. Our generation wasn't as free or as diverse as yours. And our parents? Well, their generation was so…wrong when it came to this stuff."

Wrong? She thinks they were wrong?

"Your father was only mimicking what he learned. We weren't brought up to be open-minded." She covers her heart with her hand and swallows hard. "But I know, with every ounce of my being, that he adored you."

"But…"

"Please, just hear me out. Your father didn't hate gays. He was uncomfortable with the idea. And when you told him about your…preferences, he was forced to confront other fears. Parental fears."

I bit my lower lip to try to stave off more tears.

"On the way home, he and your mom talked about you. They worried *for* you. Your father worried that your lifestyle would make your life more difficult for you. It's different for parents. We worry about how the things our children do—from getting tattoos or nose rings to sexual preferences—will impact their lives. I know you can't understand this, because your generation is so much more open with these things, but when we were growing up…" She presses her lips together and shifts her eyes toward their graves. "Things were very different. Biases were everywhere. Your father didn't want to imagine *you* facing that type of prejudice from others."

"But it's not really like that! Things have changed and it's more widely accepted now."

"No, honey, it's not like that with your generation. But your generation kind of lives in a bubble."

I can't keep my eyes from rolling.

"Not just your generation. All generations live in their own bubbles. When we were your age, *we* lived in bubbles. We still do. Only as adults we're expected to break free of our bubbles as younger generations change and evolve into things that are wildly different from what we're used to. You'll see one day, when the next generation does things that you question. This has gone on for hundreds of years. Every generation thinks the next is worse, doing things that are wrong or unsafe, or stupid." She draws her brows together. "Not that you're stupid or wrong or anything like that. I'm speaking in generalities."

"I don't understand. I'm his daughter. He should have just accepted me. He owned a house in *Harborside,* for God's sake."

She furrows her brows. "What does Harborside have to do with this?"

"What do you mean? There are tons of gays there. Why would *he* buy in that kind of community?"

Aunt Lara smiles and shakes her head. She covers her eyes with her hand, and when she meets my gaze again, her eyes soften, as does her tone.

"Honey, that's the bubble I'm talking about. To you Harborside is a diverse community because you grew up spending summers with Tristan and Brandon, and your generation is more accepting. Those lifestyles are *normal* to you because it's what you were exposed to from a young age." Lara has known Tristan and Brandon as long as we have. She usually visits us in Harborside for a few days each summer. Of course, this year everything's been different, with her recovering from her injuries and all of us trying to deal with the loss of my parents.

"It's not *normal,* according to Dad."

"Right, because your parents lived in a different bubble than you. A different bubble than me, even though they were only a few years older than I am. As far as Harborside goes, they fell in love with the romance of living on the water, the family environment, the slower-paced lifestyle. The Taproom was a great investment and a fun way for them to keep busy in the summers. Their friends weren't gay."

She takes my hand and holds my gaze. "Don't you see, Delilah? Your generation's bubble and your father's generation's bubble coexisted on the same plane but saw things very differently. They never saw Harborside as a gay community. To them it was a family community. A place to spend time with you and Wyatt, where you could build memories, which you have. Great memories."

I try to process what she's said. Try to see it from her point of view, and I guess it kind of makes sense.

"So you're saying that I see it as diverse because I'm immersed in my friendships. My *bubble*."

"Yes, exactly. Your parents' friends were straight. They saw Harborside completely differently. They saw Brandon and Tristan as two boys in a sea of thousands of families. You see Brandon and Tristan as two gay men in a pool of a diverse younger generation."

"But they looked at me like I was such a disappointment."

"Not a disappointment." Aunt Lara nodded, and her eyes became hooded, even more worried. "Honey, your parents, your father specifically, didn't know how to handle it. He was only human. He needed time to come to grips with it."

"My mom looked at me funny, too."

She shrugs, nods. "They were a little stunned. You were their baby, even if you're all grown-up. They worried about you."

I steal a glance at their headstones and feel as if my father's sitting right there watching me. But the eyes I see staring back at me are no longer judgmental. They're worried.

Oh, Daddy.

I reach for Aunt Lara's hand, and she squeezes mine.

"He used to tell us that same-sex marriages were wrong." I lift my eyes and meet her sad gaze. "I spent years feeling ashamed of myself, hiding who I was."

She shakes her head. "I'm so sorry, Delilah. I wish I had known how you felt. I wish they had known when they had more time with you, to digest it and process it and move forward. They never would have wanted you to suffer in silence. When we stopped for gas on the way home from your graduation and your mom emailed you, your father felt terribly guilty for whatever look he gave you. He said he looked at you like his father would have looked at him, and he hated himself for it."

"Wait. What?" My heart leaps to my throat. "What email?"

Her brows knit together. "They sent you an email when we stopped for gas. They said they needed to apologize. Didn't you get it?"

I stand and run toward my Jeep. I hear her calling after me, but I keep going. After graduation we took pictures, packed up our room, and after my parents drove home, Wyatt and I went to a party. That was the night we caught Cassidy's boyfriend cheating and Wyatt beat him up. Later that night we found out about my parents' accident. I haven't even thought about checking email since school ended. I never used it for anything other than school stuff.

I click on the email app on my phone, and sure enough, there's an unread message from my mom's email. I'm afraid to click on it.

Aunt Lara catches up to me.

"Why didn't she text me?"

"I don't know. Did your mom text often?"

I shake my head. "No. She always called." I look up at her, clenching my phone in my hands. "I'm afraid to read it."

"Want me to read it first?"

I shake my head. "No, but do you mind staying with me while I read it?"

She puts her arm around me, and a minute later I gather enough courage to read the message.

Delilah,

We can't believe you're all grown-up. Graduated! Dad and I are so very proud of you. Watching you and Wyatt walk across that stage was one of the proudest moments of our lives. You have both grown into such loving, strong adults. We love you so much, and we owe you an apology for reacting so poorly to your news. We are very sorry. Your father and I have been thinking about how much courage it took for you to tell us that you were a lesbian. (See? I can type it. I can even say it.) And that stunned look in your father's eyes is fading. Mine, too, if there was one.

You've probably figured out that we're not perfect. We have hurdles of our own to overcome in order to fully support you. Skeletons to deal with, harshly ingrained biases to try to navigate past, but we love you, Delilah. We're going to try our best to be as supportive as we possibly can, and even if it's hard for us for a while, please don't take that to mean we love you any less than we did before you told us. You took us by surprise, but let's talk about this after you celebrate your graduation.

Things are so different for your generation. Thank goodness for that, right? Know we love you and we're trying.

Happy graduation! Drive carefully tomorrow (or today, if you read this in the morning).

Love Mom (and Dad)

I read the letter three times, soaking in every word.

They wanted to try.

"I need to go back."

"To their graves?" Aunt Lara looks toward the graves.

"No. I mean, yes. I'll come back here, but I want to see Ashley."

Her brows knit together, and then her eyes widen. "Ash...Oh. Ashley?" She smiles.

I smile, and tears burn my eyes again, but they're no longer angry tears.

"Oh, Delilah." Aunt Lara embraces me and strokes the back of my hair, like my mom used to do. "They loved you so very much."

I draw in a deep breath. "Thank you for coming, Aunt Lara. I think I need to apologize to Dad. I kind of told him I hated him."

"I guess I don't blame you. Want me to come?"

I shake my head. "I can meet you back at the house."

This time I remember every step across the grassy lawn toward my parents' graves. I notice the umbrella of trees to my left, the stone bench farther down the path, and the recently placed flowers at neighboring graves. As I sink to my knees, I feel every piece of dirt and grass pressing into my skin, and when I read my father's headstone, I don't think the word *conditionally* is missing.

You wanted to try.

I need to try, too.

"I'm sorry, Dad. I guess our *bubbles* were in different places, but I'm a good person, and I hope you really did know that. I love you and Mom so much."

CHAPTER TWENTY-EIGHT

Ashley

THANKS TO BRANDON, I find Delilah's parents' house without getting lost. He programmed the address into my GPS. My heart is jackhammering as I drive down her road. The houses here are monstrous compared to my parents' house. It's kind of intimidating. Delilah isn't pretentious at all, but as I pass the manicured lawns, expensive cars parked out front of stone Colonials with massive pillars running two stories high and yards bigger than three of our neighbors' yards put together, I can't help wondering what she thought as she drove down our street. I recheck her address, and my stomach sinks when I don't see her Jeep in the driveway.

What if she's already left Connecticut?

I park in front of her house and grab my phone from the passenger seat. There's a text from Brandon. *Text me so I know you arrived safely.*

Good timing.

I respond quickly. *Just rolled in, safe and sound.*

His response comes in a few seconds later. *Good luck!*

I press Delilah's speed-dial number and listen to it ringing, hoping she isn't upset that I came without calling. I hear loud music and turn as Delilah's Jeep pulls up alongside my car.

"Hey!" Her eyes are red, like she's been crying. "You're here." She looks down at her passenger seat and turns down her radio, then holds up her ringing phone. "And you're calling me."

I end the call, happy that she's not upset with me. "I had to see you."

"I was just going to get my stuff and drive home to see you! Let me park. Hold on."

I scramble out of the car as she parks and remind myself not to jump into her arms. This is her neighborhood, and a very conservative one at that. I'll only make things more uncomfortable for her if I'm too eager. She comes around the side of her car and—my heart swells with emotion. She's so beautiful, and she's smiling. Smiling! Her hips sway with newfound confidence, and she's wearing her boots, which makes me so happy, given where we are right now. I shove my hands in my pockets to keep from reaching for her.

She opens her arms and pulls me into an embrace. "God, I missed you. I'm so sorry."

I stay stock-still for a second, wondering if she realizes that we're standing where anyone can see us. She's hugging me like she wants to climb inside my skin, and it overwhelms me. Fresh tears spring to my eyes, and I can't resist wrapping my arms around her. "*I'm* sorry. I should have told you about the texts."

"No. I shouldn't have overreacted. I'm sorry. I'm sorry for everything. For making you feel like our relationship isn't everything in the world to me, when it really is. For letting my father make me feel like I needed to hide it from the world. I was no better than him, and I'm sorry."

She's still holding me close, and when she draws back and

looks into my eyes, she keeps her body pressed to mine.

"Ashley, so much has happened today, all of it good, but…"

She searches my eyes, and the air between us shifts, warms. She seals her lips over mine, and for a second I'm too stunned to return the kiss. She presses her hand to the back of my head, keeping me close. Her tongue snakes over my lower lip, urging my mouth open, and I give in, finally, blissfully falling into our kiss.

I hear a door open, and when our mouths part, Delilah's lips curve up in a gratified smile.

"Oh, sorry." A woman starts to close the front door of the house.

"Wait." Delilah takes my hand and leads me up the walk. "Aunt Lara, this is my *girlfriend*, Ashley Carver."

Lara covers her mouth with her hand. The wrinkles around her eyes tell me she's smiling. "Ashley, I couldn't be happier to meet you." She pulls me into her arms. "Would you like to come inside?"

Delilah reclaims my hand. "We will, in a few minutes. I want to take her over to the cemetery first."

"Oh, okay." Lara's eyes are wide with surprise and a hint of skepticism, matching my thoughts.

"It's nice to meet you," I finally manage, still in shock by Delilah's turnaround.

"You, too." Lara waves as Delilah leads me back to the Jeep.

She starts the engine and leans across the front seat, taking me in another mind-blowing kiss.

"I'm so glad you're here, and I will never—*ever*—deny our relationship again." Delilah puts on her seat belt, then reaches across me and clicks mine into place while I sit in stunned silence. "I don't care if people stare or disapprove. The more I hide my feelings for you, the more I perpetuate the biases of older bubbles."

"*Older bubbles?*"

"Generations." She laughs and shakes her head. "Bubbles," she says under her breath.

"Delilah...What changed?"

She stops at a stop sign and sets her confident green eyes on me.

"Everything."

Delilah

I PARK AT the cemetery and step from the Jeep, then walk around to the back and unwrap the package that I bought on my way back to my parents' house before finding Ashley there. I hadn't intended to use it until I was back at Harborside, but I'm done waiting.

"What are you doing?" she asks as she comes around to my side of the Jeep.

I tuck the item into my back pocket. "Nothing." I wrap my arm around Ashley's waist and lead her away from the Jeep. She tries to peek at my back, but I lean backward and block her view.

"Stop looking, Little Miss Need to Know."

She laughs.

I love her laugh.

I want her to laugh again just so I can hear it and watch her eyes light up.

Until now I was dipping my toe into the water of our relationship. Now I've finally taken the plunge. And it feels so good

I think I might burst.

"Did someone give you magic *coming out* pills? Because that was one hell of a toe-curling kiss you gave me in front of your house," Ashley says as we cross the grass toward my parents' graves.

I pull her closer. "I couldn't help myself. I hope I didn't embarrass you."

That earned me the laugh I crave.

"The last few months have been really hard, but not nearly as hard as the last twenty-four hours. I think I went through every stage of grief at once."

She leans her head on my shoulder. "I'm sorry, Dee. I'll never keep a secret from you again. I went to see Sandy, and it was a disaster."

My stomach twists. "You saw her?"

Ashley nods. "Brandon went with me."

"Brandon?"

"Don't ask. I wanted to tell her off, and I did, but as I was yelling at her, I realized that it was me who had hurt you, not her. I'm the one who didn't share her texts with you. I didn't want you to worry."

We stop walking in front of my parents' graves, and she continues her confession.

"If I'm being completely honest, I was probably also keeping them to remind myself that I didn't want to be anyone's dirty little secret again."

"Oh." *No, no, no. Please don't tell me you don't want us anymore.* I drop my eyes, and she steps in closer, lifts my chin.

"Delilah, I'm not going anywhere. I may have been keeping the texts as reminders, but all they did was piss me off. I admit that I don't like holding back my feelings for you in public, because I feel more for you than anything I've ever felt for anyone in my entire life. You can rest assured that I will never leave you because of that. You've become my best friend, the person I want to share my life *and* my bed with. I want to be the one you call when you're happy or sad, the person you trust to love you no matter what. I want to wake up and see your sleepy face, and I want to sit on the dunes with you while you teach me to sketch and I mess up because I'm too busy staring at you. No pressure. No ultimatums. When you're ready to own our relationship, I'll be right here by your side, waiting for you."

"Ash…" I blink several times to keep from crying. I've cried enough for a lifetime. "I'm ready." I face my parents' graves. "Mom, Dad, this is Ashley Carver, my girlfriend."

Ashley squeezes my hand.

"I love her. I love the person she is and the person she wants to be. I love the way she makes me feel, and when I'm with her, I'm proud of who I am."

I wipe a tear from Ashley's cheek with my thumb, then place my hands on her cheeks and gaze into her eyes. I want her to feel my love for her, to know it's real and true and that I'm done pretending I'm not her girlfriend.

"I love you, Ashley, and I hope this is loud enough for you to hear me."

I take the microphone from my back pocket, turn it on. She and I both smile as I speak into it.

"I love you, Ashley." It doesn't amplify my voice. Ashley's eyes are wide, and her jaw is hanging open. Her fingers slip into my front pocket and hold on tight. I turn the microphone over in my hands.

"Um, Dee?"

"Wait. Let me try again." I turn it off, then on again. "I love you, Ashley!" Even when I yell, it doesn't amplify my voice.

She leans in close and whispers, "I think you need a speaker."

We both burst into laughter.

"I heard you loud and clear, you big dork!"

"Ha! You have a dorky girlfriend. What does that say about you?"

"That I'm the luckiest girl around."

When her lips touch mine, I want to argue that she's wrong, that *I'm* the luckiest girl around. But I don't break our connection—and I have a feeling nothing ever will.

EPILOGUE

Delilah

I NEVER THOUGHT that anything good could come from losing someone I loved, and don't get me wrong, I'd do anything to have my parents back in my life, even with all the guilt they left me with. But that's not going to happen. I'll never be able to take back my thoughts of wishing my parents didn't exist, and I can never relive the years I kept my desires a secret. I can't go backward. None of us can. But sitting on the beach watching a roaring bonfire with Ashley cuddled up beside me, surrounded by our best friends, I know I have them to thank for how far I've come.

I don't wish I could have a do-over.

I just want to do things right as we move forward.

Cassidy's singing a Matchbox Twenty song while Brandon plays the guitar, and Wyatt's sitting beside her, looking at her like he loves her more than life itself. And I know he does.

"So, you're really moving out?" Tristan sips a beer and hands the bottle to Charley. They're sharing a blanket across from us.

"Yup. And you get to help me move." After I got back from Connecticut, I stopped by Ashley's apartment complex and turned in my rental application. They called this morning with the good news. I am now the proud renter of a one-bedroom apartment.

I feel Wyatt's glare. He's still not sold on the idea of me living alone, but he's trying to give me the space I need.

"Wyatt, she'll be okay." Brooke reaches over and pats his leg. "How did you ever make it when she lived in the girls' dorm the first year of college?"

Wyatt rolls his eyes. "I think I was worse than my parents. I went by every day to make sure she was okay."

"When Jesse and I went away to school, I think my mom celebrated." Brent laughs.

Jesse pokes the fire with a stick. "She might have celebrated you leaving, but she missed me."

Brent gives him a playful shove.

"We have some rules to work out. Nightly check-ins, things like that." Wyatt's lips quirk up, and I know he's teasing.

"Yeah, like *Brandon* gets a key in case he needs a place to stay." Brandon holds out a hand and Wyatt high-fives him.

Ashley wraps her arms around my waist. "I'll make sure she's safe, Wyatt."

Wyatt gives me a look of approval. I never realized how heavily the way I hid my feelings weighed on him. I smile to let him know I understand, and I place my hand on Ashley's— because I want to.

"Are we ready?" Wyatt stands and pulls Cassidy up beside him. She grabs her camera.

"Yeah, as ready as we're going to get." Ashley and I stand, and everyone else follows suit.

We all walk toward the deck. Wyatt drapes an arm over my shoulder.

"You okay?"

"I'm better than I ever thought I would be." I reach for Ashley's hand. "Much better."

"You know that even when you live at that apartment complex, you can call me anytime, right? I'll drop what I'm doing and come over." Wyatt's voice is so serious it's a little startling.

"Wyatt, you know I'll be fine, don't you?"

He nods. "It's a twin thing." He leans in close and whispers, "I'll miss you."

I smile and hug him close. "I'll miss you, too."

Wyatt reaches for Cassidy's hand as we walk up the stairs onto the deck, where Jesse and Brent have already begun untying the balloons from their tethers. They give each of us a handful of ribbons as the yellow balloons bob above us. Wyatt and I were going to have a goodbye ceremony for our parents, but we decided instead to have a ceremony to celebrate the start our new lives.

"Army, you care if I go first? I kinda want to get the sappy stuff over with." Brandon looks up at the balloon and shakes his head.

"No, man. Go for it," Wyatt answers.

Cassidy lifts her camera to her eye and snaps pictures as Brandon prepares to speak.

Brandon holds the ribbons up over his head. "Here's to new digs, new loves—for you guys, not for me—and to a whole hell of a lot of partying." He releases his balloons and they float up toward the clouds.

"They're so pretty," Charley says. "Brooke and I want to release ours together. Is that okay?"

"Absolutely." They hold their balloons up and both close their eyes.

"To a year full of hot guys and great grades for me," Charley says, then looks at Brooke, who adds, "And a successful party-planning business."

We all cheer as Cassidy snaps picture after picture.

Wyatt nods to Jesse.

"To the success of the Taproom and our new restaurant, which is still nameless." Jesse releases his balloons and nods at Brent.

"To massive waves and safe rides." Brent watches his balloons rise.

"Tristan? You want to go next?" Wyatt asks.

"Sure, Army." Tristan holds up the balloons, and his eyes roll over each of us.

"To good friends and good times."

"Loser," Brandon teases.

Tristan elbows him, and they fake punch each other in the gut and laugh, while Cassidy captures it all on film.

"Wy?" I offer for him to go next.

He takes Cassidy's hand. She hands the camera to Charley. "Do you mind?"

"Not at all." Charley gets the camera ready. "Okay."

They hold the balloons between them and gaze into each other's eyes, and as I watch them make their wish, I realize I'm not pining for someone I can no longer have. I am finally capable of giving Ashley the love she deserves, no matter where we are. It won't always come easily, and I know I'll still get nervous sometimes, but I also know she'll be right here by my side.

We both look up at the balloons. We haven't discussed what we want to say when we release them. We both thought we'd know when the time was right.

I know.

"To moving forward."

I don't see the balloon rising toward the stars, and I don't see the look of happiness that I know is on our friends' faces. But I *feel* it all as I kick that fictional closet door open and take a giant leap out, gather Ashley in my arms, and press my lips to hers.

Ready for more Harborside Nights?
Fall in love with Tristan and Alex
In Tempting Tristan

Tristan

LIVI BURSTS THROUGH the door from the outdoor dining area of the Taproom, the restaurant and bar where we work. She slaps a drink order on the bar and scowls at me and Charley, the other bartender. "There's a storm brewing outside, but it's nothing compared to how much I hate you both right now."

We were in for heavy rains, but hopefully they'd hold off until after closing time. I glance at the order. "Because of two rum and Cokes?"

She rolls her pretty green eyes. "No, Tristan. Because the hottest man on the planet just parked his motorcycle and he's heading in here. All of my female customers are drooling, and I'm sure you'll see a flock of them coming in any minute now. Meanwhile, I'm stuck outside and soon I'll have a pier full of empty tables." She grabs a handful of napkins and waves them at me with a smirk. "Drool rags."

"Dibs," Charley says as she whips up a cocktail.

I laugh and hold my hands up. "I'm on a hiatus from all things male, so be my guest." My ex, Ian, is a self-absorbed ass, and I was an idiot for letting him treat me like shit. Which is why I'm taking a break from men—even if it kills me. It's been weeks since we broke up and I moved into my buddy Wyatt's house. Wyatt and his twin sister, Delilah, own the Taproom. They inherited it when their parents were killed in a car accident a little more than a year ago.

"I'm sure he's straight anyway," Livi says. "The guy swaggers like a stud."

"Hey, gay guys can swagger like studs," I tease.

"I know that." Livi peers out the pass-through window to the outside seating area and tosses her blond hair over her shoulder. "You'll see what I mean. He's a total badass."

I tend to my customers as the girls discuss the *badass hot guy*, and when the front door opens, I can't help but let my eyes drift over. Livi and Charley fall silent, ogling what truly might be the hottest guy on the planet. Linebacker shoulders fill the doorframe. The godlike creature is carrying a shiny black motorcycle helmet in one very large hand. His white T-shirt is stretched so tight across his chest I can see every ripple of his shredded abs, and his deliciously defined biceps are seriously struggling to be set free from his short sleeves. *Tear, baby, tear.*

He steps inside and runs a hand through his dirty-blond hair. Deep-set, brooding eyes slide over the customers sitting at the bar, sweep over Charley and Livi, and finally land on me. Charley whimpers, and Livi makes a sound in the back of her throat, both mimicking what I'm feeling, though my mouth is too dry to make a sound.

He swaggers, full of hard-core attitude, to the vacant stool at the end of the bar, giving me a clear view of his perfect ass—and catching the attention of nearly every woman, and several of the men, in the place. My cock twitches, reminding me it's been way too long since I've gotten laid.

The pretty brunette seated next to Hot Guy leans in close, says something, and he flashes a crooked smile, which softens his hard edges but doesn't take anything away from his rough vibe. His hand cruises through his hair again, and he slaps a sketchbook on the bar. Pulling his massive arms up onto the bar, hc nearly knocks into the pretty brunette. He apologizes and pushes his stool farther way.

Livi groans and shoves another order pad in the back pocket of her jeans as I finish making her order. "I swear I'm going to go to bartender school."

"Hands off. I have dibs. Besides, you have that pen pal from overseas," Charley reminds her.

"Jason is my best friend, not my pen pal. And you don't sleep with best friends, especially when they're a million miles away." Livi lost her mother to cancer when she was fourteen, and although she doesn't talk about that time of her life much, I know Jason has been there for her ever since. She takes her drinks and heads out to serve her customers.

Rusty, one of the waiters, sidles up to the bar, shaking his head. "The new guy has my female customers' panties in a bunch. Table four wants to send him a drink with the message" —he speaks in a high-pitched tone—"'We'd like to take *you* for a ride.'" He scoffs. "Lucky bastard."

"Oh, no, they are *not*." Charley turns her back to the bar and pushes her boobs up so they practically tumble out of her tight black V-neck shirt. She's usually a Levi's girl, but tonight she's wearing skinny jeans. I wonder what's up with that. "I'm on *him*." Charley waggles her dark brows. "I mean, I'm on *it*."

"What is with you tonight?" I have to ask. This pushiness is new. She's usually the girl who assumes hot guys are all hung up on themselves and barely gives them the time of day.

Charley sets her eyes on the guy who's got *my* briefs in a bunch. "Just feeling competitive."

I serve a few customers, keeping an eye on Charley's flirting. Harborside is a close-knit beach town, but it's also a college town, which makes it a party town. We get aggressive and handsy transients from time to time, and more than once Wyatt and I have had to step in.

Charley's pulling out all the stops, leaning over the bar, touching Hot Guy's hand. She's beautiful, funny, and smart, studying marine biology and working two part-time jobs. She has a nose for bullshit, and her patience for stupidity hangs by a very thin thread. Given the amount of time she chats the guy up, I assume he's got more than looks going for him.

She turns to fix him a drink as I tend to a group of scantily clad women waving me over. I toss my bar rag over my shoulder and flash my own pearly whites. "What can I get you ladies?"

"Your phone number?" the redhead says with a giggle.

Tips are tips and flirting's the name of the game. "Barking up the wrong tree, sweetheart. But if I were straight..." I say coyly and take their order, ignoring their offers to *turn me straight*. If I had a buck for each time I'd received that ridiculous offer, I'd be rich.

Charley nudges me as she fills another drink order. "He's not giving anything up. All I found out was that he just got into town last week." She shrugs. "He's no dummy, though. The guy's got brains and brawn. A wicked combination. He seems nice, but very closed off. It's yet to be seen how rough he is. He might be lock-you-up-in-the-basement rough, or maybe he's just sexy-as-sin rough."

"You can tell that much from, 'Hey, wanna hook up?'"

"*Tsk.*" She places her hands on her hips, and with a snap of her chin she tosses her brown hair over her shoulder with an impressive amount of attitude. "You know me better than that. I *did not* ask him to hook up. I was just checking him out and staking claim. *In case* I'm interested. But he's so focused in that sketchpad, I can't get him to give me the time of day."

I steal a glance at the guy, who's watching us intently. "Seems like he's into you," I say, and before she can respond, a loud group of girls comes through the door and flocks to the bar. I assume they're the customers Livi mentioned. The fact that they're just now coming in means Livi took her sweet time taking care of their checks. Hopefully she has a slew of new customers to take care of. I know she needs the tips.

The rest of the night is a mad rush of keeping up with drink orders and overzealous girls vying to pick me up. I can't help but notice Hot Guy's occasional snicker at my dismissal of the girls' advances.

Livi whips in from the pier for *one more glance* a few times instead of using the pass-through window, and whispers with Charley. Charley touches base with the hot guy, giggling and flirting, as do several of the women who are standing around him. He smiles, comments here and there, then turns back to whatever's got his rapt attention in that notebook.

As we near closing time, customers clear out, and Hot Guy is still sitting at the end of the bar in deep concentration. A bearded guy who had parked himself at the bar for the last half hour is standing by the door, watching Charley.

"Char, what's up with that guy?" I nod to the guy by the door.

She traps her lower lip between her teeth and waves to the bearded guy. "Can you close out the notebook guy for me?"

"Sure," I say, reassessing the bearded guy. "I thought you hated beards. What's up?"

"Don't laugh." She leans in close, her hair tumbling forward, curtaining her face as she whispers, "Blind date."

We've worked together for a long time, and I know Charley has her pick of guys. "Why? And on a Tuesday night?"

"Why does the day of the week matter?"

I shrug.

"The kind of guys I'm meeting on my own haven't really been my type." She smiles at the guy by the door. "Brian has a master's in natural resources. I think I can overlook the beard for a guy I've got something in common with. He seems nice enough, right?"

"I guess, but if you had this blind date set up, why were you flirting with him?" I nod toward the guy at the other end of the bar.

She sighs. "If you must know, ever since my sister fell in love with Sam, I've been hoping to find the same kind of relationship. Sam Braden was a bit of a bad boy before he and Faith got together, so I thought maybe…"

She looks back at the guy by the door, who definitely has kinder eyes than the broody biker. "But I'm not sure bad boys are my type. I'm more of a nice, smart, no-skeletons type of girl.

And Mr. Mysterious over there"—she nods to the guy with the notebook—"hasn't cracked under my flirtatious pressure, so I'm thinking his skeletons might be too big to keep contained. But I would never know that unless I tried, now, would I?"

She pats my chest and I set my hand on hers, holding her there while I eye Brian one more time. "Fine, but it's still a *blind* date. How'd you meet him?"

Charley presses her lips into a thin line.

"Please tell me you didn't meet him on Tinder."

"No! Geez, Tristan." Her cheeks flush. "He's one of Brooke's friends."

Brooke Baker owns an Internet café on the boardwalk called Brooke's Bytes. I've been friends with her for years and I trust her judgment explicitly. "Okay, but keep your phone on and call me if you need me. In fact, text me when you're home for the night so I know you're not lying bloody in an alley somewhere."

She rolls her eyes. "Ian has no idea how badly he messed up by losing you. Not that he deserved you in the first place." She reaches up and hugs me. "I'm not leaving until we close, but I promise I'll text you. Even though I think you should spend less time worrying about your friends and more time finding some new guy to take that jerk's place. The right guy is going to be very lucky to have you."

My gut clenches at the mention of my ex. I should be over all the shit he did, but some hurts run too deep to be easily cast aside. Unfortunately, almost everything Ian did was hurtful, from ignoring me to making me feel like an imposition. Man, I sound like a pussy. My self-esteem definitely took a pounding, but I'll never put myself in that situation again. I shove those thoughts aside for the hundredth, and hopefully the last, time.

Charley heads toward the bearded guy, and I make my way down the bar. The blond guy's still laboring over his notebook. His jaw is tight, and his eyes are narrowed in concentration.

I grab the empty bottle in front of him. "Last call. Can I grab you another beer?"

"Sure, thanks." He's too engrossed in whatever he's drawing to spare me a glance, but he's got one of those in-control voices that makes *me* want to thank *him*.

I bring him his beer, and he lifts intense admiral-blue eyes that connect with mine and momentarily steal my breath. When he flashes that sexy crooked grin, heat flares between us, and I wonder if he's bisexual. Or maybe just curious. We get our fair share of those around here, too. Straight guys looking to experiment for a night. *Not my thing.*

"Thanks, man," he says, and reaches a hand across the bar. "Alex."

His handshake is firm and his hand is rough, like he does manual labor. My sex-deprived brain moves straight to how those strong, rough fingers would feel wrapped around my cock.

Wyatt comes through the door with his girlfriend, Cassidy, tucked beneath his arm and calls out my name, rescuing me from my ridiculous straight-guy fantasy.

"Be right there," I tell Wyatt.

Wyatt kisses Cassidy and heads into the stockroom.

Alex knocks back half his beer in one gulp and tears a piece of paper from the back of his notebook. He quickly scribbles on it, folds it in half, and passes it across the bar to me. "I've got to go. Would you—"

I snag the note. He's clearly not gay and looking only for a favor. "Sure, I'll give Charley your number."

There's no mistaking the seductive darkness staring back at

me. My entire body electrifies.

"It's not for her," he says in that commanding voice that makes every part of me stand at attention. "It's for you, Tristan."

Did I tell him my name? He probably overheard it. Either way, it sounds hot rolling off his tongue.

He rises to his feet, our hands still touching. When he reaches for his helmet, our physical connection breaks, but the tantalizing heat remains.

"Call me." Alex takes a few steps away and looks over his shoulder. That mind-numbing grin sends another blast of heat below my belt. "See ya around, T."

Wyatt comes back into the bar and sets a bottle of champagne on the counter. "What's up with Alex?"

I'm still trying to process that Alex isn't straight. The endearment he used, and the way he said it so confident and casually, as if we were old friends, makes my mind stumble again. *T*?

"You know him?"

"Wasn't that Arty's grandson, Alex Wells?" Wyatt asks. "I only met him once a few years ago, but I'm pretty sure it's him."

Arlene "Arty" Bindon was a local sculptor who lived in a bungalow down the beach. We'd met a few years ago when I was out running. Unfortunately, she passed away over the winter. She was a tiny woman, about five feet tall, with frizzy gray hair that always looked windblown. From the moment we met I was drawn to her sassy nature and creative outlook. She reminded me of my own grandmother, who passed away when I was just a kid. Arty and I became close, and I checked on her when we had storms, brought her groceries every so often, and sometimes I drove her to appointments in town. She talked often about her grandson, who was in the military. She used to say, *He's a good boy, like you.*

I glance down at Alex's number, seeing the brooding biker with new eyes. "I thought he was just passing through."

"Maybe he is." Wyatt drapes an arm over my shoulder as Brandon comes into the bar, guitar in hand, followed by Delilah and her girlfriend, Ashley, and two of our other friends, Jesse and Brent Steele. Brent's also carrying his guitar. "Are you done, or do you want to talk about Alex some more? Because I have huge news."

"Sorry," I say, shaking my head to clear it and noticing, for the first time tonight, Wyatt's big-ass grin. "Huge news? Cough it up already."

Wyatt laughs. "Finally! Cassidy and I got engaged. It's time to celebrate."

To continue reading, buy
TEMPTING TRISTAN

Have you met the Remingtons?

DEX REMINGTON WALKED into NightCaps bar beside his older brother Sage, an artist who also lived in New York City, and Regina Smith, his employee and right arm. Women turned in their direction as they came through the door, their hungry eyes raking over Dex's and Sage's wide shoulders and muscular physiques. At six foot four, Sage had two inches on Dex, and with their striking features, dark hair, and federal-blue eyes, heads spun everywhere they went. But after Dex had worked thirty of the last forty-eight hours, women were the furthest thing from his mind. His four-star-general father had ingrained hard work and dedication into his head since he was old enough to walk, and no matter how much he rued his father's harsh parenting, following his lead had paid off. At twenty-six, Dex was one of the country's leading PC game designers and the founder of Thrive Entertainment, a multimillion-dollar gaming corporation. His father had taught him another valuable lesson—how to become numb—making it easy for him to disconnect from the women other men might find too alluring to ignore.

Dex was a stellar student. He'd been numb for a very long time.

"Thanks for squeezing in a quick beer with me," he said to Sage. They had about twenty minutes to catch up before his scheduled meeting with Regina and Mitch Anziano, another of his Thrive employees. They were going to discuss the game they were rolling out in three weeks, *World of Thieves II.*

"You're kidding, right? I should be saying that to you." Sage threw his arm around Dex's shoulder. They had an ongoing rivalry about who was the busiest, and with Sage's travel and gallery schedule and Dex working all night and getting up midday, it was tough to pick a winner.

"Thrive!" Mitch hollered from the bar in his usual greeting. Mitch used *Thrive!* to greet Dex in bars the way others used, *Hey.* He lifted his glass, and a smile spread across his unshaven cheeks. At just over five foot eight with three-days' beard growth trailing down his neck like fur and a gut that he was all too proud of, he was what the world probably thought all game designers looked like. And worth his weight in gold. Mitch could outprogram anyone, and he was more loyal than a golden retriever.

Regina lifted her chin and elbowed Dex. "He's early." She slinked through the crowded bar, pulling Dex along behind her. Her Levi's hung low, cinched across her protruding hip bones by a studded black leather belt. Her red hoodie slipped off one shoulder, exposing the colorful tattoos that ran across her shoulder and down her arms.

Mitch and Regina had been Dex's first employees when he'd opened his company. Regina handled the administrative aspects of the company, kept the production schedule, monitored the program testing, and basically made sure nothing slipped through the cracks, while Mitch, like Dex, conceptually and technically designed games with the help of the rest of Thrive's fifty employees—developers, testers, and a host of programmers and marketing specialists.

Regina climbed onto the barstool beside Mitch and lifted his beer to her lips.

"Order ours yet?" she asked with a glint in her heavily lined dark eyes. She ran her hand through her stick-straight, jet-black hair.

Dex climbed onto the stool beside her as the bartender slid beers in front of him and Regina. "Thanks, Jon. Got a brew for my brother?"

"Whatever's on tap," Sage said. "Hey, Mitch. Good to see you."

Mitch lifted his beer with a nod of acknowledgment.

Dex took a swig of the cold ale, closed his eyes, and sighed, savoring the taste.

"Easy, big boy. We need you sober if you wanna win a GOTY." Mitch took a sip of Regina's beer. "Fair's fair."

Regina rolled her eyes and reached a willowy arm behind him, then mussed his mop of curly dark hair. "We're gonna win Game of the Year no matter what. Reviewers love us. Right, Dex?"

Thrive had already produced three games, one of which, *World of Thieves*, had made Dex a major player in the gaming world—and earned him millions of dollars. His biggest competitor, KI Industries, had changed the release date for their new game. KI would announce the new date publicly at midnight, and since their game was supposed to be just as hot of a game as they expected *World of Thieves II* to be, if they released close to the release for *World of Thieves II*, there would be a clear winner and a clear loser. Dex had worked too hard to be the loser.

"That's the hope," Dex said. He took another swig of his beer and checked his watch. Eight forty-five and his body thought it was noon. He'd spent so many years working all night and sleeping late that his body clock was completely thrown off. He was ready for a big meal and the start of his workday. He stroked the stubble along his chin. "I worked on it till four this morning. I think I deserve a cold one."

Sage leaned in to him. "You're not nervous about the release, are you?"

Of his five siblings—including Dex's twin sister, Siena, Sage knew him best. He was the quintessential artist, with a heart that outweighed the millions of dollars his sculptures had earned him. He'd supported Dex through the years when Dex needed to bend an ear, and when he wasn't physically nearby, Sage was never farther than a text or a phone call away.

"Nah. If it all fails, I'll come live with you." Dex had earned enough money off of the games he'd produced that he'd never have to worry about finances again, but he wasn't in the gaming business for the money. He'd been a gamer at heart since he was able to string coherent thoughts together, or at least it felt that way. "What's happening with the break you said you wanted to take? Are you going to Jack's cabin?" Their eldest brother Jack owned a cabin in the Colorado Mountains. Jack was an ex–Special Forces officer and a survival-training guide, and he and his fiancée Savannah spent most weekends at the cabin. Living and working in the concrete jungle didn't offer the type of escape Sage's brain had always needed.

"I've got another show or two on the horizon; then I'll take time off. But I think I want to do something useful with my time off. Find a way to, I don't know, help others instead of sitting around on my ass." He sipped his beer and tugged at the neck of his Baja hippie jacket. "How 'bout you? Any plans for vacay after the release?"

"Shit. You're kidding, right? My downtime is spent playing at my work. I love it. I'd go crazy sitting in some cabin with no connectivity to the real world."

"The right woman might change your mind." Sage took a swig of his beer.

"Dex date?" Regina tipped her glass to her lips. "Do you even know your brother? He might hook up once in a while, but this man protects his heart like it carries all of the industry secrets."

"Can we not go there tonight?" Dex snapped. He had a way of remembering certain moments of his life with impeccable clarity, some of which left scars so deep he could practically taste them every damn day of his life. He nurtured the hurt and relished in the joy of the scars, as his artistic and peace-seeking mother had taught him. But Dex was powerless against his deepest scar, and numbing his heart was the only way he could survive the memory of the woman he loved walking away from him four years earlier without so much as a goodbye.

"Whoa, bro. Just a suggestion," Sage said. "You can't replace what you never had."

Dex shot him a look.

Regina spun on her chair and then swung her arm over Dex's shoulder. "Incoming," she whispered.

Dex looked over his shoulder and met the stare of two hot blondes. His shoulders tensed and he sighed.

"It's not gonna kill you to make a play for one of them, Dex. Work off some of that stress." Sage glanced back at the women.

"No, thanks. They're all the same." Ever since the major magazines had carried the story about Dex's success, he'd been hounded by ditzy women who thought all he wanted to talk about was PC games.

Regina leaned in closer and whispered, "Not them. Fan boys, two o'clock."

Thank God.

"Hey, aren't you Dex Rem?" one of the boys asked.

Dex wondered if they were in college or if they had abandoned their family's dreams for them in lieu of a life of gaming. It was the crux of his concern about his career. He was getting rich while feeding society's desire to be couch potatoes.

"Remington, yeah, that's me," he said, wearing a smile like a costume, becoming the relaxed gamer his fans craved.

"Dude, *World of Thieves* is the most incredible game ever! Listen, you ever need any beta testers, we're your guys." The kid nodded as his stringy bangs bounced into his eyes. His friend's jaw hung open, struck dumb by meeting Dex, another of Dex's pet peeves. He was just a guy who worked hard at what he loved, and he believed anyone could accomplish the same level of success if they only put forth the effort. Damn, he hated how much that belief mirrored his father's teachings.

"Yeah?" Dex lifted his chin. "What college did you graduate from?"

The two guys exchanged a look, then a laugh. The one with the long bangs said, "Dude, it don't take a college degree to test games."

Dex's biceps flexed. There it was. The misconception that irked Dex more than the laziness of the kids who were just a few years younger than him. As a Cornell graduate, Dex believed in the value of education and the value of being a productive member of society. He needed to figure out the release date, not talk bullshit with kids who were probably too young to even be in a bar.

"Guys, give him a break, 'kay?" Regina said.

"Sure, yeah. Great to meet you," the longer-haired kid said.

Dex watched them turn away and sucked back his beer. His eyes caught on a woman at a booth in the corner of the bar. He studied the petite, brown-haired woman who was fiddling with her napkin while her leg bounced a mile a minute beneath the table. *Jesus*. Memories from four years earlier came rushing back to him with freight-train impact, hitting his heart dead center.

"I know how you are about college, but, Dex, they're kids. You gotta give them a little line to feed off of," Regina said.

Dex tried to push past the memories. He glanced up at the woman again, and his stomach twisted. He turned away, trying to focus on what Regina had said. *College. The kids. Give them a line to feed off of.* Regina was right. He should accept the hero worship with gratitude, but lately he'd been feeling like the very games that had made him successful were sucking kids into an antisocial, couch-potato lifestyle.

"Really, Dex. Imagine if you'd met your hero at that age." Sage ran his hand through his hair and shook his head.

"I'm no hero." Dex's eyes were trained on the woman across the bar. *Ellie Parker*. His mouth went dry.

"Dex?" Sage followed his gaze. "Holy shit."

There was a time when Ellie had been everything to him.

She'd lived in a foster home around the corner from him when they were growing up, and she'd moved away just before graduating high school. Dex's mind catapulted back thirteen years, to his bedroom at his parents' house. "In the End" by Linkin Park was playing on the radio. Siena had a handful of girlfriends over, and she'd gotten the notion that playing Truth or Dare was a good idea. At thirteen, Dex had gone along with whatever his popular and beautiful sister had wanted him to. She was the orchestrator of their social lives. He hadn't exactly been a cool teenager, with his nose constantly in a book or his hands on electronics. That had changed when testosterone filled his veins two years later, but at thirteen, even the idea of being close to a girl made him feel as though he might pass out. He'd retreated to his bedroom, and that had been the first night Ellie had appeared at his window.

"Hey, Dex." Regina followed his gaze to Ellie's table; her eyes moved over her fidgeting fingers and her bouncing leg. "Nervous Nelly?" she teased.

Dex rose to his feet. His stomach clenched.

"Dude, we're supposed to have a meeting. There's still more to talk about," Mitch said.

Sage's voice was serious. "Bro, you sure you wanna go there?"

With Sage's warning, Dex's pulse sped up. His mind jumped back again to the last time he'd seen her, four years earlier, when Ellie had called him out of the blue. She'd needed him. He'd thought the pieces of his life had finally fallen back into place. Ellie had come to New York, scared of what, he had no idea, and she'd stayed with him for two days and nights. Dex had fallen right back into the all-consuming, adoring, frustrating vortex that was Ellie Parker. "Yeah, I know. I gotta…" *See if that's really her.*

"Dex?" Regina grabbed his arm.

He placed his hand gently over her spindly fingers and unfurled them from his wrist. He read the confusion in her narrowed eyes. Regina didn't know about Ellie Parker. *No one knows about Ellie Parker. Except Sage. Sage knows.* He glanced over his shoulder at Sage, unable to wrap his mind around the right words.

"Holy hell," Sage said. "I've gotta take off in a sec anyway. Go, man. Text me when you can."

Dex nodded.

"What am I missing here?" Regina asked, looking between Sage and Dex.

Regina was protective of Dex in the same way that Siena always had been. They both worried he'd be taken advantage of. In the three years Dex had known Regina, he could count on one hand the number of times he'd approached a woman in front of her, rather than the other way around. It would take Dex two hands to count the number of times he'd been taken advantage of in the past few years, and Regina's eyes mirrored that reality. Regina didn't know it, but of all the women in the world, Ellie was probably the one he needed protection from the most.

He put his hand on her shoulder, feeling her sharp bones against his palm. There had been a time when Dex had wondered if Regina was a heavy drug user. Her lanky body reminded him of strung-out users, but Regina was skinny because she survived on beer, Twizzlers, and chocolate, with the occasional veggie burger thrown in for good measure.

"Yeah. I think I see an old friend. I'll catch up with you guys later." Dex lifted his gaze to Mitch. "Midnight?"

"Whatever, dude. Don't let me cock block you." Mitch

laughed.

"She's an old…not a…never mind." *My onetime best friend?* As he crossed the floor, all the love he felt for her came rushing back. He stopped in the middle of the crowded floor and took a deep breath. *It's really you.* In the next breath, his body remembered the heartbreak of the last time he'd seen her. The time he'd never forget. When he'd woken up four years ago and found her gone—no note, no explanation, and no contact since. Just like she'd done once before when they were kids. The sharp, painful memory pierced his swollen heart. He'd tried so hard to forget her, he'd even moved out of the apartment to distance himself from the memories. He should turn away, return to his friends. Ellie would only hurt him again. He was rooted to the floor, his heart tugging him forward, his mind holding him back.

A couple rose from the booth where Ellie sat, drawing his attention. He hadn't even noticed them before. God, she looked beautiful. Her face had thinned. Her cheekbones were more pronounced, but her eyes hadn't changed one bit. When they were younger, she'd fooled almost everyone with a brave face—but never Dex. Dex had seen right through to her heart. Like right now. She stared down at something in her hands with her eyebrows pinched together and her full lips set in a way that brought back memories, hovering somewhere between worried and trying to convince herself everything would be okay.

Her leg bounced nervously, and he stifled the urge to tell her that no matter what was wrong, it would all be okay. Dex ignored the warnings going off in his mind and followed his heart as he crossed the floor toward Ellie.

To continue reading, buy

GAME OF LOVE (The Remingtons, Book One)

MORE BOOKS BY MELISSA

THE REMINGTONS
Game of Love
Stroke of Love
Flames of Love
Slope of Love
Read, Write, Love
Touched by Love

SEASIDE SUMMERS
Seaside Dreams
Seaside Hearts
Seaside Sunsets
Seaside Secrets
Seaside Nights
Seaside Embrace
Seaside Lovers
Seaside Whispers

The RYDERS
Seized by Love
Claimed by Love
Chased by Love
Rescued by Love
Thrill of Love

BILLIONAIRES AFTER DARK SERIES

WILD BOYS AFTER DARK
Logan
Heath
Jackson
Cooper

BAD BOYS AFTER DARK
Mick
Dylan
Carson
Brett

SEXY STANDALONE ROMANCE
Tru Blue
Wild Whiskey Nights

HARBORSIDE NIGHTS SERIES
Includes characters from the Love in Bloom series
Catching Cassidy
Discovering Delilah
Tempting Tristan
Chasing Charley
Breaking Brandon
Embracing Evan
Reaching Rusty
Loving Livi

More Books by Melissa
Chasing Amanda (mystery/suspense)
Come Back to Me (mystery/suspense)
Have No Shame (historical fiction/romance)
Love, Lies & Mystery (3-book bundle)
Megan's Way (literary fiction)
Traces of Kara (psychological thriller)
Where Petals Fall (suspense)

ACKNOWLEDGMENTS

With each Harborside Nights character, I fall more deeply in love. Delilah and Ashley were no different. I'd like to thank my readers for your continual support and encouragement to stand behind writing what I feel passionate about and not caving to industry pressure. Your emails, social media messages, and Street Team enthusiasm and efforts are beyond any support I could have ever imagined.

I feel it is important to share this message again (originally published in *Catching Cassidy*). I want to share with you the feedback I received before writing this series. I was warned not to write about gay and lesbian couples unless I wrote under a pen name. I was told it would upset my readership, and upsetting my readership is the last thing I want to do. However, hiding behind a pen name is sending a message I don't believe in. I trust my readers, and because I have such faith in their love of *love* and their enjoyment of my storytelling abilities, I proudly wrote these stories under my own name. For readers who do not wish to read about same-sex relationships, those books have been clearly marked with "LGBT" on the retailer pages, and the covers reveal the nature of the relationships. I can assure that, as always, the stories are written with raw emotions and real issues.

Heartfelt gratitude goes to my incredible editorial team: Kristen Weber and Penina Lopez, and my proofreaders: Jenna Bagnini, Juliette Hill, Marlene Engel, and Lynn Mullan, for bringing readers the cleanest read possible. Elizabeth Mackey, thank you for this beautiful cover!

And to my own hunky hero, Les, you know...

www.MelissaFoster.com

Melissa Foster is a *New York Times* and *USA Today* bestselling and award-winning author. Her books have been recommended by *USA Today's* book blog, *Hagerstown* magazine, *The Patriot*, and several other print venues. She is the founder of the World Literary Café, and when she's not writing, Melissa helps authors navigate the publishing industry through her author training programs on Fostering Success.

Visit Melissa on her website or chat with her on social media. Melissa enjoys discussing her books with book clubs and reader groups and welcomes an invitation to your event.

Melissa's books are available through most online retailers in paperback and digital formats.

Lightning Source UK Ltd.
Milton Keynes UK
UKHW02f1835080318
319104UK00001B/101/P